After
the
Rain

Mary McCarthy

POOLBEG

Published 2012
by Poolbeg Press Ltd.
123 Grange Hill, Baldoyle,
Dublin 13, Ireland
Email: poolbeg@poolbeg.com

A catalogue record for this book is available from the British Library.

ISBN 978-1-84223-588-1

Typeset by Patricia Hope in Sabon 10.75/15

Printed and bound by CPI Group (UK) Ltd, Croydon, CR0 4YY

www.poolbeg.com

About the Author

After The Rain is Mary McCarthy's fifth novel. She has also written: *Remember Me, And No Bird Sang, Crescendo* and *Shame the Devil*. She taught English and French for thirty-four years in St Mary's, Glasnevin. She has one son, Dara, who works as a Vatican tour guide. She lives in Dublin.

Acknowledgements

The following gave me insightful advice and encouragement in the writing of this book: Pauline Gildea, Antoinette Larkin, Alil O'Shaughnessy and my agent, Jonathan Williams.

I am lucky to have a terrific family. Thanks to you all, especially Dara, a great son and a wonderful man of whom I am so proud. Thanks to my brother, Desmond McCarthy, for his ongoing loyalty and care and to all my nieces and nephews and their beautiful children. Their visits always are a delight. The McCarthy clan is in good hands!

Since my cancer diagnosis in March 2012 I have been very fortunate in the huge support I have received from my friends. Thanks to those who have given up their time to stay with me: Assumpta Broe, my niece Shiofra, Loretto my lovely sister-in-law, Meggan King who is like a daughter to me, Pauline Gildea, a friend in a million, Anne Murphy, Eileen O'Reilly, Antoinette L and the supporting cast! Thanks, Roman, for tending my garden!

Thanks to those who have given me regular lifts to the hospital: Frances Blackburn, Pauline, Eileen, Eilis and Anne among others.

Huge thanks to Bernie Brennan and Nuala Collins

who walked my dog on a daily basis when I couldn't. Doggie people are a breed apart! Thanks to my other 'park friends', especially Claire F, Connie, Barbara, Trish and Sonali.

I have enjoyed the company of so many pals who have visited regularly, taken me out for lunch or dinner (or cooked for me!) and cheered me with their good humour. I would like to thank them all, especially Maeve Kelly, Olive Loughran, Liz Tierney, Carole Downey, Suzanne Mahon and Therese Aird.

I really appreciate the friendship of: my former classmates Mary Begley, Breda Haugh, Mary Fenton and Mary Melvin; my university pals Nora Bates and Brid Fitzgerald; Margaret Lennon and my former colleagues from St Mary's, Glasnevin. I worked with wonderful people for thirty-four years and the staff were like a second family – too many of you to name, but you know who you are!

Thanks to my neighbours for their help, especially the Laceys, the Cairds, Murph and Mo, Mary Moss and Helen Walsh. Glad you're nearby!

Thanks to all of my Facebook friends whose kind words keep up my spirits!

I owe a huge debt of gratitude to the oncology unit in the Bon Secours Hospital: Oscar Breathnach and his team, the nurses and all the staff, particularly Myra who kept me going with her entertaining chat and her delicious sandwiches! Thanks to you all for making the journey easier!

Thanks to Aoife, a little girl who has brightened my life.

I would like to thank Poolbeg Press for publishing this novel: Paula Campbell, Kieran Devlin, Sarah and all the staff. Gaye Shortland, my editor, has done a wonderful job and has put up with my technological shortcomings! The publication of *After the Rain* has given me a bright new focus. I'm delighted to be back!

Last, but definitely not least, where would I be without the unconditional love and devotion of my beautiful Belgian Shepherd, Benni? Love that dog!

For Dara and the future!

Prologue

"This flat would freeze the balls off a brass monkey."

Jackie shivered, her pale skin puckered in goose-pimples. She stretched out one hand and pulled up the borrowed silky eiderdown, which kept sliding down the side of the bed. They hadn't enough blankets for the night's icy temperatures so she'd piled coats and jackets over herself under the cover.

Her husband Sam, wearing two jumpers and a reefer jacket, was hunched over the inadequate one-bar electric fire, studying. From the double bed, she gazed longingly at him. He was intent on his textbook, oblivious.

He was magnificent – smooth skin, jet-black hair, and muscular body – nothing like the gauche, silly boys who had taken her to the pictures and then expected a grope in the back row: greasy, freckled, boring blokes who could barely string together a coherent sentence.

Jackie turned in the bed and closed her eyes, thinking back to when she had started work in Belton's Bakery. One September day Sam Jones had walked into the

1

crowded shop and queued deliberately for her. He'd asked for an apple tart – flaky pastry if she remembered correctly. There was no accounting for how romance could start. "Is it freshly baked today?" He'd spoken in a bass, refined voice. It was his American lilt and mellow tone that had first attracted her. She couldn't believe her luck when he called back the next day and the day after.

"Luck, me arse!" commented Chrissie, the other shop assistant, a widow in her sixties who had ten grandchildren, two-great-grandchildren and claimed to have had three lovers since her husband's death. "Men are my particular field of study, love. My education was the streets of this city and I can tell you that I learned a darned sight more about life than anything you'd find in one of them fancy books. A medical student, you said? They're the worst – dazzle you with seductive words. Words to wangle their way out of anything, not to mention wangle their way in!" She tittered. "There's not a man born yet who has the ability to shock or surprise me. You, on the other hand, and if you don't mind my saying so, are an innocent abroad."

"I don't know what you mean, Chrissie."

"Listen to her, will ya? You think mister-me-man is here to admire your puff pastries, do ya? Believe me, sunflower, he has more things on his mind than cream buns! You'd want to watch them foreigners, love. Fast movers, I'm telling ya. A friend of me sister went out with a Spanish Don Juan and before the poor girl could stub out her fag he was into her knickers – in like Flynn – and sure you can guess the rest. Twins she had, to add insult to injury, and what about yer man, José or whatever-the-hell his name was, what did he do? Upped and went back to Madrid to train as a matador. A matador! What a load of bull, I said to the sister!"

"Sam's not like that, Chrissie," Jackie had assured her.

"They're all like that, chicken, given the chance. They don't think with their brains, if you catch my drift!"

"Sam's different."

Chrissie shook her head and went to box some éclairs for a customer.

Their first date at the National Gallery was followed by another and a visit to Trinity to see the Book of Kells. Sam behaved like a gentleman, his manners impeccable. He brought her to the Abbey theatre and to the Gate, which she preferred, when his finances allowed but mostly they went to the cinema because it was cheaper.

They ate fish and chips in cheap cafés but it didn't matter where they ate, where they went or what they did because Jackie was love-struck. They chatted for hours on end, discussed politics, history and literature and he was amazed by her knowledge. They went for walks in the Phoenix Park or along the canal bank where Sam read her the sonnets of Patrick Kavanagh. Jackie was smitten.

"Maybe you're on to a good thing after all, love," Chrissie admitted reluctantly. "He speaks real well, doesn't he? He has nice manners and his gleaming American teeth would light up a dark alley. Hasn't he a gorgeous smile?"

He hadn't smiled in a long time, Jackie reflected now. The pressure was mounting as the final year's medical exams loomed. Their future depended on these exams. They lived on a pittance, despite the generosity of her sister Emer and her mother. Jackie was now unemployed, having been asked by the boss to give up her job in the bakery once her pregnancy became obvious.

Ronan, her brother, had offered no help whatever. Not that that was surprising – she hadn't spoken to him since the night of the horrible row nearly three years before when she'd announced her engagement. He'd refused to come to her wedding. That had been a great blow. Jackie had hoped Ronan would give her away.

Jackie missed her dad and neither she nor Emer had truly got over his sudden death from a heart attack shortly before the wedding. This had estranged Ronan further, because her brother believed Jackie's engagement to Sam had in some way exacerbated her father's illness. Emer, by contrast, had been generous to a fault. Her sister had organised and paid for the wedding, which was incredibly kind, considering she'd just started her new career as a librarian. Her sister's salary was good but not that good. Jackie guessed that Emer had borrowed for them as well as putting all her meagre savings into the wedding. Their mother had been supportive too, despite her deep grief.

Her belligerent brother was the trouble. The thing Jackie most regretted now was that Ronan had never set eyes on his beautiful baby niece and she hadn't seen his new baby daughter either. This had gone way beyond a sibling spat.

Jackie was determined to sort it out: to do something to heal the breach. Emer had advised her to let sleeping dogs lie, but then Emer was like that. She just accepted things – a real fatalist. She ignored what she didn't like, had been like that since they were kids. Jackie had never met anyone who could turn a blind eye as easily as Emer could.

Jackie couldn't let it rest. It wasn't right for the next generation to be alienated from each other. Both sisters blamed their sister-in-law for the feud. Della had her claws fully embedded in their brother and when she was introduced to Sam, she'd taken an instant dislike to him and hadn't hidden her antipathy. Della had refused to attend all family gatherings after the row and Ronan had followed suit.

If it hadn't been for Emer's financial support, she and Sam wouldn't have been able to afford the rent on this little one-bedroom flat. Sam's family was not in a position to help. Anyhow, they were so far away. Although the flat was dark and damp and dingy, it was their home.

Married for nearly two years now, Jackie was still besotted with Samuel Jones and would have put up with anything for his sake: separation from her brother, losing her job because of the pregnancy, the disapproval of her sister-in-law, suffering cold and even hunger at times. She didn't care what others thought.

When baby Avril came along, their love of the child overrode all financial problems.

"She's fast, God love her. This cold isn't getting to her at all. As snug as a bug, aren't you, pet?" Jackie peeped into the pink cot beside the bed. A little clump of black curls was barely visible above the pink and blue cover. Emer had bought all the baby's bedclothes, clothes, pram and cot. Jackie didn't know how she'd ever make it up to her sister.

Avril slept on, her breathing even and low. Her tiny daughter was a constant source of wonderment to Jackie. Eight months old, she was pretty and dainty, comical at times, with her huge range of facial expressions and as bright as a pin, already beginning to stand on her own and chanting the usual baby lingo.

Sam got up, came over and sat at the edge of the bed. He took his wife in his arms and kissed her long brown curls.

"Jackie, I'm sorry."

"For what?"

He motioned around the room. "For this. You deserve better."

"There is no better for me," she mumbled into his shoulder. She lifted up her face to his and kissed him, full on the lips.

He gently explored her mouth, his tongue sliding between her teeth and licking the soft insides of her cheeks. The flickering in the pit of her stomach grew more intense, but he drew away.

"Come to bed," she whispered.

He sensuously stroked her upper arm. "Soon. Real soon. I have to finish this chapter."

"Come to bed now!" She blew into his ear.

He laughed and pulled back. "I have to finish this. I must do well in these exams. In time everything will change for us. I promise I'll get us out of this hell-hole."

"It's no great shakes, Sam, but I don't mind it here. The people are all right."

His eyes narrowed. "There are things you don't know and –"

"I do know, darling, I do."

She was aware that her husband wasn't accepted in the neighbourhood. Everything about him set him apart, not least his education. A young gang of thugs from the next block of flats had it in for him – ignorant, unemployed louts who had nothing better to do with their time than to taunt and provoke him.

He kissed the tip of her nose. "I must get back to the books."

"You're a swot!" she laughed.

"I have to be." He mussed her hair playfully.

"You're no fun!" She lifted her blue wool jumper and flashed her small pink breasts.

He leaned over and kissed each of her erect nipples. "I'd love to jump into bed and make mad passionate love to you right this minute."

"Then do," she implored.

Sam hunched his shoulders.

She pulled down her jumper and pouted. "No fun at all."

"I really need to finish reading this tonight. I've no choice."

She relented, sorry for needling him. "OK, but don't overdo it. You look all in."

He turned her hand over and lightly kissed the wrist. "I suppose a cup of coffee is out of the question?"

"There's no milk. I used the last of it for Avril's bottle."

"I'll take it black."

"No, you hate it black." She pushed back the mountain of covers and coats and emerged fully clothed from the bed. "I'll pop down to Hickey's and get a bottle. We'll need it in the morning, anyhow."

"Forget it. I don't want you wandering around out there in the dark. It's not safe."

"It's only nine o'clock. The shop's five minutes away."

"No, honey, that gang may be around."

"Fat chance. They've got their dole and they'll be in the pub till closing time. I'll be perfectly safe."

"It's too cold to go out."

"Mother of Moses, will you stop fretting? You're a worse fusser than my mother." She took him by the hand, led him back to his chair and made him sit. "Now, hush up and finish that chapter." She kissed the top of his head. "I'll be back in a jiffy with the milk. After your coffee, I'm going to drag you into bed and ravish you, so, sleepy or not, you'd better be ready."

He grabbed her waist and pulled her close. "I'm always ready for you!"

"You horny thing! Right, release me! I'm off."

"Jackie, it's too cold to go out. Please stay. I don't give a damn about the coffee. Go back to bed, please."

"Stop worrying, will you?"

"I don't trust that gang."

"Those yobbos? I'm not afraid of them, Sam. Mindless morons, that's all they are." She leaned down and nuzzled his neck.

He stared up at her. "I'm serious. It's far too cold for you to be out. You're prone to getting bronchitis. And it's foggy."

"What's bugging you? Those idiots or the weather?"

"Both. Stay here, please."

She shook her head defiantly.

"I want you to stay in." He hugged her waist harder. "Do as I ask for once."

"No deal. To be honest, I fancy a coffee myself."

"There's no arguing with you!"

"Exactly!"

She pushed him away, went to the door and took the old heavy army overcoat from the peg. Her former boss in the bakery had given it to Sam. She was tall so it fitted her quite well although it was far too big on the shoulders. "I'll wear this for protection! See you in a sec, worry-wart!"

Smells of fried food wafted up the corridor when she opened the flat door. In this building at every hour of the day and night there was always someone cooking. "Be ready for me when I get back!"

She accidentally left the flat door ajar and he heard her laughing all the way down the stinking stairwell to the front door of the squalid building. The door banged loudly behind her. He went to the window and saw her crossing the street, the wind whipping the ends of the huge coat round her thin ankles. She turned, looked up at him watching her, as she knew he would be, and waved. Then she blew him a kiss and turned the corner.

"Thanks, Mrs Hickey. No, that's all." Jackie checked her purse for loose coins, hesitated, then reconsidered. "I'll take a packet of Marietta biscuits as well. Thanks."

"There ya go, love. How's himself?"

"Bleary-eyed. Studying as usual."

"God help him." Mrs Hickey closed the till. "Sure you'll be on the pig's back once he's qualified."

"I hope you're right, Mrs Hickey."

"And how is that precious lamb of yours?"

"Great. Talks non-stop – gibberish of course but she's comical. As good as gold."

"Ah, the creature! Enjoy them when they're babbies, love. They grow up all too soon."

"That's what my mother says, Mrs Hickey. Thanks. Goodnight."

"God bless. Take care."

The bell chimed as Jackie clicked the door shut after her. Mrs Hickey took off her apron, threw it behind the counter and went to lock up when her husband came in from the back kitchen.

"Are you closing? It's not nine yet."

"May as well. There's nothing much doing tonight. It's too bloody cold for anyone to venture out."

"I thought I heard talk. Was it that Jones one again?"

"Do you mean Jackie?"

"The little trollop."

Mrs Hickey made the sign of the cross. "How can you talk like that? Your mother would turn in her grave if she could hear you."

"I'm not the only one who thinks she's a slut. Carrying on and living here openly with that son of a bitch –"

"Stop it, Harry."

He shook his fist threateningly. "If only I was a few years younger, I'd take him on myself."

"What did Sam Jones ever do to you? He minds his own business. He's a clever man and a hard worker."

"Why can't he do a man's job then?"

"He's going to be a doctor. What's more important than that?"

"No time for doctors; never had and never will. He has

10

some nerve coming over here with his uppity ways, lording it over the rest of us."

"Sam is not uppity at all. He's always polite and friendly and he loves that little baby. I've never seen a grown man dote so much on a child."

"The bugger should go back to where he came from!"

"Not another word!"

Harry Hickey's eyes glistened with hatred. "He'll never belong here, not in a million years. He's a blight on our little community. He should be strung up and –"

"Shut up!" His venom horrified her. "You've no right to think such appalling things, never mind say them."

"I can think what I want, woman."

Jackie left the shop and stuffed the empty purse into the right pocket of the big overcoat and the biscuits into the left. She gripped the cold milk bottle in her hands. It was foggier than she had realised; the night was frosty and the paths slippery so she'd have to watch her step. She blew onto her hands. She should have worn her gloves, even if they were ripped.

Picking her way slowly, she began to cross the main road, unaware of the headlights glaring behind her. The roar of an engine made her whip around. A car emerged from nowhere out of the smog. She squinted blindly into the bright headlights.

"Stop, stop!" she shouted.

The car kept coming. Instead of braking, it gathered speed. Had they not seen her? Was the dark green of the army coat making her invisible in the gloom of the night? She held up the milk bottle as a defence weapon.

11

"Stop! Stop!" she screamed.

The car lunged forwards. She tried to manoeuvre out of the way on the icy road. Her nerves and her legs let her down. Try as she might she wasn't able to move quickly enough.

She heard the shriek of brakes and a loud crunch before she realised the car had ploughed into her. She was hurled backwards onto the hard bonnet. She glimpsed grinning faces behind the windscreen. Another lurch forward and Jackie felt herself flung off into the road.

The milk bottle flew out of her hand and smashed in smithereens near her lacerated body, its contents spilling out, seeping under and into her streaming brown curls. The milk fused with blood and spread over the hard concrete.

Agonising pain seared through her. She couldn't feel her legs. Something sour filled her mouth. Blood, she thought, oh, God, it's blood. She lay rigidly on her back, her neck twisted and her left arm trapped, mangled, under her body.

Jackie was too terrified to budge. Excruciating pain engulfed her. She bore a grotesque resemblance to a rumpled rag doll, sprawled there on the dirty street as a solitary star way above twinkled down from the inky blackness of the sky.

She saw its brightness shimmer, grow fainter and fuzzier, then nothing.

"Shite! It's not him," a voice rasped. "Quick, get the fuck out of here. It's a woman. Jaysus, we hit a woman."

"Wha'?"

"It's his bitch," the front seat passenger hissed. "It's not him! It's her, his woman. For Christ's sake, put the boot down. We have to get outa here before the cops arrive. Put the shaggin' boot down."

"She might be badly hurt," the driver pleaded. "We can't just –"

"Hurt, me bollix! She's dead. Look, she's not movin'. What are ya waitin' for, ya gobshite? Come on. Fuck it, come on."

The car screeched off up Dorset Street, heading towards the back roads of Santry, up past the airport and out into the open country and freedom.

Sam Jones tidied away his books. He hoped the water in the shower down the landing would be warmer than it had been of late. The landlord was a skinflint and stinted on the electricity in the building. Wouldn't it be wonderful to have his own bathroom as he'd had in the States?

He glanced at his watch. Jackie should be back any minute and then he'd shower and try out the new aftershave his mother had sent for his birthday. He'd make love to his beautiful wife. Tonight, he promised himself, he'd excite her to more than one climax. They were good together, physically as well as every other way. He said a silent prayer of thanks to God for finding this woman for him. He was blessed.

Sam tiptoed to the cot and checked his baby daughter. Gently, very gently so as not to disturb her peaceful sleep, he pulled up the cotton sheet and the pure wool blankets she'd kicked off.

He heard sirens in the distance.

1

January 10, 2008

Dorgan, Emer, [54] after a long illness, died
peacefully at home in the loving care of her family.
Removal tomorrow 5.30 p.m. to Christ the King
Church in Cabra. Funeral Mass at 10 a.m. Friday and
then to the crematorium in Glasnevin Cemetery.
R.I.P.

"Ronan! You'd better read this!"

Della Dorgan, her voice more than usually edgy, passed
the *Irish Times* to her husband, who was engrossed
watching Sky News on the high-perched TV above the
kitchen table. "Look, look there."

"Hmm?"

"Read it. Five names down. The death notices. Look."

Her husband slid his glasses from the top of his shiny,
balding head onto his nose. He lit a cigar and started to
read the paragraph, slumped in his chair, slipped off the
glasses and closed his eyes.

"Ronan?" His wife prompted.

He went rigid. After a couple of seconds, he opened his eyes. Their expression was vacant.

"God rest her soul," his wife murmured.

He stared blankly.

"Ronan?"

He continued to stare ahead, not seeing or hearing her.

"Answer me, Ronan."

Slowly, despondently, he bowed his head.

"Ronan?"

The TV ads blared out their jarring jingles.

Della came over to his side of the table, knelt beside him and shook his arm. "Are you all right?"

In a robotic trance, he took the remote control and flicked off the television. He peered at her, long and hard. "God rest her soul . . . is that all you have to say?"

His brow furrowed. She knew that look. She stood up calmly, leaned over, took his dinner plate away from him and scraped the remains of his shepherd's pie onto her plate. She knew what he was thinking, but his facial expression and non-communication drove her berserk. She was living with a stuffed animal.

"Are you going to the funeral?" she asked warily.

"Pardon?"

"Are you going to go to the funeral?"

He tapped his fingers nervously on the wooden tablemat. "I can't believe you asked me that."

"Well, are you?"

His fingers drummed rhythmically.

"I don't understand you, Ronan."

He stayed silent.

15

"It's not my fault," she said. "I had to show it to you, didn't I? You had to be told."

The tapping was driving her crazy.

"I'm sorry to be the one to give you the bad news but you had to know. Why are you upset with *me*?"

He took up his glasses again and blew on them, a habitual gesture when he was angry, then took his napkin and wiped each lens furiously. "A kind word wouldn't have gone amiss."

"There's no kind way of giving news like that."

"Not for you," he muttered. "Sensitivity was never your forte."

"Me? You're calling me insensitive?"

"Don't start now."

"I'm not starting anything. I merely asked you a civil question. Are you going to the funeral?"

He glared at her and put his reading glasses into the open black leather case. "Naturally."

Della arched a perfectly curved eyebrow. "I won't go."

"You'll have to."

"I won't."

He snapped the glasses case shut. "She's my sister."

"Some sister."

"Stop it, Della."

She dropped the cutlery onto the stacked plates and sat into her chair defiantly.

He shoved his chair back from the table, got up slowly and began to pace. "I should have gone to see her long before now. All these years of pointless recrimination – what was it all about?"

This time she didn't reply.

He came back to the table and stubbed out the cigar in the ashtray. "Wasted years of separation."

"She never kept in touch with us, either," she lied. "Why should you feel bad? It's too late now."

"Yes," he replied softly, "it is."

"I'm certainly not going to Emer's funeral. I'm not that much of a hypocrite. I never liked her, if you must know."

"Oh, I do know." He stroked his dappled beard. "You never bothered to hide your animosity. She was well aware of your feelings for her and for . . ."

"Go on, say it. Say it – my feelings for Jackie."

He lowered his voice and spoke in measured tones. "Please don't mention her name. I've asked you never to mention her name again to me."

"She was your sister too," she snapped.

"Do you think I need reminding?"

"Yeah, well, all that was thirty years ago. We should be able to discuss it now in a civilised fashion. You'll have to accept –"

"Will I?" He walked stiffly out to the hall table and picked up his car keys.

Della followed him. "Where are you going?" She was touchy but curious.

"Where do you think? I'm going to Cabra Road to pay my respects. I realise it's too late for poor Emer, but the least I can do is to go home – to be there. I may be able to help in some way and –"

"It's not your home – not now, hasn't been for years. You won't be welcome."

"She's my sister." His eyes burned through her. "She's my sister and now she's dead. Christ Almighty, have you no compassion? What kind of a woman are you?"

"Don't shout."

"I don't know what happened. I didn't even know she was ill. I don't know who is with her there in the house. It's my fault that it came to this."

"How can it be your fault if you didn't even know she was sick?"

"I *should* have known. Common decency demands –"

"Decency is not a word I'd associate with your family."

His mind in a muddle, he was unconscious of the last barb. He struggled into his dark tweed overcoat. "I have to go over there. I'll have to help. I don't know how but –"

"You're making a big mistake, Ronan."

"Perhaps."

His fingers shook as he handled the car keys. He went to the hall door in a daze. All his actions seemed to be in slow motion.

"I may be late."

He sighed aloud in the shadowy light of the hallway. He felt deeply ashamed. There was no justification for his neglect of his sister. Stubborn pride had split them all those years before. And now Emer, his little sister, was dead. No opportunity to kiss and make up. No time to make atonement. He gulped down the knot in his throat. What had she gone through? A long illness, the paper said. Was it cancer, like their mother had? He hoped she hadn't suffered. Mostly he hoped that she hadn't been alone in her final days.

He turned back to make a last bid at civility. "Della?"

His wife wasn't there: no goodbye, no peck on the cheek, no parting hug of comfort or reassurance. She had gone into the sitting room and turned on the big plasma

TV. He could hear the familiar *Coronation Street* signature tune.

He knew with that customary sinking feeling that the bottle would be opened before he reached the car in the driveway. He was glad she'd be in bed when he got back, if he came back tonight at all. He wouldn't want any further discussion about Emer with his wife – a bitter woman still carrying a grudge.

2

Della took the remote control and turned down the sound. She couldn't concentrate on Weatherfield's latest trauma. Ronan was crazy to have gone over to Cabra tonight, showing up like a smacked puppy. Who did he think he was?

What if someone in Cabra Road informed him that Emer had phoned him? How long ago had it been? Three months? Four? Emer wouldn't have told anyone, would she? Not when she hadn't heard anything back. The family rupture must have been embarrassing for her. She had caused it, after all. Who would she have told? That friend of hers, that . . . Della grasped for a name but none came.

Ronan, haring off tonight. He was such a wimp. Della picked up the newspaper. She wouldn't lift a finger. The way Emer had spoken to her that dismal day would forever be etched on her brain. Now Ronan, the less-than-dutiful elder brother, riddled with remorse, had decided to reappear, thirty years too late, his tail between his legs.

Would he offer to pay for the funeral? Or had Emer saved for it herself? She wasn't exactly a worldly woman, never had any real respect for money. She couldn't have any savings if she'd continued to be the spendthrift she once was. No, Ronan would offer. Guilt money. She'd lay a bet on it. He'd fork out to help salve his conscience, spend *their* money on his sister. It wasn't enough that Emer had inherited the family house. Now she'd cost Ronan his hard-earned cash to pay for a fancy funeral. And it wasn't only Ronan's money, was it?

Something funny struck Della. Who was going to give the homily? It should be one of the family. In the old days it was always the priest – platitudinous words mouthed in reverent tones, delivered in that ingratiating clerical voice, pitched high and on a monotone. Excruciating for the congregation, who shuffled in their pews and wondered who the hell the priest was talking about.

Who wrote those saccharine scripts? Was there some secret scribe who composed ready-made sermons? Did the bereaved pay per word? Inoffensive words, mild and carefully penned, paying tribute to the person's good deeds, charitable works, hard work and love of family.

And Emer? Good deeds – a moot point. One person's notion of good deeds was another's definition of interference. She would be considered charitable by some, Della supposed. She had vague memories of Emer's fundraising for the children's hospital, the reading classes she gave for the local kids in the library and her involvement in adult literacy.

Then there was the care of her mother and her devotion to her sister, as Ronan had pointed out on more than one occasion, but she'd been amply rewarded for that, in Della's view, by getting the Cabra house. That must be worth a fair few quid despite the fall in market prices. Who'd inherit the house? It was rightfully Ronan's now.

Hard work? Her sister-in-law had been hard work right enough – cantankerous, opinionated, but as for her career she'd settled for a soft option – stacking a few shelves every day and stamping books. Librarians had hardly been busy in the last few years. Sure most people had their own personal libraries at home with the Internet. Emer had no ambition when she was young. But who was going to say that publicly?

And love of family! What family? When had any of them last seen her? Spoken to her? Ronan hadn't set eyes on her in decades.

January 9th . . . peacefully at home in the loving care of her family.

Whose loving care? Had she finally got a partner or children? No, this city was small, they would have heard. So, who was this *family*? Hadn't she and Ronan been at loggerheads? Who had been in the house with her? How many would show up now for the funeral? That niece, maybe? But wasn't she in the States?

After a long illness.

Heart trouble like her father? Cancer like her mother? That was a distinct possibility. All her life she'd puffed like a demented dragon. Della thought it was probably emphysema. Lousy disease. So, Emer had finally experienced what suffering was, had been forced to learn tolerance. That must have been difficult for someone so spoiled and sheltered. She hadn't a clue what real living was about –

no husband to care for, no children to rear – yes, maybe she had been good to that American niece, but that was at a distance. That's the way she had lived her life – at a distance.

She'd given up that guy – what was his name – Brendan Foyle or Brian or – ? No, it was Ben, Benjamin Fogarty. She remembered now because he'd reminded her of Dustin Hoffman in *The Graduate*. Only Ben Fogarty was tall. He was strikingly handsome and, frankly, she had never understood what he'd seen in Emer.

What had happened to him? She thought she remembered Ronan telling her that Ben had taken off – New Zealand or Australia or somewhere exciting. Dublin in the 1970s was not exactly full of opportunities for enterprising people with ambition. He'd emigrated for a better life and apparently had wanted Emer to go with him but of course she'd refused – chosen to stay in her comfort zone in Ireland.

The late Emer Dorgan. Passed away, gone to a better place. Maybe she was there already, bossing the blessed and arguing with angels, driving the saints insane.

They'd tried to help out after Jackie's horrible death but Emer had kept them all away, didn't want their assistance, she'd said. Emer had gradually detached herself and her mother from their lives. Not that Della had given a damn – she had her own mother and father – but it was hard on Ronan. So much for family!

Emer would have friends among her work colleagues, no doubt. Della knew that there was a scattered staff, moving from one library to the next, all knowing each other and no doubt gossiping too – a community of librarians. Maybe her colleagues had helped at the end.

"Nobody deserves abandonment!" Isn't that what Emer had screamed that fateful night long, long ago? Certainly, nobody should die alone, Della reflected, but Emer had wanted to be left alone. She'd said that and she meant it, no matter what Ronan maintained now, but she wouldn't be left alone in death. This was Dublin. People would turn up in their droves. Aged neighbours from the Navan Road – God, how many of them were still creaking around? Anybody Emer had worked with, known even superficially, sons and daughters of acquaintances, anyone who had ever met her, however briefly, would turn up at the church. That was the tradition. It didn't matter how much you bitched about, ignored, belittled, scorned or insulted the person in life – in death you said nice things, you patted backs, you swapped stories, you mouthed inanities and you smiled in false sadness at all and sundry.

Della decided to pour herself a large vodka. She turned off the TV, puffed up the new suede couch cushions and sat in the dusky twilight, regretting now how tartly she had spoken to her husband. She couldn't apologise because she'd only spoken the truth, but she didn't want any more unpleasantness.

No doubt Ronan would go into one of his huffs. He could keep up the silent treatment for days. Did she want that? He might be stingier with the money too. Maybe she could force herself to apologise? If he inherited the Cabra house, it was half hers.

She should think this through. She had to live with him. Why make life harder for herself? She *would* sit up and wait for him, apologise and offer condolence – even prepare a light late-night supper. That would mollify him. He wouldn't be home for hours yet so she might as well relax and put on some music.

She glanced along the shelves above the stereo: CDs of all the classics, Beethoven, Schubert, Bach, Handel, Schumann and Mozart. Ronan's precious collection secretly bored the pants off her. Now, where had she stored that Sting album? Suddenly, stacked behind the Gilbert and Sullivan collection, she spotted the Frank Sinatra tape that Emer had given them for their first wedding anniversary. That was fitting in a weird way. She took it out of its cracked plastic cover, put it in the tape deck, turned up the volume and the familiar words echoed around the room: *"And now, the end is near . . ."*

She raised her glass to the ceiling and sneered. "Here's to you, Emer – your swan song!" She filled her glass to the brim – no mixer required. She preferred the sharp taste of the undiluted spirit, didn't have to pretend to lace it with white lemonade, as she did when Ronan was around. She downed the lot in three gulps.

Perhaps she would go the removal after all. Perhaps she'd phone Carla and Ian to come to their aunt's funeral – not that they knew her. They hadn't set eyes on her since they were toddlers. But Ronan would like his children to attend the funeral of his sister. Etiquette.

"And for a bank manager, decorum is imperative." She spoke aloud in mock obsequiousness.

She poured herself another drink, larger this time, not bothering to go to the kitchen for ice. It was actually nicer at room temperature.

OK, she'd phone her daughter in the morning and in

an effort to persuade her to come, she'd offer to pay for the flight from London. Ian would attend if she asked him. He could easily afford time off from his restaurant in Temple Bar. He had an excellent manager ready to take over. Maybe he could bring his eldest with him? Greg could be taken from school for a few days. He was ten now, old enough to attend, and Emer was his grand-aunt. Hardly grand, Della brooded. She didn't even know of Greg's existence.

Della felt suddenly magnanimous. The drink had helped to sweeten her. She would do the right thing: support her husband, put on a good show. She would rinse in the mahogany hair colour she had bought in the chemist's. Her roots needed touching up and she hated the way her snooty hairdresser refused to give her the colour she wanted, maintaining that the dark colour was too severe for her face. Whatever happened to clients' preferences?

In the morning she'd put on her best suit, the maroon one with faux-fur collar and cuffs, and face them – whoever they were. At least she wouldn't have to face Emer. Della stared out of the sitting-room window at the hushed evening traffic and wondered about the coming days.

Funerals are a big deal in Ireland, she thought. Death doesn't scare us. We understand ritual. We have faith – or alcohol. At times of death, people like to help, to feel useful. They come from far and wide to attend; bring cakes and sandwiches, make stews, casseroles and trifles. It's a big party where they chat and drink and reminisce: a *wake*. They stay up and wake the dead, for days sometimes. Emer had attended her fair share. She wouldn't be *waking* now. Never again.

Della swirled the delicious liquid around the Waterford tumbler. She took another soothing sip. The question remained – who was going to give the homily and what the hell was going to be said?

3

After-work commuters had gone and traffic on the quays had eased. Ronan Dorgan adjusted the heating dial in his Mercedes to *cool*. Beads of sweat dotted his forehead, but he was aware that this could be anxiety. He managed to get into the right lane for his turn, drove over O'Connell Bridge, admiring, ahead of him, the sight of the prettily lit spire, which towered above Dublin's main street, although the street now looked bare without the Christmas lights and decorations, recently taken down.

How everything had changed here in Dublin, and not everything for the better. From his youth he remembered the weekend trips into town. At first he and his sisters had stuck to the northside: shopping in Henry Street, coffee in Caffola's Café at the top of O'Connell Street. Then in their late teens they'd braved the challenge and crossed the Liffey to the – what they then considered very stylish – south-side Dandelion Market with all its exotic, trendy clothes and hippies selling their wares amid the floating whirls of hash. He'd bought a poncho once but it hadn't suited him. He'd passed it on to Jackie.

Jackie – his younger sister with her dark wavy hair and statuesque figure – had been truly beautiful. That girl had brains to burn but had given up her studies to work in a cake shop. She'd sacrificed an academic career for the lure of cash, clothes and a social life. She could have had her pick of men but she'd chosen – he gripped the steering wheel tightly and swerved to avoid a cyclist. He tried to concentrate on his driving.

In their early teens, Jackie and he used to make fortnightly visits to the Carlton Cinema and the Ambassador. Emer had been too young at that stage. Both cinemas were long gone, supplanted by the Multiplexes, which had sprung up all round the city and the suburbs. Jackie was long gone too.

Now Emer.

A terrible heaviness welled up in his chest, forcing him to breathe harder and faster. He turned the car into Parnell Square: his schooldays in Scoil Mhuire, chanting Latin to the sound of the swishing straps of the Christian Brothers. He was lucky: he had never suffered brutality at their hands because he'd been a good student: never mitched off to the slot machines nearby or the flicks; completed all homework tasks; hadn't asked awkward questions and had been a model of correctness and propriety.

Ronan reached Phibsborough and drove on past the stately Gothic church. More memories surged. His granny had lived in a terraced house in Munster Street: his lovely, elegant grandmother, who had taught in St Peter's National School, opposite the church, before he was born. She had long retired by the time he came along. He thought back on her kindness. She always bought sweets and treats for himself and his sisters: Cadbury's threepenny plain chocolate bars, pink and yellow rosebud sweets, sticky toffees, black-and-white-striped bulls' eyes and, on her pension day, she gave them big shiny brown pennies for the pictures.

The old Bohemian Cinema, or the fleapit as it was known locally, allowed the kids in free if they brought empty jam jars in lieu of payment. The State was slightly more upmarket but shabby and dirty in comparison to the luxury of cinema complexes now.

He and his schoolmates, Pete Jordan and Gary O'Mahony, played cowboys and Indians. In summer they had adventures on homemade wooden rafts on the Tolka and on the Canal. Gary's granddad was 'away with the fairies' and they regularly used to trick him out of money, which they then spent on fags they'd smoke up lanes and alleyways.

Another life.

He was a grandfather now himself. What would his grandmother think if she knew he was on his way to pay his respects to his dead sister whom he had been estranged from for so many years?

Ronan reached the Navan Road. It hadn't changed significantly. Redbrick bay-windowed houses with long front gardens lined both sides of the wide street. He pulled up outside the house where he had grown up.

The front garden was well maintained; grass trim, bushes neatly manicured. The tall lilac tree his father had planted still stood proudly to the right of the sitting-room window. Emer had taken good care of the place.

There were lights on all over the house and he saw shadows of people moving around downstairs. More people arrived and scurried up to the front door, carrying bottles and other offerings. He couldn't see who, but someone was there to receive and welcome people.

The family home.

He turned off the headlights, switched off the ignition, undid his seat belt and slouched over the steering wheel. He wanted to cry. He couldn't.

4

Ronan became aware of a light tapping on the passenger side of the car. He pressed the release button to lower the window.

"May I help you?" A refined voice seeped through the mists of his mind.

A dark young woman was peering in at him. Her accent was American.

"I'm sorry if I'm bothering you, only a neighbour spotted you in your car and was concerned. Are you OK? Have you come for the wake?"

He nodded dumbly.

"Pardon me for saying this, but you don't seem well. Is there anything I can do?"

Ronan looked helplessly at her. She was beautiful. His niece. She didn't recognise him. "I'm sorry for staring," he blurted. "When I saw you standing there beside the car I was . . . overcome."

What was he wittering on about? She must think him

daft. There was something surreal about this whole thing. She had appeared out of nowhere, come up to his car and addressed him as a stranger would. His niece, his long-lost niece. She didn't know him, but then why should she?

He felt lost, confused.

"I apologise," he mumbled.

She smiled reassuringly. "No need."

"Oh, there is every need," he rushed on. "I didn't mean to be impolite. I'm . . . I'm not quite myself."

"Would you like my husband to take a look at you? He's a doctor."

He shook himself out of his stupor. "Not at all, I'm fine, honestly. I'm f-fine." He'd started to stutter. Was he losing his mind?

"Would you like me to phone someone? Your family?"

"No, no." He mopped his brow with a newly pressed white handkerchief. He definitely did not want her to call his wife.

The young woman stared at the gleaming white hankie and it reminded her of her father. He was the only man she knew who insisted on using them. Maybe it was an age thing. This guy seemed to be in his late fifties or early sixties, with a balding head and silver moustache and beard. Was he . . .? Could it be? Something about him was familiar, but she didn't trust her judgement because for the last few days nothing made sense.

"I'll be recovered in a minute," he said. "Maybe I could trouble you for a glass of water?"

"Of course. You're very pale. Come in and see Emer and then you can rest for a while, just until you feel a bit better."

"I . . . I've had a shock tonight. It's just a reaction." He got out of the car slowly.

The young woman looked harder at him. She saw a flicker of something familiar in his eyes, but again it was fleeting. "Follow me. I'll take you in to see Emer and then I'll get my husband to take a look at you."

He was about to protest again that he didn't need a doctor when she led the way across the path and opened a front gate – the gate to his childhood home! He inhaled quickly but she had walked ahead and didn't hear or notice.

"There's a big crowd in the house. I know I must seem a bit distracted but the truth is I'm . . . I'm heartbroken but I . . . my husband says I'm 'high' and he says that's normal, that some people get slightly hysterical, you know. It's adrenaline pumping or something." She turned back to him. "We're having a wake, although my aunt didn't want one – didn't want any fuss at all – but you can't prevent people from visiting. To tell you the truth she was more of a mother than an aunt. She –"

He staggered.

Alarmed by his demeanour, she grabbed his arm. "Are you ill?"

"My dear girl . . ."

Her stomach somersaulted.

"Oh, Avril!" he burst out.

She gasped. "Ronan?"

He clung to her arm.

She released his grip and backed away from him. "Did you know? Did you know she was dying?"

"I only found out this evening."

He took a step towards her but she stiffened.

"You left it a bit late."

He raised his eyes from under his silver eyebrows and looked sheepishly at her.

He moved forward and clasped her hands tightly in his own. "I know."

His niece, avoiding the host of people assembled in the front room, led him down the hallway towards the back room where, she said, Emer was laid out in an open coffin. Memories and images swamped him as, with a heavy heart, he followed. There had been many parties here all through his youth when his parents often had open house. Relatives and neighbours regularly came for singsongs on Sunday nights and 'card nights' on Wednesdays. The house was often full. No locked doors, no formal invitations, no dinner parties, just casual callers and 'visiting'. There had been no alcohol consumed on these occasions but pots and pots of tea – coffee was also a rarity – and plenty of sandwiches, biscuits and cakes.

His mother looked down on him from the photo placed high on the wall in the hall. Her lovely smile and laughing eyes held no hint of scolding but the picture unnerved him. Before her long illness, she had been a jolly woman. He remembered how she'd pull funny faces behind his father's back when the latter was lecturing them on unacceptable behaviour. She hid household bills from him when he was in a bad mood. She humoured him and her children, and her greatest concern was to have a nice dinner for them each night, for them to be warm and well and happy. They could do no wrong in her eyes. He thought with fondness of how nightly she used to smear her face in cold cream and, with hairnet clamped on her grey curls and false teeth sitting in a glass on the bathroom shelf, she would announce she was ready for a bout of bedtime fun. She got amusement from every simple thing: her Bingo nights, walks with the next-door neighbour, taking the bus out to Howth for a Sunday stroll. The photo brought it all back.

Ronan stepped further back in time. He saw himself again as a small blond boy, dressed in short grey pants and V-necked blue jumper, sitting on the bottom step of the stairs playing with a red yo-yo his father had given him. The image was so vivid that he emitted a low groan.

Avril turned to him. "Are you sure about this?"

He looked as if he were about to faint.

"Maybe this is a mistake?" she asked.

"Please go on."

When they reached the back room, Avril lowered her voice. "You don't have to do this."

Through the crack of the door he caught a glimpse of white candles and white flowers. "I do. I must see Emer."

His niece pushed open the door and walked ahead of him into the candlelit room. Two old ladies knelt, one at either side of the coffin, which was raised on some kind of dais. The women were finishing a decade of the rosary. They made the sign of the cross and stood up to leave. They smiled at him on their way out but he didn't notice. His eyes were riveted on the snow-white silk where his sister lay, eyes closed, blonde hair neatly arranged around her pallid face. She had shrunk beyond recognition.

Avril nodded encouragement at him, withdrew quietly

and shut the door. She wondered again if she had done the right thing letting him in. Had he any business to be here? He'd been absent from his sister's life for so long. What would Emer have wanted?

Ronan cautiously approached the coffin. Lying there, docile in death, she was the image of their late father. His youngest sister, the kid, the baby, the butt of his childhood pranks, his little 'Emu' as he had nicknamed her, was lying there, perfectly still.

Her face had aged, thinned and ravaged by disease, but there was an aura of serenity about her. The candlelight created a yellowish waxen glow.

Ronan placed his trembling hand on her cold stiff fingers, and he suddenly recognised their mother's black rosary beads entwined around them. No longer able to contain his grief, his body convulsed, wracked by sobbing.

5

Dejected, Ronan sat at the oak kitchen table. He recalled with disarming clarity the old, yellow oilskin tablecloth with the garish red flowers, which was always in use to safeguard the wood when they were kids. This table was his mother's proudest possession because it had come from her family home in Meath. Despite its protective covering, the years and constant usage had taken their toll and had a detrimental effect on the table's polished surface. He was glad to see that it had been restored to its former glory.

He remembered family meals here: the squabbling, the laughter, the pokes from his mother prompting him to eat up his carrots, the glares from his father when he interrupted one of his sermonising speeches about mastication and digestion. The old man had had a point – maybe if he'd heeded his father's advice, he wouldn't now be suffering from an ulcer.

Ronan was present again in the kitchen where he'd

grown up but he might as well have been on Mars. He felt removed.

"Please have this." Martin, the throat specialist, the man who was married to his niece, handed him a brandy.

He shook his head.

"It will do you good."

Ronan took the glass and put it on the tablemat at his elbow. He had no intention of drinking it, but felt too overwhelmed to argue. The drink would have stuck in his gullet. Anyhow he had to drive home soon.

"Avril is just seeing the last of the visitors to the door."

"Would Emer have wanted a gang of people here? She liked her privacy."

"She loved people. We'd never have gone against her wishes but we knew it was just that Emer didn't want to put people under an obligation to come. She hated being a bother." He said this in a tone that hinted strongly that of all people on earth, Ronan, her brother, should have been aware of Emer's magnanimity. "Emer touched so many lives and people needed to come. They trickled in here all day in twos and threes and some came alone. She was highly thought of."

Ronan, picking up on the tone of recrimination, lowered his gaze.

"It wasn't just friends who came either. Many of her clients turned up: older people in the area who saw the library as a refuge. You wouldn't believe the number of country people who drove here tonight to pay their last respects to your sister, people who'd moved to the city and had found it hard to settle in. Emer had been a source of comfort to them, they told Avril tonight. Young people from the local schools constantly asked Emer for help with their projects and there was a call from the nearest school principal telling Avril that the students wanted to form a guard of honour at the funeral. Avril turned her down politely; Emer wouldn't have liked that much fuss."

Ronan sat dumbly.

Martin continued: "Emer taught the so-called 'New Irish' – the immigrants – the basics of computing. They used the library's Internet facilities, as a way of keeping in touch with loved ones far away. She took a personal interest in each of them. The cleaning lady at the library, Mrs Lynch, regaled us with all sorts of funny stories and with tales of Emer's huge kindness. Avril had always known that Emer was devoted to her job but we had no clue of what exactly she had done for everyone. And of course she had many friends."

"She was very popular when we were young," Ronan finally managed to say.

"Her closest friends are devastated. Maggie is crushed."

"Maggie?" Ronan repeated dazedly. "Is she still around?"

Martin seemed irked by the notion that any friend would have deserted Emer. "Maggie got Emer through the worst times. She cheered Emer with her chat. She encouraged Emer to eat. She was fantastic."

Ronan mumbled something.

Another awkward silence ensued.

Martin wondered if he had gone too far in his tribute. The continuous barking of next door's dog began to grate on his nerves. "Avril will be back in a moment."

"I know what you must think of me," Ronan said stiffly.

"This is not the time. I don't want my wife any more upset than she already is."

Ronan bit his lip. "I'd like to be a help, not a hindrance. I know it's too late to help my sister but I'd be very happy if Avril would let me pay for the funeral."

Martin stood up to clear away glasses and plates. He did his best not to stare in disbelief at this sad specimen stooped at the table. This man had caused such hurt to his sister and he probably didn't even know it. Now he had the audacity to offer money. Martin tried to keep his voice dispassionate. "You'll have to discuss that with my wife."

Avril wouldn't hear of it. She thanked him for his offer but assured him that Emer herself had left plenty to cover the cost of the funeral.

"She wanted to be cremated," Avril explained. "She hated the idea of going into the earth. Emer never liked the dark or the cold." Avril's eyes misted. "She asked for a simple ceremony and afterwards her ashes to be strewn on the sea off the pier in Howth. She loved it there." She fixed her gaze on him. "So did your parents apparently."

Two buses there and back. They'd never enjoyed the luxury of a car. They'd buy ice creams and wander down by the harbour. His mother had always dreamed of living near the ocean.

"Whatever Emer wanted," he whispered.

Avril clenched her hands on her lap. She was physically and emotionally exhausted from the day. She had so much to do the next day: organise the flowers and discuss the music for the gospel group who had volunteered to sing at the removal and the mass, ask Gerald Moore, the priest, about the readings. Emer and he had discussed all those details. She'd planned her own funeral. What guts did that take? Avril also had to contact the undertaker again. He would phone the cemetery to finalise the time for the cremation. They'd be allotted a slot and if they missed their time they'd have to wait in line, she'd been told.

Ronan sat and stared. Avril didn't know what to say or do to get rid of him. He had turned to stone.

They had to get to bed for a few hours' sleep. Avril wanted to lie in her husband's arms and have a good cry in private. Martin was the only one who understood the depth of her sadness. Of course her father would understand but he couldn't be here. Emer's funeral would bring back too many bad memories for him.

"You're not drinking your brandy, Ronan." Maybe this would galvanise him into some kind of action.

"I'm driving."

"Right."

"I don't drink much these days." His wife drank enough for the two of them, but there was no need to share that piece of information.

"One wouldn't do any harm," Martin said. "It would warm you up. This is not easy for you."

"For any of us," Avril murmured.

Ronan, finally getting the hint, stood up shakily. "I've imposed on your time for long enough."

Avril felt a stab of remorse as she noticed how pathetic he looked and sounded. She shot a look to her husband in appeal.

"I don't think you should drive yet," Martin advised. "You seem a bit shaky."

"Perhaps a strong cup of tea or coffee?" Avril suggested, kicking herself at the same time for prolonging his inconvenient visit. "There's a pile of sandwiches in the sitting-room. Are you hungry?"

To their consternation, Ronan broke down. He wept into his crossed arms. His whole body shook.

"You can't let him go like this," Martin whispered to Avril. "He's not fit to drive."

"I know, I know," she hissed and stood up anxiously. "What about the spare room for tonight?"

"I think so."

Martin came over and put an arm around her, leading her into the hall, out of earshot.

There, he faced her and quietly asked, "But how do you feel about him staying?"

She shrugged.

"Don't do anything that will make you uncomfortable," Martin advised, kissing her forehead. "Why should we put ourselves out for him?"

Avril hugged her husband. "He's Emer's brother. It's what she would have wanted."

"You think so?" He sounded dubious.

Avril considered only for a second. "Yes, I do."

Avril showed Ronan into the spare bedroom, unaware that this was his boyhood territory. The old ornate wallpaper had been painted over many times in the intervening years and the room was now a pale peach with matching peach curtains and duvet. The floor had been recently sanded and polished.

"It's a lovely room," Ronan said. "I must thank you for your graciousness, Avril."

43

"You're my uncle," she reminded him. "Why wouldn't I be good to you?"

They both knew the reasons.

She turned on the radiator beside the bed. "It's chilly in here." She drew the curtains and switched on the bedside lamp. "I'll go and get you a pair of Martin's pyjamas." She couldn't suppress a small grin. "They might be a bit too big."

"You're very kind." He sat on the bed. "You know the really tragic thing is that I don't know you and I didn't know Emer – not since we were young anyhow."

"She was the best," Avril said.

"I wish I had known her in adulthood. We used to be close before . . ."

Avril hesitated. "It may not be too late."

"I beg your pardon?"

"There is one way you can get to know your sister again. Hang on. I'll be back in a minute."

Increasingly puzzled, Ronan stood up, took off his charcoal suit jacket and draped it over a chair. He was bone-weary and grainy-eyed. He noticed a picture above the bed. It was a print of Trinity College that he had bought for his parents with his first pay at the bank. His mother had loved this picture. She'd always wanted him to study English there but, although he loved the theatre and all things literary, he had wanted money and success and Della didn't think that the academic route would guarantee that. He had always intended to join an amateur drama group or to write a play, but the steady flow of promotions and commitment to the job had taken over his life. It was Emer who had entered the groves of academe.

"I'm sorry, Mum, I let you down." He was amazed to hear himself talking to the picture.

Avril came back into the room, a black book under her arm.

"I was just talking to my mother," he explained self-consciously. "You must think me crazy."

"Not at all. I've always talked to mine."

"Jackie would have been proud of you."

Avril stood, trying to figure out this man before her. He was nothing like she'd expected. She knew he was important in banking circles but you'd never guess that now by his demeanour. Beyond that she knew very little. He was her flesh and blood but she had only the vaguest memories of his sporadic visits to Cabra Road when she was a child. He was not around at all during her granny's last months and at the funeral he had been cool and standoffish. That had truly upset Emer, she remembered.

A baby's cry broke the silence. Ronan's eyes widened.

"My daughter," Avril gushed. "Grace. It was Emer who named her. She lived to see her born and that was her last wish. She's nearly six weeks old. Martin and I both love the name: Grace Emer Liston."

Ronan crossed the room and, in a gesture not at all typical of him, embraced her.

She held him then at arm's length. "I'll introduce you to your grand-niece tomorrow. I don't want to disturb her now. If we're lucky she'll sleep till six in the morning and then it's feeding time. She's a hungry little thing."

"Babies are a full-time job, or so my wife informed me. I have a son and a daughter and a grandson."

"My cousins," Avril said ruefully. "I'd like to meet them."

"Sad to say but I was never really close to my children. They grow up so quickly and now . . . they're gone. I left all the domestic stuff to my wife. I was always too busy with my job. It was a mistake."

Avril nodded.

"I intend to rectify that," he said.

"I want you to have this." She handed him the book. "Allow me to present your sister. Read this and you'll get to know her all over again."

He glanced down at it

"Read the cover," she persisted.

"*Red Poinsettias.*"

She clapped her hands excitedly. "Look at the poet's name."

"Emer Dorgan! Good God, Emer still wrote poetry?"

"All her life. A local publisher just brought this out."

"Remarkable." He traced his sister's name with his finger. "Truly remarkable."

"You'll enjoy the poems," Avril said with great pride. "Many of them are based on her childhood memories. They'll be your memories too."

"Did she write about Jackie?"

"Yes."

"Her death?" he asked tentatively.

"Yes, and your mother's, but the poems aren't glum. They're more a celebration of life. She wrote about happier times too when you were young on holidays."

"In Blackpool," he whispered, "many moons ago." He hesitated. "I suppose she wrote about me as well?"

Avril ran her tongue quickly over her upper lip. "She wrote about her alienation from you, but the poem isn't bitter, Ronan. Emer wasn't acrimonious."

Jackie, Emer and himself – three siblings born into the one family, but every child has a different childhood, different perceptions and experiences. He stroked the book lovingly. "Says who?"

"What?" Avril started.

"Says who?" he repeated. "When we were kids and we'd argue, Emer's retort was always 'Says who?' Funny, isn't it?" He paused. "Did Emer suffer?"

"I think she did. That time when she phoned you she –"

"She telephoned me?" His face paled. "At the bank?"

"I think it was your home she rang. She wasn't sure if you were still there or if your number had changed."

"I have the same number since I got married. When did she phone?"

"I can't say exactly. After we came back from Clifden, around the beginning of September, I suppose. She left a message on your answering machine and when you didn't return her call, she –"

"I never got the message," he said, aghast.

"Perhaps whoever heard the message didn't realise how important it was –"

"Perhaps."

It was obvious there was more to it and it was clear he couldn't discuss it.

"I'm sorry Emer had a hard time."

"She never complained. Her specialist was super. So was the hospital but we wanted her to stay here with us – I'm a nurse after all and Martin gave her great care."

"The stories about some hospital conditions are horrific at the moment," Ronan replied. "I'm glad she didn't have to endure indignity."

"In the last few weeks she became very ill and Martin,

in conference with her doctor and the oncology team, upped the morphine dose. She went in and out of consciousness in the last few days. Before that, she was alert and in good form – she pretended a lot, put on a good act. She was a true stoic. When Grace was born, she was exhilarated. Then her poetry book arrived. Her illness was terrible and there were some awful days but it wasn't all doom and gloom. We have many happy times to remember."

"Had she been ill for long?"

"She had symptoms for a good while before she saw the doctor."

"She dreaded the diagnosis, I'd bet. She went through so much with Mum. I want to thank you, too, for everything you did for my mother. I shirked my duty. I should have been here." When Avril didn't reply, he added: "You were only a teenager then."

"Granny Dorgan was a gutsy lady," Avril said. "I have a perfect image of her sitting at the piano and playing 'Bye Bye, Blackbird' and Emer and I dancing and messing around. She played all Gracie Field's songs too. 'Sally in our Alley' was her favourite party piece. Granny loved that piano."

"It's not still here?" he asked hopefully.

"No. Riddled with woodworm. Emer was sorry to part with it. That summer when I helped out with Granny Dorgan, I made up my mind to be a nurse. Looking after the sick is an honour."

What could he say? What help had he been? He cleared his throat. "When was Emer diagnosed?"

"She outlived the time the doctors predicted, I know that. Let me see. It was just before Martin came to Dublin for his interview. That was over six months ago. It was the scariest day of her life, apparently, and she was alone with the specialist hearing the news. She'd chosen to go in on her own. She was independent and stubborn, right to the end."

"Stubbornness is a family trait."

"Indeed." Avril's voice softened as she recalled her aunt's slow demise. "I'll begin there, shall I, the day she was diagnosed? During the time we spent together in recent months, Emer told me a lot and Maggie and Noelle both talked about those awful days so in a way I feel as if I went on the whole journey with Emer – she said I did."

"Yes, tell me from the start."

"That day, the day she was told she had cancer, was the worst day of all. Nothing had ever frightened her so much in her life before, she said. It was early June. It was humid and oppressive but raining, Noelle said. She'd driven Emer to the hospital. Yes, it was a murky day last June . . ."

Ronan listened intently as Avril began to tell him the story of his sister's last months.

6

June 2007

"My estimation would be about three months, possibly longer. It's not something that can be pinpointed with accuracy."

The oncologist carefully studied his patient's reaction. Her shining blonde hair framed her face. Although he knew she was in her mid-fifties she looked much younger. Her eyes were the bluest he'd ever seen. This woman must have been a stunner in her youth. Her illness, however, had begun to affect her skin colour; the greyish tinge was noticeable despite the carefully applied foundation.

Emer Dorgan gulped, paused and then cleared her throat nervously. "Three months?" The expression on the specialist's face indicated that she hadn't misheard.

"In or around. Not possible to apply a specific time limit."

Emer felt the familiar choking sensation rising.

Mr Noonan made an effort to keep his voice upbeat. "With chemotherapy, somewhat longer perhaps."

She swallowed hard.

"There's no certainty. I'm sorry."

"And if I decide against chemo?"

"As I said, about three months, Emer."

He sniffed, apologetically, she thought. Or maybe she had taken up enough of his expensive time? She couldn't interpret his tone.

"It's just an opinion, but it's based on the results of the ultrasound and the CT scan." When she said nothing, he felt compelled to continue. "Every case is different. You are free to get a second opinion. I would prefer if you did, in fact."

So, she was now a *case*. "No."

He leaned forward a little over his desk. "No?"

"No second opinion. I came to you because you're the best."

He raised an eyebrow. "I'm not God."

"Good job. I don't believe in him, her or it."

Mr Noonan's expression was inscrutable. "I can promise I'll do my very best for you. We'll put up a fight."

"A fight?"

"A positive attitude is a must."

"That's a tall order."

He nodded gravely. "I realise that. But if you adopt a fighting spirit we can –"

"You make it sound like a battle."

"Yes, Emer, and we have to plan our strategy."

"I thought the enemy had already advanced too far."

"Why lie down under attack? We have weapons."

She wanted to shout at him to stop this ridiculous repartee. She didn't need to: her look said it all.

He twiddled his pen between his long fingers. "First things first. I recommend that you begin your treatment as quickly as possible."

"I appreciate your opinion, Mr Noonan, but no. No treatment."

"Oh?"

"No chemotherapy, at any rate. I am not going to subject my body to unnecessary torture for a measly amount of extra time. We don't even know how much longer I have, do we?"

"No, but –"

"Three months it is then."

The specialist had to allow that this woman was different, as feisty a patient as he had ever met. Yet there was a huge vulnerability about her also. He wasn't sure how to proceed.

The room began to spin. *Three months*. Now that Emer had said the words herself, it was different. She owned them. Her words, not his. It was real, horrifyingly real.

Emer Dorgan, fifty-four years old, had been given a death sentence. Mr Noonan, painfully polite, talked on in soothing tones but his utterances meant nothing now, just muffled humming sounds emerging from a foggy haze somewhere far away. Vision blurred, her heart pounded deafeningly in her ears.

Words. Words. Earnest expression of concern: lips moving, eyes gently focused on her, hands clasped in his lap like a choirboy. All he needed was the surplice.

Her heart was pumping. Louder and louder.

Words, words and more words, emitted slowly, softly,

carefully, his voice hypnotic, but she managed to block out the meaning as he described, in effect, her death.

Faster and faster, temples throbbing away.

Her body shuddered violently despite the stifling heat. White dots shimmered before her eyes. Then the room zigzagged back into view. Her heartbeat slowed and fluttered.

"I'm sorry, Emer, I truly am. I had hoped for a better prognosis."

What now? What was she supposed to say? Was there some kind of etiquette for such moments? He moved back his chair gracefully, uncrossing his long legs, unfurling his long body till he stood tall. Now what? Was it her turn?

She moved to stand up and shake hands with the specialist but she swayed and lost her balance. She clung onto the back of the black leather chair.

"Sorry, I'm clumsy . . . I can't seem to . . ."

"It's all right." Mr Noonan, eminent oncologist, rushed from behind his mahogany desk and took her arm to steady her. "Sit down. Sit a while to regain your composure." He leaned over and with his free hand picked up the phone. "Ms Reilly, please bring in some tea. Hot sweet tea."

He replaced the receiver hurriedly and gripped her waist to assist her to a standing position. "It takes time to assimilate all this."

Emer's breathing became laboured.

"Slow deep breaths. That's it." He took her wrist gently and felt her pulse. He slipped his arm around her waist and led her back to the chair.

She dropped into it and her head fell forward onto her

chest, bizarrely reminding him of a large cotton puppet his sister used to play with half a century before. He felt a deep sense of uselessness and it hit him hard, as it had done intermittently during the past few years since his wife's death.

"Mr Noonan . . . I . . . I can't think. I can't . . ."

She lifted her head and her glazed eyes bore into his. Then she lowered them and stared helplessly at the carpet.

Finally the reaction he had been waiting for: fear. "It's entirely understandable, Emer. Try to inhale slowly. Take deeper breaths if you can. You are in shock."

"I was half-expecting it," Emer murmured, breathing harder. "I always try to prepare myself for the worst."

"Some people do."

"The funny thing is that usually I succeed but you can't help hoping for . . . you know . . ."

He knew only too well.

7

For weeks Emer had been preparing herself for what she considered to be the inevitable. She had gone through crippling trepidation, followed by a refusal to think about it at all. Then she found the website and was shocked by what she read there.

When the choking sensation got unbearable, she was forced to seek medical attention. Friends suggested a hernia or an ulcer: something safe, something non-threatening.

She feared the worst.

Then the terrors of the dark followed: long sickly-coloured meandering corridors leading to antiseptic white rooms, herself trapped in a bed hooked up to blood-filled tubes, prodded with sharp needles. Cries of agony and morphine-induced raving as the faces of strangers in white coats loomed over her and finally the coffin stood dark and ominous and lonely as mourners in ritual black filed by to the accompaniment of dirges.

Her nightmares had always been grisly.

These images raided her nightly sleep, tossing her troubled mind into paroxysms of panic and finally frightening her awake, heart palpitating, body lathered in sweat.

Emer had sunk deeper and deeper into a slough of depression but she managed to hide it from friends. They would think she was overreacting.

She had known her symptoms were serious.

Her GP had been marvellous – kind, very understanding and above all efficient. Luckily, Emer had medical insurance. That speeded up the waiting period to see a specialist, but time wasn't in fact on her side. If the cancer had spread, as the oncologist had just told her it had, to her liver, there was no long-term cure. Stage 4 was serious.

Mr Noonan was the only person on the planet now who fully understood her predicament, who had the necessary information to tell her what she needed to know. As such, she felt some sort of weird affinity with him, although she wasn't sure she liked him.

"This is it, isn't it, Mr Noonan?" She wanted honesty, however brutal that might prove.

The specialist nodded.

"Jesus, I'm afraid. I think I'm about to faint. I thought I'd be braver. I'd steeled myself, at least I thought I had but . . . I *am* afraid."

"Of course you are."

This was difficult. Usually he would consult with the spouse or partner or some family member, at this stage, to find out the mental state of the patient. Emer was single and middle-aged and, as far as he was aware, had no children. She had an air of being very strong and self-possessed but, in his opinion, she should not be on her own hearing this news.

What she clearly saw as independence he saw as isolation. Yet he had no right to surmise about her life. She had demanded an honest assessment. He couldn't give her false hope.

Emer, waiting for him to continue, felt waves of nausea pass over her. Beads of sweat broke out on her brow. The damned heat. She gulped for air and pressed the thumb of one hand into the palm of the other, in an effort to remain focused.

"Time is of the essence. We must start treatment."

"No, I told you. No treatment."

"I can help you. I can't cure you but I can alleviate your symptoms. I do understand what you're going through."

She scratched her eyebrow. A bluebottle flew in the open window, buzzing noisily around the desk before alighting on a gilded mirror. They both ignored it. A sudden gentle breeze caressed her cheek. She was glad of the air.

"I suggest laser treatment. You've complained of difficulty in swallowing. We can remove part of the tumour to allow food to pass easier down the oesophagus."

Emer's fear was mounting. "Sounds painful."

"More uncomfortable than painful, but it's done under local anaesthetic and you don't even need to stay in the hospital."

"I couldn't bear anything going down my throat. I'm gagging as it is."

"We can sedate you as we did for the oesophagoscopy. You won't be fully conscious."

"I'll think about it."

"It would relieve your discomfort."

"When could it be done?"

"The sooner the better."

"Pity you can't zap it all away and we could pretend it never happened, Mr Noonan."

"Unfortunately, it has spread. It's a nasty business when it's this virulent."

"My mother died from cancer. It was awful." Emer's eyes avoided his. "I'm a coward, Mr Noonan. I don't think I can face that pain."

"There are drugs to control the worst of it. I buried my wife five years ago from cancer of the colon."

Emer tried to imagine how he – an oncologist – must have felt to lose a loved one to cancer. He was an expert, brilliant in his field from all she'd heard, and he had to watch his wife die and not be able to cure her.

"So, I know what you're experiencing," he went on.

Emer stared dumbly at him.

"You're not driving today, are you?"

Emer shook her head.

"Would you like us to call you a taxi?"

She blinked in bewilderment.

The secretary, entering the surgery with the required cup of hot sweet tea, interrupted gently. "There's a friend in the waiting-room. She's driving Ms Dorgan home."

"That's good." Mr Noonan went back to sit behind his desk. "Are you still against the chemo? I want to reiterate that it may only give you a few extra months and the sessions can be harsh. Debilitating."

"What's the point?" Emer finally managed to ask. Her voice seemed unfamiliar to her: a stranger's voice coming out of her mouth. Her tongue had thickened, making her mumble. An invader had infiltrated, assailed her body and her mind, incapacitating her. Cancer was on the warpath, as this man had made perfectly clear. It had crept up resolutely and insidiously and was even now, as she sat there helpless, eating away at her innards.

"I can't give you advice as such, just talk you through the possible procedures." Mr Noonan took out a writing pad from his desk drawer and scribbled an address from a little card. "You might find counselling of some value. This person I'm recommending is very good."

"No, thank you." Emer was polite but firm.

"Still, if you change your mind," he persisted, handing the note to her.

Not wishing to be rude, she tucked it into her handbag, accidentally upending the cup of tea, which fell and spilt all over the plush carpet. Emer, mesmerised, stared at the blue-flowered pattern being saturated. The stain spread out, getting bigger and bigger, soaking the woven bluebells.

"I'm so sorry," she gasped.

"Don't trouble yourself, please," Mr Noonan said calmly. "It's of no consequence. Let me get you another cup."

She began to visualise the scalded flowers screaming, withering, drowned in tea. She felt an enormous urge to cry. "No tea, thank you."

She had to get out of this office, away from these creamy walls and blue-flowered carpet and expensive mahogany furniture. Most of all, she had to escape from this soft-spoken messenger of death. A scythe had begun to take shape behind his shoulder.

"I'll see you next week, Emer. In the meantime you will have to try to come to terms with this."

"I wish I knew how."

"Facing death requires mammoth strength, but I can see you have courage. We will make it as easy as possible for you."

She wanted to vomit.

"I want you to read all the literature I gave you. It's helpful. Carefully consider your options –"

"Options?" Emer blurted. "I have options?"

"Of course. There are different courses of action we can take and we do have several –"

"We?"

He lowered his eyes. "You. You do have several choices. I want you to discuss things with your family –"

"They don't know."

"You didn't tell them about your tests?"

"No."

He tried to cloak his incredulity. "I see."

"I live alone."

"But you have some family?"

"Both my parents are dead."

"Siblings?"

"My sister died years ago. I do have a brother."

"Grand."

"We're not on speaking terms."

He looked blankly at her.

"I have a niece, my late sister's child. We're close."

"That's good."

"But she lives in the States."

He became a little testy. "Friends?"

Emer managed a weak nod. "Yes, I do have friends."

"You'll have help then."

"You said *you'd* help me." Why was she being so caustic?

"I meant someone to talk to, to –"

"To give me comfort?"

"Ms Dorgan, I am merely . . ."

His using her surname meant she had rattled him and that had not been her intention. She was ashamed. "Mr Noonan, I'll be OK. I have people I can rely on."

"Good, good. You shouldn't spend too much time on your own."

"Are you afraid I might try to top myself?"

If this was one of her jokes, it was in bad taste.

"You will need care at a time like this. You're angry now and rightly so –"

"I'm not." She kept her tone even.

He knew better. Her anger would turn to bitterness and then to a huge helplessness. She would need support, although she would find that hard to accept, he realised.

"I value my independence. I need to get back to work too."

She was a librarian, he knew, and obviously a dedicated one. "Work? No, I don't think so."

"I'm not an invalid yet."

"I agree, but no work for a while. You need time to adjust."

"Can you give me a cert for this week?"

"And the next. My secretary will give it to you on the way out." Her ambition to get back to work was a good sign, he thought. Maybe work would help her? But she wouldn't be able to continue much longer.

She stood up to leave, slightly steadier on her feet, and realising she'd overstepped the mark, made an effort at last-minute civility. "Thank you, Mr Noonan. You have been very kind. I realise that giving information like this isn't easy for you. I'll see you next week and let you know what I've decided."

With a formal little bow, she left the room.

Alex Noonan felt like a schoolboy who had disappointed a teacher. This woman had had a most unsettling effect on him. It wasn't that he was unused to dealing with serious illness and death; too often he had to be the one to give the bad news.

He loosened his tie, went to the open window and drew in long breaths of fresh air. He hated this part of his job. He was supposed to be a healer not a harbinger of doom. He wished there was something he could have said, some hope he could have offered her, some new wonder drug, but the cancer had spread to the lymph nodes. She had chosen to ignore her symptoms for too long; having started in her oesophagus it had now reached the liver. She had about three months, six at the outside. She presented herself as a confident woman who wanted to take control of her life and her choices. She appeared courageous and outspoken; nevertheless, she was a vulnerable human being who had just received the worst possible blow.

8

"Give her my apologies, Anita, and reschedule her appointment, will you? I'll check in with you later."

Noelle Geraghty swept her brown fringe from her eyes, turned off her mobile phone and, conscious of the disapproving frown, apologised to the woman beside her in the crowded hospital waiting room. She had confirmed that all was well in the salon and informed Anita that she was taking the rest of the day off. It was vital to have a good manager in this business. Anita had joined the salon as a young stylist and Noelle had taken her under her wing, encouraging the young woman to take extra courses in management. She gave Anita more and more responsibility as time went by. Noelle believed in delegation.

Buying her own hairdressing business had been a huge undertaking, but she loved being her own boss. One advantage was taking charge of her time; another was the financial security it had given her since the rancorous break-up of her childless marriage the year before.

Noelle got up anxiously when her friend emerged from the specialist's room. "Emer, you were in there for ages. Is everything OK?"

"Have to go to the loo," Emer mouthed as she rushed by. "Will you wait here, Noelle?" It was more of a plea than a request.

Noelle sat down and took up the *Irish Times* Simplex Crossword again. She was worried.

Emer dashed into the toilet. She promptly threw up the salad she had half eaten at lunch. Her chest heaved with the effort and the tightness in her throat was suffocating. Another churning and she vomited again. She sat down on the toilet seat and put her head between her legs. The polished tiles undulated beneath her. Keep calm, keep calm, she told herself. She didn't want to alarm Noelle. Gradually her breathing returned to normal and she managed to stop shaking.

She stood up cautiously, flushed the toilet and came out of the cubicle. There was nobody around. She went to the wash-hand basin, carefully scrubbed her hands and splashed her face with cold water. Its iciness stung. When she looked in the mirror a startling image stared back at her: dark circles under her sunken eyes, mascara smudged, blonde hair a mess. She had left the house perfectly groomed, having made an extra effort to look well.

Bad news certainly worked fast. Puckering up her lips determinedly, she reached into her handbag for her make-up pouch.

Noelle negotiated her new Saab into the outside lane of traffic to make the right turn into Dorset Street whose gridlock was manic as usual. She had offered to bring Emer to the hospital but she hated driving in the city. Road works were a continuous headache.

The arrival of the Luas, Dublin's newest transport system, reminiscent of the old trams but speedier and more attractive, was intended to have alleviated matters on the south side of the city. It had done nothing to appease irate motorists on the north side where traffic was grinding slowly to a standstill.

"How did it go?" Noelle asked tentatively.

"A laugh a minute."

"Emer, stop acting the maggot!"

"He was a gentleman to his manicured fingertips. The higher the status, the more genteel, I always say."

That was no answer. Noelle glanced in the rear-view mirror and signalled left.

"Where are you going? This isn't the turn." Emer was glad of this excuse to change the subject.

"I thought we'd go on into town and have a meal somewhere. It will save you cooking."

Emer checked her watch. "You need to get back to the salon."

"No worries, Anita can cope. I'll show my nose later."

"Poor Anita," Emer said. "Don't you think you're taking her for granted, Noelle?"

"Don't be worrying. She's living the life of Reilly on the wages I give her."

"She's left running the show a lot. It's your business, not hers. She doesn't have a vested interest in the salon."

"She's a manager. She's paid to manage. Now, where to eat?"

"I'm not very hungry." Emer adjusted her seatbelt. The thought of food made her nauseous.

"Would you like to go for a drink?"

"Not really, Noelle. I'd prefer to go straight home if that's OK with you."

Emer, painfully aware of the tension in the car, didn't know what to do or say to make her friend more comfortable.

Noelle pulled up at traffic lights and turned to Emer. She had to try again. "Did you get the results?"

"It's complicated."

"What did he say?"

"The usual medical jargon. He gave me leaflets and stuff. I have to see him again next week."

"Not an ulcer?"

"No."

Noelle kept her eyes on the road.

Emer looked out of the passenger window. Her throat muscle contracted.

"Will you be getting treatment?"

"I suppose so."

Noelle tapped the accelerator impatiently. "Was he in any way positive?"

He was positive all right. Positive she was going to die. "I have options," Emer said quietly.

"Are you waiting for a particular shade of green?" Noelle shouted at the driver in front. She lurched off as the light changed and indicated right at the next turn. "Options. What does that mean exactly?"

Three months or six months, Emer thought. That's what it meant: three months of steady deterioration with a quicker end, or six months of protracted medication and intervention, hair loss, weight loss and personality loss.

When she realised that Emer was struggling for a reply, Noelle altered her tone: "You look knackered. This isn't the time to talk and I didn't mean to interrogate you. You can tell me in your own time." She paused and bit her lip. "Whatever I can do –"

"I know that, Noelle. Thanks."

Noelle turned on the radio. News, weather, traffic reports. Emer felt the tears pricking, burning her eyeballs. If she could just hang on for a few more minutes she'd be home: home where she could run to her bedroom, fling herself on the bed and bawl her eyes out. Fear gnawed at her stomach. She was afraid she was going to puke again, spew out all over Noelle's new car. She needed the release of tears. Suddenly and unexpectedly she missed the loving arms of her mother.

9

Emer shifted around in her double bed and squinted at the glaring red digits on her clock radio. 7.45 p.m. She had slept for over five hours.

She mulled over the day's events. After being dropped home, she had waved hastily at Cheryl next door. The neighbour was spraying her roses but she had waved and looked perplexed when Emer had rushed by, not stopping for their usual chat. Emer had pushed her key in the front door lock and dumped her handbag on the hall table. She had taken the stairs two at a time, plunged into her bedroom, pulled the curtains, shutting out the world, hit the pillow, fully dressed, wept bitterly for what seemed like ages and then had fallen into a coma-like slumber.

A sliver of weak evening sunlight shimmered in the gap of the curtains. She experienced an intense moment of happiness as the sun encouraged her to move. Was she going mad? How could she feel happy, even for a moment? Euphoria – that must be what it was.

Better get up. If she remained in bed she would succumb to the dreaded doldrums. The sombre mood would hit all too soon, no matter what she did. Let it come whenever and she'd deal with it, but she refused to meet it halfway.

The June nights didn't darken until ten o'clock and until recently Emer loved this. She would pop into her car, drive out to the coast and take a power walk, the Beatles on her MP3, loud in her ears, egging her on. She hadn't done this for months.

She hauled up her sleepy body and sluggishly edged out from under the duvet, feet feeling around on the floor for her slippers. Her heavy head drummed and she was perspiring profusely again. She hoped she'd find some aspirin in the dresser drawer downstairs. What she craved was a stiff drink. A whiskey and Diet Coke would hit the spot. It didn't much matter now whether it was Diet or not. Weight was no longer an issue, except for losing it, that is.

Time was slipping away, hour by hour, minute by minute. She couldn't afford to waste any. She had to make plans. She resented having to spend any time in that hospital. Not now when she believed they couldn't do much to help her. Those erudite doctors and specialists and medical experts couldn't help her now. The illness was too far advanced.

She was now the next *case*, another bloody statistic. But why blame them? She had felt the twinges, the choking sensations and the discomfort. For months she'd noticed the weight slipping away but she'd ignored it, refusing to acknowledge the fact that she was seriously ill.

She hated sickness, detested visiting doctors or hospitals or clinics. She'd had enough of lotions and potions, powders and pills, when she'd looked after her mother. She didn't want this house doused in disease again.

So, what could she do? Nothing for it but to accept the inevitable. It was almost a release to admit she was defeated.

She smiled sardonically at her gaunt image in the mirror as she combed her hair. She thought about how, in the last few years, since she had hit fifty, she'd tried to live a healthier life: packed in smoking, started to walk more, watched what she ate, cutting back on the booze and on fatty foods. Maybe her body was so *cleansed* that the cancer had quicker access? What was more likely, obviously, was that it had started by then. She had begun her fitness regime too late.

She decided to put on make-up. Idiotic, really, as she wasn't going out but she was repelled by the pale face that sneered back at her. Paint an inch thick. Wear a cosmetic mask. Where was the harm? Perhaps she should go to the pub for a few hours? And do what? Pretend that this wasn't happening?

What if, after a few drinks, she blubbered and blabbed it all to someone. Noonan had advised her not to spend too much time on her own, but whom could she call?

Should she phone Ronan? And say what? 'Hi, it's been a long time. How are you? How are the family? Me? Oh, I'm dying of cancer, thanks.' Why should he care? When had they last seen one another? Their mother's funeral, not since then. They'd been frostily polite, nothing more, no sharing of experiences, no mutual understanding. And then there was Della, simpering smugly from the second pew, impeccable hairdo, designer clothes, and perfect body drenched in Dior.

Yet, Ronan was her brother and blood was . . . Was it, though? And she hadn't a clue about him or his life. His kids were grown up and must have flown the nest by now. She hadn't been close to this nephew and niece because Della had maliciously alienated them at the time of the row. And what a row it had been – a humdinger. They'd blamed Emer for everything, cut her off completely.

As he always did, Ronan had bowed to his wife's will. He had adamantly refused to take part in what he considered a charade, a travesty. He'd acted like a thick.

They had lost their beloved Jackie in the aftermath. Ronan had blamed Emer as if it were inevitable, as if one act had automatically led to the other. The cruel words he had spat at her had left an indelible mental scar. He hadn't seemed to care that she was his only sister now. He had chided his mother but he'd denunciated Emer, needing to apportion blame instead of providing support.

Emer was not responsible for the awful tragedy. She had done the right thing, the only decent thing. All the old anger and disappointment welled up inside her. She would not be phoning her brother.

Emer came downstairs and checked her answering machine. Three missed calls; she had slept through them all.

The first was Noelle: *"Hi, hon! I hope you got some rest. I'm off out to meet Uncle Ger, but I'll text you later. I can call over in the morning if you like. Let me know if you need anything. I can come over any time. Later tonight if you need me."*

Noelle sounded frantic. Emer had obviously freaked her out on the drive back. It wasn't fair to keep her in the dark like this, particularly after she'd been so helpful. She'd ring her tomorrow. Next message.

Maggie. Oh my God, Maggie.

"Dory, how did the hospital go? I tried your mobile. Ring me."

Dory, a shortened form of Dorgan, was Maggie's pet name for her since they'd been kids in primary school. Maggie had been her closest friend for almost fifty years. Nothing could ever erase the shared secrets, the confidences, the advice given and taken, the laughs, the tears, the troubles halved, the mutual trust.

What could she possibly say to Maggie?

The third call was Avril ringing from New York: *"Hi there, darlin'. How you doin'? Dyin' for a chat. Martin says howdy. Will give you a bell tomorrow night."*

How would she tell her lovely niece, this gorgeous girl she loved as a daughter?

What about her work colleagues? She had many good friends in the library service where she'd worked for over thirty years. And neighbours who had always been so friendly and helpful, some of these had known her parents and family through two generations.

And her clients, as she liked to call them. Deborah Dixon with her dyslexia – what would happen to her? The little ten-year-old was on a waiting list for extra help at school, but God only knew when a support teacher would be appointed. Emer had made out spelling charts, games and crosswords for her and tutored her every Tuesday. She couldn't let Deborah down.

Was giving news like this fair on any of them? How would they react? With compassion and sadness, of course, and goodwill, plenty of goodwill, they would want to help. Could she bear it? All the kindness, the charity, the pitying looks?

Noelle and Maggie knew that something was up, but they didn't yet know the details. Could she keep it like that? Could she delay their knowing? And what about when she did manage to tell them? Noelle would take over. She wouldn't mean to but she would. Organising everything was part of her life's blood. She'd offer to move in and live here with Emer, possibly insist.

Maggie had her husband and daughter to consider, but that had never stopped her from helping before. She had been invaluable when Emer's mother was ailing.

But this was different. Emer was dying and that was a desolate prospect because, no matter who was with her, she had to face it alone. It separated her from everyone she knew. It marked her as changed, unlucky, unfortunate, and pitiful.

She couldn't endure their pity. They would offer wisdom, consolation and prayers. Prayers – it was definitely too late for them. Emer didn't have the comfort of the opium of the people. When death impended didn't we all view it as a misfortune, a tragedy that befell others, as if it didn't concern us except as supportive spectators, as if we were luckier, somehow immune? Her sister-in-law would react like that. She wouldn't be confiding in Della.

We're all dying, Emer tried to tell herself. She just

happened to know when, or at least, that her death was imminent. She had the opportunity to prepare and get her affairs in order.

She wasn't ready to die. She had too much to do: early retirement, travel, taking up art classes, doing a Masters degree, setting up a reading group.

Too late now.

She blotted her lipstick and checked her face in the mirror: not bad at all although the dark mauve of the lipstick made her look a bit spectre-like. She put on her loose kaftan to hide her thinness. She decided she looked quite attractive in a stick-thin-insect type of way. If she looked fairly presentable, people wouldn't guess how ill she was. She would be able to enjoy herself a little while longer and maybe she'd be able to spread a little joy before . . .

Could she keep the news to herself? Was she strong enough? Couldn't she accomplish some of the things she wanted to? She'd shortlist the vital ones. She couldn't control her illness and the length of time she had left but she could damned well control the here and now.

How bad did she feel? The choking sensation was worse than ever. She would take the medication Noonan had prescribed. What else? A bit weak, a bit shaky and she had a raging tension headache. She'd go downstairs and take two painkillers. The whiskey might not be a clever idea but she didn't care. No need to worry about overindulgence in alcohol. It's not as if she had enough time to develop an addiction.

And how would the illness develop? She'd become weaker and weaker. She wouldn't retire to bed and wait for death. As Dylan Thomas advised, she'd rage against the dying of the light. As long as she had some strength, she'd live each day as fully as she could manage.

She could try some homeopathic cures. How about acupuncture or herbal remedies? Her diet could be looked at, too. The doctors could do their thing but she could do hers. She didn't have to yield to their predictions? With a strong will she could defy or at least postpone death. Couldn't she?

What did those damned doctors know in any case? They weren't infallible. What if Noonan had got it all wrong? A misdiagnosis? It happened all the time. You read about cases like that in the papers. Wasn't some young guy operated on wrongly for cancer? They'd removed his stomach and it was all a huge mistake. Other women had got the all clear for breast cancer when they should have started treatment. Mistakes were all too prevalent.

She stroked the thin skin on her neck. Her collarbone protruded. How would she hide her final deterioration? She could pretend she was going away on holiday for a few weeks. She could say she needed a change of scene and was off to visit Avril in New York. Everyone would believe that.

The phone rang.

She stared at the number that came up. Cheryl from next door, probably wondering what the hell was going on since she'd spotted Emer's manic sprint up the garden path.

She ignored the ringing. Cheryl was a decent individual: a good neighbour, helpful and kind, but a bit of a gossip, and Emer wasn't ready to talk now. She didn't feel any impulse to pick up the receiver. You'd think that the warm sound of a human voice would cheer her up, but no. She couldn't muster up the energy to explain anything. She certainly couldn't indulge in chit-chat. Let it ring. She'd drop in to see Cheryl in the morning and make up some story.

Now, she had to make plans.

The kitchen was cool, dark and damp. She hated it. Over the years she had promised herself to have it gutted and overhauled. She'd planned it all in her head: cherry wood presses, a stainless steel built-in oven, a hob, a dishwasher. Maggie had agreed that the old house needed a makeover. Time for some luxury in Emer's life. Too late – were those two words going to take over?

Maybe not. What if she just upped and left? She could go on the Internet and find a nice cruise. The Mediterranean maybe? She could go into town, buy a whole new wardrobe – wonder of wonders Size 10 again – and take off to the great blue yonder if she wanted. Why not? Wasn't it as easy to pop your clogs in the South of France as it was in dear old Dublin?

She poured a large whiskey into a glass and added the Coke. She watched it bubble, sniffed the amber liquid and breathed in its aroma. Lovely.

She picked up the *RTÉ Guide* to plan her night's viewing and tucked it under her arm. She plonked her reading glasses on her head and, carefully balancing her glass, she went into the sitting room, flicked on the television and settled back into the sofa.

Then she burst into tears.

10

The January Spanish sun suited Emer perfectly, not too hot or dazzling. Maggie brought more coffee on a tray out to the terrace. There was nobody at the pool and they had the large garden to themselves, so they could enjoy a leisurely breakfast of fresh croissants from the nearby bakery. Pity it was too nippy for a dip, Emer thought. The Christmas visitors had already returned to their homes and most of the apartments stood vacant. Then the pool disappeared and they were at the beach but the sky turned black and a wind arose and Maggie had to run after her towel – but it wasn't Maggie at all. Who was this woman who turned to her, glowering?

Weird.

The TV guide fell off her lap and Emer shook herself out of the dream. Ah, it had been heaven for a moment but then it had turned dark. She hated dreams like that. Thinking of those wonderful holidays with Maggie brought back such happy memories. She took a sip of her whiskey, lay back and closed her eyes again. Daydreams could be therapeutic too. She could conjure up images and scenes at will, had always been able to. Maybe that's what helped her to write. She was able to recall in vivid detail one particular morning on the terrace . . .

"It's bliss here, Maggie, so peaceful."

"It is nice, isn't it?" Maggie stirred her coffee.

"Nice doesn't come close. Elviria is a lovely district, just the right distance from Marbella. It's much more quiet and residential than I'd expected. It's so relaxing, I could stay here forever."

Maggie beamed. "Glad you said that. You're our first visitor and I was afraid you wouldn't like it. You know, some might think it too chic. People who want the authentic Spanish experience would live away from the tourist trail. Didn't a friend of yours buy a house up in the mountains?"

"Mmh, in a quaint little village called Competa. Anne loves going there and a gang from work usually goes with her. I have an open invitation but I haven't taken her up on the offer yet. The drive there is super scary, I hear, winding up high along narrow country roads with a sheer drop on one side. Even the description gives me vertigo! But according to Anne, the village is the 'real Spain'."

"We wanted an apartment near a beach. This place is an investment as well as a holiday home, so Joe and I wanted somewhere easy to reach and I like to be near the sea when I'm away."

"Me too. Nothing like the cooling breeze and night strolls. I've always liked the beach. I love going for walks on the Bull Wall . . . Will you ever forget that crazy holiday we had in Torremolinos – Jenny, Noelle, yourself and myself? Four loose women on the prowl and that was long, long before the days of *Ibiza Uncovered*."

Maggie laughed. "You met some Waterford guy, remember? And I think Jenny ended up with a Spanish Don Juan. And the French guy Noelle shifted was a hunk. Come to think of it, I was the only one who didn't hook up with a holiday Adonis."

"You were saving yourself for Joe!"

"Jaysus! I had my fair share of doomed romances before I married Joe. Do you realise that holiday was over twenty-five years ago?"

Emer certainly did realise. It was after her brother-in-law Sam had left Ireland and gone back to the States, taking Avril with him. Emer had then broken up with her boyfriend, Ben Fogarty, because he'd wanted to emigrate to Australia and she'd felt she couldn't abandon her mother at the time. Emer had had enough of shock, separation and sadness and that holiday was intended as a temporary relief to help her get her head together.

"Those were the days, or so we thought at the time. We were quite innocent really," Maggie said. "By today's standards, anyway."

"We should take the bus out to Torremolinos just to revisit our inglorious past!"

"I'll pass, thank you, Dory. I'm quite content to sit and read, saunter down to a nice restaurant for lunch, have a siesta in the afternoon and dress for a quiet dinner in the evening."

"With a few glasses of wine."

"Naturally! The bright lights and cavorting crowds don't have the same appeal now. I'm glad I'm finished with all that running around and worrying about my skin and my figure and do I stand a chance with the fella I fancy? There's a lot to be said for middle age. I'm happy now to relax, eat and drink and get pleasantly plump."

"Speak for yourself, Mrs Walsh. You're not turning into a smug married, are you? There's life in this auld one yet! I haven't given up the ghost. A nice toy boy or a rich widowed accountant – I'm not fussy."

"You with an accountant? Don't think so somehow. I can still see you in those long flowing skirts you used to wear and your dangling earrings dating a fuzzy-bearded jazz musician or a portrait artist or someone vaguely bohemian."

"When you put it like that, I think I'll pass too."

Maggie grinned and put on her sunglasses.

"I could sit on this patio for ever. You and Joe made the right decision. It has everything you could want here."

"Easy maintenance is a must. I've no intention of cleaning or doing repair jobs when I'm supposed to be relaxing."

Emer shaded her eyes to have a better look at the garden. "I've never seen such red poinsettias – and I've never seen them growing in the ground before."

"These were planted especially for Christmas."

"They're so pretty. It's a pity they won't last, isn't it?"

"When they're finished, Julio will be back to plant the spring flowers so there's always something in bloom."

"Always something in bloom, what a lovely thought! And the gardener is called Julio? You're joking!"

"No, that's his name."

"Does he croon?"

"Now that you mention it, I do hear him singing at his work but he's no Iglesias."

"Wonderful gardener, though."

"Yes, he is. There's a caretaker too, a cleaning service and a lady from the agency rents it out when we don't want to use it. You're welcome to come out with me any time. When you take early retirement, you can come in September or March or whenever you choose. There's quite a lot of sunshine even in the winter, as you can see, and you'll get cheaper flights off season."

Emer tinkered with the radio but all she could tune in were the Spanish stations. "What's the plan for today?" she asked.

"We can chill out here for a while and, if you fancy it, we'll pop down to the beach for lunch. There's a good restaurant right beside the waves. They do lovely snacks. I'd love a big creamy mushroom omelette and a side salad."

"Yum!" Emer put her empty cup on the patio table, whipped off her T-shirt, loosened her swimsuit straps, fixed herself more comfortably in the lounger, lay back, closed her eyes and felt the warming rays on her face . . .

Maggie loomed above her.

Emer opened her eyes. "God, where –? What's going on?"

"You were miles away, Dory. Sorry if I startled you."

She'd escaped to another world and another time for only a few brief moments, she realised with a sinking feeling: looking back on that wonderful holiday the year before last, when she'd been happy, healthy, or thought she was, enjoying herself and relishing the camaraderie of her oldest friend. When she'd been light-hearted and carefree – before the symptoms had manifested themselves, before the blasted diagnosis.

"I let myself in with the spare key you gave me. What's going on?" Maggie glanced at the whiskey bottle on the table. "Are you drinking on your ownio?"

Emer shook her head. "I only had one. I was going to phone you but I must have fallen asleep again. I've been snoozing most of the day, which is weird considering I'm normally a lousy sleeper."

"What did Noonan say? I've been going bananas. I phoned your landline twice and texted you about five times. Then I rang Noelle but she'd gone out with her uncle, the priest. Are you OK? What did he say?"

Emer looked away.

"Tell me, for God's sake."

"You don't want to know, Maggie."

"I do."

"I can't talk about it."

"Emer, please."

"I can't."

Maggie stood stiffly, priming herself. "Is it serious?"

"You could say that."

"Cancer?"

"Yes."

Silence.

Emer bent forward and rested her head on her folded arms. She wanted to crawl off the couch and disappear through a crack in the polished floorboards.

Maggie took a deep breath. "Is he going to operate?" She moistened her lips with her tongue.

Emer buried her head further. Her shoulders shook.

"Oh, God." Maggie plonked down on the sofa and put her arms around her friend. "Go on, grit your teeth. Tell me."

Emer gripped Maggie's hand tightly.

"There's nothing you can't say to me, Emer. Nothing at all. You're not to be afraid to –"

"I *am* afraid, Maggie."

"OK."

"I'm paralysed with fear."

Maggie stroked her back. "OK."

"I don't think I can handle this. I feel –"

"I know, I know."

"No, you don't."

"*Shh, shh.*"

"You don't know. How could you?" It sounded like an accusation. Emer recoiled at her own anger.

Maggie kept on stroking and making little hushing sounds, cooing, like a mother to a small baby.

"I'm in bits, Maggie. I'm in bits."

"It's all right, take it easy."

"I'm sick with fright. I'm . . . I –"

"*Shh,* Dory. We don't have to talk."

Emer sat up straight and stared terror-stricken at her friend. "I intended to say nothing. I was going to try and pretend it wasn't happening. I thought I might go . . . I don't know – somewhere. Anywhere. I have to get away. I feel trapped."

"Away?"

"For a while. Till I get my head around this."

"Do you want to go away? I can go with you."

"Really?"

"Yep, I'm free for the summer. We can go anywhere you want. We can go to the apartment if you like."

Emer started to weep.

"That's it. Have a good cry." Maggie held her close as Emer heaved and gulped back sobs.

"I don't know what I want. I don't know anything any more. It's pointless. What's happening to me?" Emer hiccoughed and tried to hold her breath but the shuddering, heaving cries consumed her. "I'm falling asunder – losing it."

"Emer, you're not losing it. You'll weather this storm and I'm going to help you."

"Not this time. You can't. Nobody can."

Maggie fished in her handbag, drew out a tissue and handed it to her.

Emer blew her nose violently. "Sorry. Sorry. That's all I seem to say these days. Sorry, sorry, sorry. I'm pathetic."

"You're not."

"I am."

"I need to hear everything. I want to hear it all, Dory, every word he said. I know you're afraid –"

"I'm scared shitless."

"I'll pour us both a drink. Are you on medication?"

"What does that matter now?"

"Will alcohol not make you sick?"

"Mags, I *am* sick."

"I meant it could make you puke."

"I don't care. I feel like getting sloshed."

Maggie mixed the drinks and handed her one. "Come on, Dory. Spit it out."

"You'd better rephrase that."

"Ever the old wit, eh? That hasn't changed anyhow. Right, big sip, deep breath and tell me everything."

"I don't think I can, Maggie. I find it hard to spell it out."

"I'll prompt. You went in to him and he gave you the test results. Then what did he say?"

"It's a bit of a blur. It's like it's happening to somebody else, as if I'm acting a part but I've no script." Emer shook her head, unable to continue.

"Buddies forever, right? Just say it quickly and then it's out there." Maggie took her hand again.

Emer bit her lip. "It's not good, Maggie."

"Not good?"

"No."

As Emer told her all, Maggie's heart sank. Her thoughts darted all over the place as the dreaded words spilled out. Cancer. Stage Four. Three months. No, no, no, she wanted to bawl and scream. She wanted to yell at God and the world and the universe. She wanted to rage that it wasn't fair, it wasn't fair for this to happen.

She gripped Emer's hand tighter.

11

Noelle Geraghty sat at a downstairs table with her Uncle Gerald in Toscana in Dame Street. As the waiter took their order, Gerald studied his niece. She seemed preoccupied.

"I thought Jenny looked marvellous when I met her for coffee this afternoon," he said. "She told me you went to the concert hall last week."

"Yeah, my birthday treat for her, a jazz concert. I enjoyed it but it's not really my thing."

"Isn't it?"

"I was a child of the sixties – rock and roll and rhythm and blues – but I love classical as well."

"Me too, oh me too." To Noelle's horror, Gerald started to hum the Toreador chorus from *Carmen*.

She didn't appreciate the grins and sniggers from the table beside theirs. "We must get tickets for some of the lunchtime concerts, if you're free."

"I'd love that," Gerald said.

"I'll get their programme, shall I? I enjoyed the

concert, although I wasn't expecting to. The orchestra was superb – fantastic sound and one of the guest singers was Duke Ellington's son."

"Very impressive. Jenny is good company."

"It gave us a chance to catch up. We're both so busy."

Gerald Moore had been a Jesuit priest for over fifty years and had served on the missions for as long as Noelle could remember. He was now retired, back in Dublin, and was involved in parish work. Noelle loved this man, her late mother's youngest brother, and had seen a lot of him since his return. He was warm, wise and very amusing, entertaining her with stories from his colourful past. Meeting him was always a pleasure. She valued his opinions and was often surprised by his particular take on the world.

She was grateful for this chance to confide her worst fears about Emer. "Cancer I'm guessing, although she didn't say that."

"Then don't jump to conclusions."

"If you saw how she looked. I got an awful fright. I haven't been attentive enough lately. I've been up to my eyes with the salon. One of these days I'll meet myself coming back. I didn't notice how Emer was looking."

"You've had a lot on your plate."

Noelle, glancing at his starter of a huge dish of mussels, was tempted to remark that so had *he*. "I'm still reeling after the court case and all that business with Brendan."

"At least you got a fair settlement."

"True. It gave me the opportunity to pay off the loan on the salon. I hate debts. It's looking very classy now. I got a good firm of painters. I went for soft colours: beige and honey which soften the black marble and – oh, listen to me blathering on about the salon and poor Emer going through God knows what."

"What precisely did Emer say?"

"Something about options but I didn't understand and she didn't elaborate. She was ashen-faced and very quiet when she came out from the specialist."

Her uncle finished his mussels, carefully wiped the buttery sauce from his moustache with his napkin and took a sip of water. He was considering what Noelle had told him.

A waiter arrived on cue with their pasta dishes. For a few minutes the conversation stopped as they both tucked in. Her uncle had a very healthy appetite and it was a pleasure to watch him attacking his Penne Arrabiata with such relish.

"I hope I'm wrong about Emer," Noelle said. "But she looks thin and sickly. She seems to have shrunk. She must be very ill."

"That doesn't mean she can't be cured, Noelle. Nowadays they have great treatments. Keep up your heart." He winked at her. "And your faith."

He knew full well she hadn't practised her religion since she was a teenager but, every chance he got, he threw in little hints to remind her of her Catholic upbringing, although he was never judgemental.

"I know one thing: she'd been complaining about her stomach for ages and was swallowing indigestion tablets to beat the band. I kind of dismissed her," Noelle confessed. "Then she had the . . . the . . . that yoke that they stick down your stomach with a camera."

"A gastroscopy?"

"That was a month ago."

He sipped his Chianti. "And then?"

"When I asked her, she just said something had shown up and she was going for more tests. She went into the Mater Private for a few days but she didn't tell any of us at the time. She can be very evasive."

"Doesn't she have a brother?"

"They fell out. She hasn't set eyes on him since their mother died in 1993 – imagine, fourteen years ago!"

He clicked his tongue. "Families are so important," he said. "Didn't Emer have a sister who died?"

"Jackie. That was thirty years ago. She was only twenty-six."

"Now I remember. Yes, a very sad case. The poor mother was beside herself with grief." He paused to sip some wine. Then he belched.

He reminded Noelle of Henry VIII or at least the Keith Mitchell version on the TV when she was young.

"I was home on leave from the missions at the time and I went to the funeral with your dear mother, God rest her. Frightful business. Her young American husband was very cultured. A student doctor, as I recall."

"He later qualified as a chest specialist. He couldn't settle in Ireland after what happened. He went back to the States with his baby daughter."

"Who could blame him?" Gerald took a piece of bread, broke it and swirled it around his dish, mopping up the last of the delicious sauce. "He was heartbroken, poor man."

"And angry."

"Sudden death can have that effect. A shame, an awful shame. So the doctor left Ireland with an infant to rear by himself."

"His parents in Cincinnati were terrific, I believe. His mother took on the role of chief minder, leaving him to concentrate on his career. He thrived, according to Emer, and now he has his own clinic in New York. He came from such poverty and today he's a millionaire but a dedicated doctor first and foremost."

"And a good father too?"

There was a pause as a waiter arrived to clear the table and Gerald ordered dessert for himself, Noelle declining.

"Yes, he was good father," Noelle continued, "but he did have his mother as a support and Emer and her mother took Avril for the summer holidays here in Dublin every year. She was such a little darling with her dark curls and huge dancing eyes. Impeccably behaved too."

"A child always brings hope."

Noelle flinched but Gerald didn't notice. He beamed at the waiter who had arrived bearing an enormous plate of gooey dessert drowned in thick fresh cream and two coffees.

"And Emer's brother? Wasn't he married with children?"

"Ronan's wife is a bitch. She rarely visited with her brood. Della kept herself to herself and more or less separated Ronan from his family. When Mrs Dorgan got lung cancer, Avril was in her teens and she spent an entire summer here, helping with the daily care, which allowed Emer to continue to go to work. Ronan never visited – not once. Too busy. He actually sent money which Emer promptly sent back."

Gerald nodded, his mouth full.

Noelle was amazed at the speed with which her uncle ate. "I think that's where Avril got her interest in nursing. Of course her father would have preferred her to be a doctor."

"Nursing is such an undervalued career, but if you have the misfortune to have to stay in hospital, you quickly realise that it is the nurses who are the chief care-givers." He pushed the empty dessert plate away from him. "Oh, I ate too much. So, getting back to our discussion, Avril and Emer are close?"

"As thick as thieves."

"Emer was her surrogate mother, I suppose you could say. Wasn't it an utterly horrific way for a young tot to lose her mother without ever really knowing her? And then she had to cope with having her granny ill for so long. The poor unfortunate has had a hard life. Does she know the circumstances of her mother's death?"

"Not the details. That whole business was shrouded in mystery and some people doubted the truth of it being an accident. What would be the point in telling Avril that? Emer is fiercely protective of her to this day. Avril is married now."

"Married? You don't say! Where do the years go at all?"

"One of the doctors from her father's clinic." Noelle stirred her coffee. "A surgeon."

"Very fitting. A good match. The father must be delighted."

"Sam has been an attentive father, sometimes too devoted, according to Emer. I think he tends to interfere in Avril's life. It's to be expected, I suppose. Being a single parent probably made him over-protective."

The priest poured more water for both of them. "He must be relieved now that his daughter is married and settled after a lifetime of looking after her. Parenthood is difficult, but being a single father must have been very hard. I admire him, I must say. Jackie Dorgan certainly made a great match all those years ago."

"Not according to Ronan Dorgan. He and his wife vociferously opposed the marriage. Didn't think Sam was suitable."

Gerald shook his head sadly. "You'd despair of some people, wouldn't you?"

"And when the tragedy happened, they felt justified in having rejected Sam in the first place."

"They *blamed* him?"

"They blamed Emer too."

"Why on earth should they blame Emer?"

"She provided the money for a deposit on a flat. She'd been working for about three years by then. She handed Jackie all her savings. It was very generous of her. Sam was broke . . . still in medical school."

"And Mrs Dorgan? Was she against the marriage too?"

"Quite the reverse. Their mother knew Jackie was in love and she respected Sam, was in awe of him actually. No, Mrs Dorgan only wanted her daughter to be happy. Ronan raged against Emer, claimed that if she hadn't butted in there would have been no marriage and no calamity. Emer thought she was doing the right thing. She still thinks that."

"And you?" He blotted his lips with his napkin.

"Who's to say? Emer acted out of kindness, I do know

that. The marriage certainly seemed happy. A lot happier than mine, that's for sure."

"It's a shame that Jackie's death drove her siblings apart. There's nothing worse than bitterness. Bereavements should bring families together not estrange them. So, Noelle, what now? What about Emer?"

"I want to help, but I can't if she shuts me out."

"Be patient. Give her time."

"I should be doing something."

"Wonder Woman! You were always the same – rushing to the rescue. Never could sit still, even as a child. You were for ever organising things: charity sales of work in your garden, visiting the old folks in the flats, helping out with the youth club."

"I like to be useful."

"Well then, ask yourself how you can help Emer this time. Maybe the best thing you can do at the moment is nothing."

"Nothing? How can that help?"

"She might appreciate a bit of space right now."

"We can't leave her alone. It's unthinkable." Suddenly Noelle's eyes lit up. "I have it! I know what would cheer her up. Avril could come for a holiday."

"That's a good idea," her uncle agreed.

"Emer would always want to see Avril, no matter what. And I'd be happier knowing Emer wasn't coping with whatever it is she's coping with on her own." Noelle checked her mobile phone. She was upset that there was still no text from Maggie, who had promised to call over to Emer's house.

"She'll confide in her niece, is that what you think?"

"You'd never know with Emer. She's a terrific aunt and they're really attached, but I wouldn't rely on her being too forthcoming about her personal problems. She's petrified of illness since her mother's long-drawn-out battle with cancer but Avril adores her and she'd hate to be kept in the dark about this."

Almost on cue, Noelle's phone vibrated. She opened the text message.

E's news is bad. Big C. Asked me 2 tell u and sorry she couldn't tell u 2day. Talk 2moro.

Noelle shut off the phone. She took a long slug of wine. Her stomach churned. "Cancer."

"Oh, dear oh dear."

"I knew it."

Her uncle reached out and stroked her hair. "I'm so sorry."

"Oh, Ger, what can I do?"

"Emer needs family at a time like this." He took off his glasses and cleaned them with a crumpled handkerchief, a gesture that reminded Noelle of a cranky Maths teacher she'd had in school. "Avril should come."

"Emer knows her own mind. She's obstinate."

"She isn't well at the moment; she may not be thinking clearly."

"But it's not up to me to –"

"Yes, it is, Noelle. It is up to you – you and her other friends. You must all rally together to help her through this." He saw her annoyed expression. "I realise there's no need for me to be lecturing you about friendship. You are loyal and a good friend and you'll do the right thing. Can you get this niece's phone number?"

"No problem. Emer keeps numbers stored in her phone, the ones she uses all the time."

"There's your answer then."

"If I do ring New York, what will I say? I don't want to alarm Avril."

"Avril wouldn't thank you if something bad happened and nobody had had the courtesy or foresight to tell her that her aunt was seriously sick. Despite what people say, ignorance is not bliss. Not usually."

"You're right. But what –"

"Just say you're concerned and think it would be wise for her to pay a visit. She knows you, doesn't she, this Avril?"

"Knows me well. Emer and I used to take her to the zoo when she was only a toddler. I've met her often over the years."

"There you go. She'll understand your concern, be grateful that you filled her in."

Noelle sighed. "But I have to give her some consolation when I phone."

"Modern medicine – that's what you can dwell on. Every day new drugs come on the market. How many women have survived breast cancer? The statistics are very encouraging. One of our lads has just got the all clear from prostate cancer."

Noelle fiddled with her mobile.

"It may be a long haul, but she'll be fine, given the right medical treatment and help and love from her family and friends." He took her hand between his. "Noelle, chin up!"

She withdrew her hand a bit abruptly. Noelle had seen

too much of early death in the past few years. Five of her friends and acquaintances had succumbed to the deadly illness and they were all in their forties and fifties. All the cancer sufferers she knew lived on the east coast and it occurred to her that there might be a connection to their proximity to Sellafield, not that the powers that be would ever admit that.

But, as her uncle said, she had also heard of many people who had survived the disease, regained complete health and managed to live full lives afterwards. The problem was she didn't know which cancer Emer had and what was the prognosis.

Her uncle called for the bill. "Trust in God, Noelle."

12

Emer was groggy when she ambled downstairs in her white cotton dressing gown the following morning. Sunlight flooded the kitchen, Abba was playing on the radio and Maggie, dressed in a multicoloured sundress, was making porridge.

"Morning, Dory. Did you get any sleep?"

"A few hours. There was no necessity to stay last night. You're very kind, Mags, but you've your family to mind. What will Joe think?"

"Be delighted with the peace." Maggie stirred the oatmeal. "Joe won't mind in the least and I enjoyed sleeping here last night. Your spare bed is nice and comfortable and it's a relief not to have his bony elbow stuck in my ribs. Spending the night here reminded me of the old days when we'd stay out late and your mum would put me up. She was great fun, your mum."

"I dreamt about her last night."

Maggie could see Emer had been crying. Why the hell

had she mentioned Norah Dorgan? "Sit down and I'll give you some breakfast."

Emer took a seat at the table. "Mags, I appreciate what you're doing. I'm not taking any of this for granted."

Maggie turned from the cooker and opened the kitchen window. The house was stuffy. "We all need a bit of pampering now and again. Joe always brings me breakfast in bed at weekends."

"He's good to you."

"I deserve it!"

"Yes, you do, but you're lucky all the same." Emer spoke without bitterness but Maggie heard the catch in her voice.

"You had Ben, Emer. He was cracked about you."

"A lifetime ago." Emer smiled sadly. "I fell for him the day he strolled into the library and borrowed a copy of *Finnegans Wake*. He appealed to me because he was interested in books. He had a brain."

"Ya big spoofer! You fell for him because he was divine! *Dee-vine!* He had the most amazing green eyes I ever saw in my life – real come-to-bed eyes! I always thought you two would end up together. When he got married years later, I thought it was on the rebound."

"You're a riot! Ben was well over me by then. He had a new life in Australia, loved his job and the outdoors. Things worked out for the best, Maggie. It wasn't meant to be."

"He used to send you a Christmas card every year and he wrote you a lovely letter when your mum died, remember?"

"I think his marriage was a bit shaky around that time.

I'd say things weren't easy for him. Apparently the wife was sick all the time. They had a son. God, he must be in his twenties now."

"I know you never wanted your own kids, not while you had Avril. Still and all, it was a shame you didn't marry. Remind me, what did Ben do out there?"

"He and his brother set up a tour company. They expanded all over Australia. They had a staff of about five hundred the last I heard."

"Do you regret not going out there with him, Emer?"

"I couldn't have left Ireland. It was too soon after Jackie's death."

"Your mother still in mourning for your father, then the accident – a double whammy – and the rift with Ronan."

"I made my decision and I've never had second thoughts."

Maggie didn't believe her. Emer still had a certain expression in her eyes when she spoke of Ben Fogarty.

"I'm not going to waste energy wondering about what might have been." Emer clasped her hands in front of her and stretched them over her head with a big yawn.

"If 'ifs' and 'ands' were pots and pans, as your mum used to say. In any case, you did have your fair share of fellas afterwards."

Emer pulled a face.

"Ah, you don't need a man," said Maggie. "More trouble than they're worth, I'm always telling Joe. You're not on your own, Dory. You have me, Avril, all your friends and . . ."

"And?"

"Your brother."

"Ronan? Are you out of your mind?"

"He *is* family."

"A moot point."

"We'll talk about it later."

No, we won't, Emer consoled herself.

Maggie went to the kettle. "Tea or coffee?"

"Coffee, please. Need to get my eyes out of the back of my head." Emer shook her hair free from the collar of her dressing gown. "I must look a fright."

"You look fine," Maggie lied. "You *will* have support, Dory."

"I know."

"And you have something I don't have."

"Yeah, cancer," Emer groaned.

"I meant your poetry. It must be good to get your feelings down on paper."

"I wouldn't write about cancer. I'm not on some sort of crusade here. I don't see myself as a victim."

"I didn't mean it that way."

"I know you didn't, and what you said is true. Writing can be cathartic. Did you know Jackie kept a diary? She wrote all about her youthful hopes and fantasies. I gave it to Avril on her wedding day."

"All my youthful fantasies have been quashed by the bank manager," Maggie said.

Emer spooned some sugar into her cup. "Do you know what I regret if I regret anything?"

"What?" Maggie, with her half-filled mug of tea, took a seat opposite.

"That I took life so seriously. It's a mistake. I did my

duty, as I saw it, accepted everything as my lot. Too busy, or too scared maybe, to do what I wanted – afraid to take risks."

"Our generation were brought up like that – taught not to expect too much. I envy the young with their new ideas, hopes for a better future. We weren't encouraged to explore our potential."

"No," Emer agreed, "we weren't. We had to take our studies seriously if we were lucky enough to be educated, get good pensionable jobs and settle down to a life of regularity and routine. Emigration tore up this country. Jesus, growing up in the fifties and sixties in Ireland was depressing and restrictive, wasn't it? Don't envy the young. Be glad for them."

"I take my hat off to them," Maggie said with enthusiasm. "Holly, now, is a case in point. She's full of confidence. Sometimes I think her ambitions are unrealistic."

"What matters is she believes in herself, Maggie. She's making the most of her life, and time is on her side. I'd planned to do so much and now I can't. I'm sorry that I'm bitter but I really don't think it's fair."

"It isn't and you're not bitter, Dory."

"I can be – bitter about Ronan at any rate."

Maggie didn't want to pursue this. "Now, to mundane matters like eating. I'll serve you this gourmet gruel."

"I detest porridge."

"It will do you good."

"If I were a masochist, maybe!"

"You wagon!" Maggie laughed. "Try it to please me. It will build you up for the day. It's good for you. I've put in some cinnamon and raisins. They make it more palatable."

"Porridge palatable?"

"I can add honey too, if you want. Makes it sweeter."

"I don't have any honey. Come to think of it, I don't have any cinnamon either."

"I went out to the shops earlier."

"You were already out?"

"Mmh, I woke at seven-thirty, had a quick shower and grabbed a cup of tea. By the way, sorry I ruined your white towel. This stupid mahogany hair dye is lethal. I only put it in a few days ago and I honestly thought I'd washed all the –"

"Don't worry about it."

"I should have gone to Noelle for my colour. She'll go mad when she sees my mop."

"Hairdressers make far too much of unimportant things. They like to add mystique, I suppose. Don't tell Noelle I said that, though."

"No fear. When I checked on you after eight this morning, you were out for the count, so I decided to make myself useful, do some shopping. Your fridge was almost empty."

"Shopping was the last thing on my mind."

Stupid, stupid, stupid, Maggie told herself off.

Emer stared at the bowl of steaming porridge.

"I got in a few things I know you like: chicken, a pork steak, some greens," said Maggie. "I got two lovely fresh salmon cutlets too."

"Thanks a million." She'd never get through all that food; she found meat impossible to swallow and had precious little appetite.

"I noticed the laundry basket was full so I've stuck on

a wash for you. I didn't hang it out yet because we had a sudden shower. It was sunny earlier and then the rain came. Now the sun is out again. It's no wonder we're schizophrenic!"

"You've had a busy morning. I didn't hear a thing. What time is it now?"

"After twelve."

"What! I slept all that time! I've no time for dozing the day away – I'll be asleep long enough."

"A cheerful thought."

"I warned you I wouldn't be pussyfooting around this. My sense of humour may be a bit morbid from now on."

"No change there then." Maggie tapped the bowl insistently. "Come on, try the porridge."

"I thought I could trust you not to fuss."

"I'm not fussing. I'm merely feeding you."

"I'll take a few spoonfuls just to shut you up." Emer was surprised to find she actually liked the taste.

"I could scramble some eggs."

The thought of eggs! "This is fine. Thanks. God almighty, twelve o'clock. Half the day gone. What about you? What about work?"

"I told you last night, I'm off for the next few weeks, no more interviewing until August. I'm staying tonight as well and I want no arguments. I've rung home and everything there is under control. Holly got a part-time summer job in Tesco, so Joe can drop her in on his way to work."

"All work experience is good for kids. She'll be glad of the money."

"Like the rest of them, she's saving for the Debs next

year. That's all they have on their minds, not their exams. The Debs has become a bloody farce: stretch limousines, designer dresses, all-over-body fake tans, outlandish hairdos and then off they go and get pissed on expensive cocktails, staying out all night and carousing till morning. They end up looking like something dragged backwards through a bush!"

"Gallivanting!" Emer smiled. "Maggie, there's no need for you to feel you have to stay again tonight. I don't expect the world to come to an end because I'm sick."

"No arguments! We need to discuss what you want to do for the immediate future: who you want to tell, who you don't, that kind of thing and what you'd like to do, where you want to be when . . ."

"When the time comes."

Maggie went to the sink, feigning an urgent desire to wash the porridge pot. She feared her eyes would give her away. The sink was under the large kitchen window and Maggie looked out at the bleak wilderness of the back garden. "Your grass needs mowing and the shrubs should be pruned. They're very straggly. I'll ask Joe to come over at the weekend."

"You will not! There's a flier from some gardener there in the cutlery drawer. I got him before to tidy up the place. He's a good worker. I'll ring him later."

"But the expense –"

"No buts. Here, hand me over the flyer." She took it from Maggie who went back to stare out of the window.

"Do you know you have a robin?"

"Yeah. He comes every morning for breakfast. He loves fruit cake."

"Janey, I'd have thought he'd prefer bread."

"Well, this one definitely has a sweet tooth. I've written a poem about him."

"Have you?"

"The bird intrigues me he's so tame. When I walk out into the garden, he stays put on the branch, as cheeky as you like. It's as if he knows I'm a friend."

"Have you a copy of the poem?"

"There's a file in the cupboard in the hall."

Maggie went off to search and came back with a green folder. She handed it over.

"I don't know about this."

"Come on, sure I haven't a clue. Never understood all that alliteration business we studied in school. Remember Miss Cronin? That woman was a demon."

"I liked her," Emer protested as she flicked through the first few pages. "I thought she was a great teacher."

"You were brilliant at English. Cronin was always raving about your essays. 'Now, girls, you must engage the attention of the reader in your first sentence and that's just what Emer Dorgan has done. Well done, Emer, an excellent essay!' That woman did my head in!"

"Poor Miss Cronin!"

"What was that first sentence for an essay you wrote that she told us was 'absolutely marvellous, girls!'"

"I haven't a clue."

"Something about sperm. I nearly fell out of my desk when you read it to the class."

"Oh, now I remember. '*Gotcha!" said the microscopic sperm to the startled ovum*' – something like that."

"I couldn't write that in a million years." Maggie scoffed.

"Ah, I never got all that stuff about sound and imagery and rhyme."

Emer located the verses on the robin and read them to Maggie.

"Ah, it's lovely. You've captured him brilliantly."

"You have to say that," Emer protested.

"No, I don't. I have a perfect image of him in my mind: charming on the outside but underneath savage enough to survive."

"I've been watching him for ages. He's a plucky little fellow. I wonder . . ."

"What?"

"Will he notice when I'm gone?"

"Have to do a pee. Back in a sec." Maggie, face flushed, dashed out of the kitchen.

Emer's throat muscles tightened and she felt the familiar difficulty in swallowing. It was a horrible experience, as if someone were strangling her. What had possessed her to talk like that? Worrying whether a garden bird would miss her – Maggie must think she was a stupid eejit. She didn't want Maggie upset. She didn't want anyone worried or put out by this damned illness.

Maggie came back, her face newly scrubbed, a smile painted on her lips. "Now that the rain has stopped, we could go for a walk in Howth later, have our dinner there, if you feel up to it. We can walk and talk or not talk and you don't have to feel any pressure at all. OK?"

Emer was struggling with the food. "Sounds good."

Maggie took the dish away and poured a second mug of coffee. "You need your caffeine fixes. You didn't eat half of this. Will I make toast?"

"I'm not hungry."

"Is there anything you would like?"

"Anything?" Emer's face lit up. "You mean it? Anything?"

"Within reason." Maggie laughed.

"Do you promise you'll get me what I ask for?"

"Of course."

"Cross your heart."

"No, you crazy woman!"

"Humour me. Go on, cross your heart."

Maggie obeyed, carrying out the command in an exaggerated mocking gesture. "Now, enough drama. What is it?"

"Do you know what I'd absolutely kill for?"

"A large Bushmills?"

"Close. Guess again."

"A ride." Maggie giggled. "A lovely long ride with a young stud."

Emer stuck out her tongue. "What are you going to do? Go on the Internet for a *male* order?"

"I would if you wanted. We could try one of those escort agencies or the dating sites. There are loads of them."

"Why don't I put an ad in the paper while I'm at it? 'Wanted: Young handsome strapping stud to service middle-aged skinny-but-not-yet-skeletal cancer sufferer. Must be adventurous.'"

"Ooh, Dory, count me in!"

The two of them collapsed laughing into each other's arms. Maggie felt the tension in Emer's thin body, or maybe it was her own body that was rigid.

"Joking aside, what is it you want?"

"Twenty Silk Cut. I haven't had a fag since New Year's Eve of the Millennium."

"Cigarettes? Are you serious?"

"What's the harm? They can hardly kill me now, can they? I would truly love a long slow hard drag. I can feel it already, oh yes, oh yes, a pull, a lovely big pull, the nicotine hit, the smoke filling up my lungs."

"I'm on my way." Maggie grabbed her handbag. "Twenty Silk Cut it is."

"Hang on." Emer tidied the bundle of poems and put them back in their plastic folder. "No, wait. I'll go and get them myself."

"It's no trouble. I'll just pop down to the Spar."

"No, Maggie, thanks. I want to go out. I can't sit here and mope. Would you mind if we left Howth for another day? I need to drop into the library and find out how things are. I want to see about Deborah Dixon's class. I've missed the last few sessions and she needs continuity."

"Emer, should you not rest?"

"I'll be resting soon enough!"

13

From their spacious, high-rise apartment, Avril Liston and her husband Martin had a long-distance view of the Brooklyn Bridge and the East River. She felt privileged to be living in such luxury and recognised that it was thanks to her father's generosity that they could afford it and also thanks to his connections that they had been permitted to live in this exclusive block.

Many of their acquaintances had been amazed that they had been welcomed to join this somewhat snobbish elite and they didn't hide their surprise, but being the daughter of an eminent specialist had its advantages. Haughtiness was as evident in this community as anywhere else. Avril was amused but Martin hated what he considered to be pretentious living.

Avril loved the view of the bridge. Lit up by night it was splendid. She'd miss this view and she'd miss the shops, the buzz, and the daily thrill of living in New York.

Although Macy's on 34th Street was her favourite

department store, she also frequented the designer shops of Madison Avenue when she received gifts of cash from her indulgent father. And her beloved Broadway with its dazzling glamorous musicals would always be a loss. Martin, the drama buff, preferred the off-Broadway productions where, he claimed, you found the real talent.

What she wouldn't miss was the weather: the horrid humidity of the summers and the biting wind which in winter, and sometimes even in spring, whipped the cheeks and took the breath away. And air conditioning was another thing; it played havoc with her eyes, making the wearing of her contact lenses very uncomfortable. It would be great to live in a place where she could open the windows and breathe fresh air.

Now, in the midday glow, bloated and basking in the sun, Avril settled on a bench in Strawberry Fields, the John Lennon memorial section of Central Park, just opposite the Dakota building. She gulped down her hot-dog lunch, knowing that Martin would frown at her eating junk food, but what Martin didn't know wouldn't bother him and, besides, she was famished. These days she always seemed to be hungry. She swigged cola from the bottle to quench her thirst and cool her parched mouth. The day was too hot.

She placed her hands on her still-flat tummy and smiled to herself. A young dishevelled student type strummed a guitar and sang Beatles songs.

Avril's earliest memories of rainy holidays with her Irish granny were infused with 'Penny Lane', 'Eleanor Rigby' and all the other Beatles songs her aunt played over and over, humming along as she cooked dinner on the old Aga, ironed blouses or mopped the huge flagged kitchen floor. Emer's face would light up and she'd laugh and dance and swirl her astonished niece around and around.

The heat was stifling and Avril's pregnancy seemed to make her swelter more. Her light cotton skirt clung to her damp thighs. If this heat continued, she'd have to buy one of those little portable fans.

Reluctantly she got up to go. How was it that lunchtimes always flew? She'd amble slowly down Central Park West, cut through West 66th Street, and then pass the Lincoln Centre, back to the clinic on Amsterdam Avenue. It would take her about half an hour at a leisurely pace. Then she'd try Emer's phone again. She loved her weekly chat with her aunt.

Avril glanced at her watch and counted the five-hour time gap. Martin would have landed in Dublin by now and checked into the Skylon Hotel. She'd warned him not to say anything to Emer. She wanted to be the one to deliver the surprise. The last time she'd spoken to her aunt, she thought Emer sounded very tired and a bit low but it was hard to have a genuine chat down a phone line and e-mail wasn't for intimacy either. Martin assured her he'd say nothing until she had spoken to Emer.

His interview in the Bon Secours Hospital was scheduled for eleven o'clock Irish time. He'd get the job, she was sure of it. Who was more qualified or more impressive?

Her father might not approve of this temporary move back to Ireland. He would miss Martin at the clinic, miss them both, but with luck he'd be glad for them and for this new opportunity for Martin. She'd talk him around when he came for his weekly visit. He might be a bit peevish but with a nice meal and a few glasses of her special claret and her usual persuasive charm, she'd win him over to her point of view.

She could always get around her dad.

14

The Bon Secours is an elegant redbrick private hospital set in spacious grounds on an elevated site in the heart of Glasnevin, overlooking the village, the River Tolka, the rose garden of the Botanic Gardens and the church known locally as The Wigwam because of its distinctive architectural style. In recent years the hospital had extended a new wing, building a clinic. Recently, with plans to add more consultancy rooms, the owners had bought out the local florist and boutique owner, to the dismay of many of the district's residents.

Martin Liston, waiting patiently for his taxi, sat in the reception area of the hospital after what he considered had been a gruelling interview. He felt he had acquitted himself well, but had no way of knowing. This was not America. He was well qualified and had a lot of experience, but Ireland had a different culture and he knew the success of any interview boiled down to whether the board 'took to him' or not.

He felt he could have expanded a bit more on some of the issues but hadn't wanted to appear arrogant. Well, it was done now and he'd hear soon enough whether he had got the post or not. It was a temporary contract for one year and that would influence his decision in accepting if he should be lucky enough to be offered it. He would have to discuss it further with Avril.

"Doctor Liston?" the receptionist called politely. "Your taxi's outside."

He smiled his thanks and took up his briefcase. He would go back to the Skylon hotel, change out of his grey suit and into his jeans. Then he'd telephone Avril to tell her how he had got on and after that, Emer, to arrange a visit.

The phone rang and rang. Finally a tremulous whisper: "Hello?"

He didn't recognise the voice. "May I speak to Emer, please?" Maybe he had dialled the wrong number?

"I'm sorry," the rather suspicious voice replied, "she's not available at the moment. May I take a message?"

He paused. "Would you tell her Martin called. I'm in Dublin at the moment and would like to see her."

"Martin?"

"Yes, Martin Liston. I'm . . . I'm her niece's husband."

The voice faltered. "Oh, right."

Who on earth was this woman? "Pardon me for troubling you. I'll call back later." He was about to hang up.

"Wait a moment, please, Doctor Liston. Hold on."

Odder and odder. Whoever this woman was, she seemed to know who *he* was. He cradled the receiver in the crook of his neck and struggled to remove his tie. He kicked off his suede shoes and flopped down on the hotel bed. Jet lag had suddenly hit.

"Hello, Martin, is it really you? You're here, in Dublin?"

"Yes, Emer! I hope I'm not interrupting anything. Is this a convenient time?"

"What? Oh, Mags, yeah. Sorry about that. She's like a mother hen clucking round."

"Is everything OK?"

"Grand. I was having a nap. She presumed I didn't want to be disturbed. She's like a sentry; she'd be brilliant at Buckingham Palace. Of course when she realised who was on the phone, she – oh, never mind all that. So you're actually here in Dublin? I can't believe it."

"We wanted to surprise you."

"We?" Her voice rose animatedly. "Is Avril with you?"

"No, I didn't mean that. No, she couldn't make it this time. I'm here on my own on business. How are you?"

He heard the small intake of breath.

"Fine, thanks. All the better for talking to you now."

She did seem glad to hear from him but she was a bit hesitant.

"Is it all right if I call over to see you, Emer?"

"To *see* me?" she echoed inanely.

"Yes, I was hoping we'd meet up."

"Of course, but are you not going to stay here with me? I'm rattling around here on my own in this big house and I'd welcome the company."

"I'm staying in the Skylon Hotel."

"Why would you do that? You're staying with me and that's that. Why go to the expense and inconvenience of a hotel when I've a perfectly good room here for you? Grab your bag and come over straight away."

"No, really, thanks for your kind offer but the hotel is being paid for by the hospital. Oh, I haven't told you yet. I'm here for an interview."

"You're *what*!"

"Look, I'll tell you all when I see you. Avril will phone you later because she –"

"But why won't you stay with me. I have loads of space and –"

"I'm all checked in here now. It's convenient for the city and the airport, I've a nice room and the service so far is excellent and –"

"Well, if you're sure."

"I'm certain. That's settled. When would you like to meet up?"

"Tonight? Or does that suit? Maybe you have other plans?"

"No plans at all. I'll catch a cab and be over to your place about seven o'clock? OK? I'd like to take you out for a meal. Is there anywhere special you'd like me to book?"

"We are not going out to a restaurant when I've a fully-stocked fridge." God bless Mags, she thought. The idea of dressing up and going out to eat was not appealing. She was not up to it.

"I don't want to put you to any trouble –"

"It will be no bother at all."

"I'll bring wine. You prefer white or red?"

"Any colour, so long as it's alcoholic."

He laughed.

116

"I'm looking forward to seeing you, Martin."

"Same here."

Martin hung up. He stretched out on the bed and closed his eyes. There was something odd about the phone call. Emer had been as friendly and warm as ever and she sounded genuinely pleased to hear from him, but something was niggling him. She had most likely got a bit of a shock being phoned by him out of the blue like that but her voice sounded faint, croaky almost at the beginning of the conversation but then she'd kind of rallied. She was a bit breathless as well. Maybe she had a bout of flu or a chest infection and was too polite to put him off.

"Guess who's coming to dinner! Oh, Mags, what'll I do? He's coming tonight. I couldn't be rude to him and he seemed so eager and, oh God, what am I going to do?"

Mags pursed her lips. "Tell him. You'll have to tell him, Dory."

"But what about Avril –"

"Avril has to know. You'd have to tell her sooner or later and sooner is better, in my opinion." Mags said nothing about her conversation with Noelle, who had already sneaked Avril's number from the phone. This way Noelle wouldn't have to call the States. Martin could be the conduit.

Emer bit her lip. "I'm not ready to tell Avril."

"OK then, but you can tell her husband. You trust Martin. I mean, he's a doctor and all."

"He's here for an interview. God almighty, I didn't ask him a damn thing about it. He must think I'm a right gawm. Imagine I didn't have the savvy to ask him about the job? Mags, do you think they're considering a move to Ireland? They must be. Sure, what else could it be?" Emer's eyes glistened with excitement. "Avril living here?" She began to pace. "And me sick? More than sick. I'm dying. Mags, don't even think of disagreeing – I am dying." She shuddered. "This couldn't have happened at a worse time."

Maggie led her back to her armchair. "Now listen to me. You're getting agitated and that will serve no purpose. You wouldn't listen to me this morning and look at you now! You're wiped out. I knew you shouldn't have gone in to work. I told you it would be too much. You're going to have to take it easy, Emer."

"But I only went in for two hours and June was delighted to see me. She's under terrible pressure at the moment because the temp is only just trained and she's not very conscientious from what I gather. June was very grateful. I told her I'd go in again for a few hours tomorrow and –"

"Mr Noonan told you to rest."

"He told me to take my time coming to terms with the news. That's not the same thing."

"Well, how can you come to terms with anything if you're running away from it?"

"That's not fair, Maggie. I am *not* running away from it. I told you the facts and the stark reality and I told you I'm not under any illusions as to my recovery. Resting is not going to make it go away. I'm not fighting a cold here."

"But you need to conserve your energy, Emer."

"That's in short supply all right but the stint in the

library was great because it took my mind off myself for a few hours. That's good, isn't it?"

Maggie sighed, defeated. "What about Martin? What time is he arriving?"

"About seven." Emer clenched her fists. "Should I tell him tonight or what? What good would it do? Why upset him when he's probably only here for a few days? He has enough to be worrying about with the interview and everything."

Maggie shrugged.

"I'm fooling myself, is that what you're thinking?" Emer didn't give her friend a chance to respond. "He only has to look at me and he'll know. You wouldn't have to be a doctor to know there's something seriously wrong with me. He won't recognise me."

Mags opened the packet of cigarettes Emer had bought on her way home from the library earlier and handed her one. "Go on, have a puff. It might calm you."

Emer lit the cigarette, inhaled slowly and started to splutter. She gagged. "Oh, that's gross. Did you ever think you'd see the day when I couldn't smoke? Oh, that's revolting. How did I ever enjoy that filth?"

"How did any of us?" Maggie crushed out the cigarette in a long-disused ashtray on the mantelpiece.

"I'll have to be honest with Martin, won't I?"

A brief nod from Maggie.

"Well then, I'll tell him everything. He's used to this kind of thing. Probably trained how to cope with people like me."

Well for him, Maggie thought. *She* had had no training and was winging it big time. She put her arm around her friend, got her up off the chair and steered her towards the kitchen. "There you go then – he'll know how to handle you and he'll know how to tell Avril. He can make the decision what to tell her and when." Maggie rolled up her sleeves. "I'm going to vacuum the dining room and set the table for you."

"No. I can do it!"

"I know you can but you'll be busy here at the kitchen sink, chopping carrots and peeling potatoes. I left out the high stool for you so use it. No sense in standing when you can sit."

Emer laughed. "You needn't have bothered. I won't have time to develop varicose veins."

"That doesn't even merit a reply! Cook the salmon cutlets, why don't you? You make a lovely sauce for salmon, I've always loved it."

"I just mix tomato ketchup with fresh cream."

"Whatever! It's delicious. I picked up an apple tart as well so you can serve that for dessert."

"You never mentioned apple tart before. You must have been inspired!"

"I didn't come up the Liffey on a bicycle!"

This was awful. This absurd banter which had never existed before between them was widening a gulf and Maggie was all too aware of it.

Martin swirled the white wine round in his glass, his gaze fixed on the twirling lights reflected in the crystal glasses from the candles on the dining-room table. He nodded or murmured encouragingly from time to time and he smiled reassuringly at her as little by little the whole story came out.

She was pale and frightened-looking, so different from the flirty, funny lady he had met two years before at his wedding in Hawaii. She'd been the life and soul of the party, dancing and drinking and making up to his uncle. Emer had enchanted them all.

"Martin, you must promise not to tell Avril . . . not right away."

"I can hardly keep it from her."

"I just need more time to adjust to it myself before I can let her know."

"She'll come to Dublin – you *do* know that? Even if I don't get this job she'll come over to stay with you. She'll insist."

"Yes, she will. Martin, I'd do anything to spare her this unhappiness."

"I know that."

"She's the best thing that ever happened to me."

"Me too," he agreed.

They sat there staring into their empty glasses for a few moments.

"It's shit, Emer. What else is there to say? That's not very professional or profound or politically correct or even sensitive of me to say, but I think it's shit."

She was grateful and relieved for his honesty.

"I think it's shit too," she replied, her voice slurring. She was twisted, she suddenly realised – marvellously, deliciously drunk. "I'm going to open another bottle. More Chablis, I say!" She got up from the dining-room table, swayed on her feet and he guided her into the front room and the safety of the sofa.

"I'll get the wine." He was sober. He'd matched her

drink for drink but he might as well have been swallowing spring water. Her news had stunned him.

Avril was going to be heartbroken. That was the only clear thought he had. This news would consume her. Would it affect the pregnancy? Did she have to be told right away? What to do for the best? That was Martin's dilemma: what was best for Avril?

And best for Emer? She needed her niece and yet, tonight, she'd said she wasn't ready yet for Avril to know.

Naturally he kept it from Emer that Avril was expecting a child. He'd promised his wife to let her be the one to tell the good news and, anyway, it wouldn't have seemed appropriate to talk about impending birth when she was attempting to come to grips with imminent death.

On the other hand, maybe the news of the pregnancy would help Emer? She had always loved children, Avril had often told him. Hadn't she played a huge role in her niece's upbringing? Now she would have a grandniece or a grandnephew to spoil but the chances were that she wouldn't last long enough to see the child.

He opened the fridge and took out another bottle of white wine. He knew Emer had had enough, but it didn't seem to matter now. A hangover would be the least of her problems. And if it numbed her, no matter how temporary that numbness might be, that was fine with him.

He would cancel the taxi he'd booked to take him back to the hotel, stay with Emer tonight, keep her company, drink with her, listen to her, and put her to bed when she became sleepy. And he would be here for her in the morning when she woke up.

15

"The dinner was delicious, darling." Samuel Jones wiped his mouth with his white napkin, carefully smoothing the edges of his salt-and-pepper moustache. "How are you feeling, Avril?"

"Good, Dad, apart from the heat. I thought I'd pass out this lunchtime in the park. The humidity gets me big time."

"Yes, it's very oppressive. The air-conditioning is all right here? I can get someone to check it for you."

"No, it's working perfectly, thanks. The apartment is terrific, Dad. We'll . . . em, we'll miss it when we move."

"That needn't be for a long time, sweetie. You've plenty of room here for a nursery. I realise you'll want a house in the suburbs when your family grows, but there's no rush. Easy and slow, as your Grandma Jones always said."

Avril squirmed and shifted in her chair. How was she going to broach the subject?

"You're really all right?" He took her hand gently and stroked her palm, as he used to do when she was a small child.

"Fine. Just a bit uncomfortable."

"OK, let's go and sit on the couch."

She followed him. Her father, elegantly dressed in a navy pinstriped suit and pale lilac-coloured shirt, cut a dashing figure. He was six feet two in his bare feet. He had always appeared gigantic to her – big in size and big in character.

"So, Martin's enjoying the golf, is he? Have you heard from him today?" He'd poured more water for both of them and handed her a glass.

"Dad, I have a confession."

"Oh?"

Avril gulped from her glass. "He's not playing golf."

"But when he asked me for the week off he told me he was involved in some tournament or other in New Jersey."

"He's in Dublin."

"Dublin?"

"Yes."

Her father raised an eyebrow, never a good sign.

She held her breath.

He continued staring at her – more of a squint than a stare.

Avril nervously played with a cushion. She decided to take the bull by the horns. "He came for an interview."

"An interview!"

"Yes."

Sam stared harder at his daughter. She couldn't make out what he was thinking.

124

"It's in the Bon Secours Hospital, you know, on the north side of the city, near the Botanic Gardens. You know it, don't you? Seemingly they've built a large extension and have a brand new endoscopy clinic." She knew she was babbling. "It's state of the art, latest equipment and all that and it has attracted some of the top consultants in Ireland. They need another throat specialist. Martin heard about it through the grapevine and we discussed it and –"

"Did you?"

"Yeah, a friend of Martin from his college days bumped into him at that conference he attended last month and he – this university friend – has just returned from Ireland and he gave Martin the tip-off."

"How fortunate." Sam sat up straight, rather primly. "You didn't think to discuss it with me?" There was no mistaking his tone.

"Dad –"

"You didn't think it was my business?"

Avril concentrated on her clenched hands.

"It's preposterous. It really is. I gave Martin Liston his start. I set you both up in jobs at my clinic. I had intended to make him a partner once the baby arrived – a huge act of faith on my part. I suppose that's not good enough for you now. You want something else. Something you think is better –"

"No, Dad, not better, just different. We want a new start. We want to strike out on our own."

"You want to *what*?" he shouted.

She got up from her seat, came around the back of the couch and put her arms around his neck. "Dad, you know how much I love you and I appreciate everything you've done for us –"

"I don't think so, Avril. I don't think so at all."

"I know all the sacrifices you've had to make over the years. I realise how difficult it's been for you raising me on your own." She felt his shoulders stiffen. "I do love you, Dad."

"You've a funny way of showing it then. This is no way to thank me. You lied. Both of you lied to me."

She burrowed her head in the back his neck. "We didn't want to upset you."

"Ha!" He sat up straighter.

"Honestly, we wanted to spare you the worry."

"I'm not worried. I'm annoyed." His shoulders tensed again. "I thought we had a bond, Avril, that there were no secrets between us. We were always open, always considerate of one another's feelings – at least that's what I believed. I cannot understand this new departure. I'm hurt, Avril, deeply hurt. I can't believe you are capable of such ingratitude and duplicity."

Avril unwound herself from her father's neck, came around and sat by him. "Oh, Dad, it wasn't duplicity –"

"Well, what would you call it? Pretending he wanted time off for golf when all the time he was sneaking off to Ireland for a job interview?"

"Martin isn't a sneak. That's not fair."

"Don't you dare talk to me about fairness. Going behind my back is hardly fair. Stabbing me in the –"

"That's not true, Dad." Avril was angry now. "I've always done my best by you. I studied hard, made the grades and got to college. I married someone *suitable*, someone who had your full approval."

"Listen to me, my girl –"

126

"No, hear me out. Martin has always respected you. Why do you think we agreed to work with you in the clinic? But Dad, we have to move on. Martin needs new experiences, new horizons. You, above all people, must understand that. It's vital for a young doctor to get as much experience as he can."

"Bullshit! He can get it here. New York is the capital of the world!" he yelled. "Look around you. Who do you know of your age with a set-up like this? *Who?*"

Avril obediently admired the lavish room with its solid oak furniture, parquet floors, Turkish rugs and designer fine-bone china ranged in neat rows beside the crystal glasses in the cabinet.

"That young pup, who does he think he is, dragging my only child off to a foreign country without as much as a *by your leave*? And he's abandoning his excellent job in my clinic. He can get more experience here than he can in a small private hospital in Dublin. The goddamn nerve of him! This is a kick in the balls for me."

Avril stood up and stood squarely in front of him. "Maybe he won't get the job."

"And then he'll come crawling back here, will he? I'm supposed to accept that? What does he take me for?"

"It was *my* idea. Going to Ireland was *my* dream, not his."

They eyeballed each other.

"Martin went to that interview for my sake. I want to live in Ireland. I want to settle in Dublin and rear my child there."

"And why, pray tell me? I'm here. Martin's family is here. You are Americans. This is your proper place."

"I'm half Irish."

"Do you honestly imagine you will be accepted as Irish?"

"You're over-sensitive."

"Am I?"

"Oh, Dad –"

"Avril, you're making a dire mistake. Forget this nonsense."

"I want to live in Ireland. I've wanted to for a long time."

"Why?"

"It's a magical place, Dad."

He jumped up from the couch and walked to the large window, staring out at the spectacular view but not seeing it. "Oh, please, Avril, give me a break!"

"It is," she insisted. "Clean air, pure water, a slower pace of life, lovely people."

"Buzz words, brochure language."

"I love Ireland. I can't wait to get back there. My mood lifts every time I get off the plane and land on Irish soil."

"Get the shillelagh off the wall, why don't you?"

"Dad –"

He turned huffily. "Utter crap. I never took you for a fool, Avril."

"I'm not." His bitterness and his strong language upset her. He was normally so polite, so correct, so controlled. "What's wrong with loving a place?" she argued. "What's wrong with wanting to know your neighbours, to be able to stop and chat, to have time to enjoy the simple things – a cup of tea with the next-door neighbour, a drink in a local pub? When I'm in Ireland I always have a sense of something deep, something spiritual, something Celtic, I suppose."

"God give me patience! Rainy grey days, that's what I remember about Dublin, and smoke from the factories and people with snotty noses sneezing and wheezing in damp raincoats queuing for the dole. The poverty was palpable."

"Thirty years ago maybe. This is 2007 and Ireland is doing well, and anyway material things are not what I'm after. It's not always raining there, either. They have a kind climate – no tsunamis, no hurricanes, no tornadoes. What's a little shower of rain? I love the weather in Ireland – the rain, the soft winds, the mists on the mountains. I love it all, Dad. What's wrong with that?"

"Economic booms don't last. You're describing Shangri-La, not Ireland of the twenty-first century and definitely not Dublin, with its exorbitant house prices, narrow-minded conservatives, dreadful transport system – possibly the worst in the world – and a healthcare service in severe crisis. In my opinion they're heading for a crash. Maybe you imagine Martin as some kind of crusader who can fix the ills of the Irish?"

"What if I do? You used to think it was noble to be of use to others."

"You both can be of use here where you belong." He crossed the room but this time chose the armchair opposite her to sit in. He tried to repress the tremor in his voice. "You have a deeply flawed over-romantic view of Irish people too. They're not all the friendly, helpful, perfect paragons who invite you in to tea at the drop of a hat.

They are a race of people, like any other, with all the human frailties of greed, meanness, bigotry and cruelty." He took out his immaculately laundered handkerchief and blew his nose. "I can bear testimony to that."

"Meaning?"

"Forget it."

"No, what do you mean, Dad?"

"Just be aware, Avril, that any problems you encounter here you will also meet there – possibly more problems, financial ones at any rate. You are doing well here in New York. Why change and why now? I'd like your baby to be born here. I want my grandchild to be close by. Why do you want to go running to a place you don't know apart from holidays?"

Avril folded her lower lip under her top teeth for a second or two as she built herself up to say what she knew would hurt him. "I feel a genuine connection to Ireland. My mother was Irish."

"Leave your mother out of it."

"No." She was defiant.

"Ireland killed your mother."

She was stunned. "How can you say that? Chance killed her, an unfortunate accident. It happened in Dublin but it could have happened here or anywhere else on the planet."

He drummed his fingers impatiently on the wooden arm of his leather armchair. "I don't want to talk about the accident and I don't want to discuss her."

"Her? Why can't you say her name? You can't even say her name – it's hurtful to me, Dad." This time she wouldn't be put off by his evasiveness. "*I* want to talk about my

130

mother. Why do you always avoid the subject? I need to talk. I have to know about her."

"It was a long time ago and in the past." He lowered his voice. He came back and sat beside her again on the large sofa. "Your mother is with the angels. Leave her in peace."

"I've no desire to disturb her peace, but what about mine, Dad? All my life I've wondered about her. There are so many unanswered questions. You never talk about her." She clasped his hands in her own. "You don't keep photos of her. There's no sign of her in your home. It's as if she didn't exist."

"I loved your mother with my whole heart and soul, with all my being. Then I lost her." He appealed to his daughter with a piteous look in his soft dark eyes. "Why would I have inflicted my suffering on you? You were an infant, an innocent, barely eight months old when she died. I thought it better to say nothing to you. I didn't accept her death. Not then and —"

He stopped suddenly and withdrew his hands, retiring back to the comfort of his self-imposed shell.

"And now?" she prompted.

"What's the point in raking over past pain? She's gone. I miss her. You don't remember her."

"And that's my pain!" Avril cried. "I have no picture of her in my head. Oh yes, Emer has shown me all the photos of her in Dublin and she gave me photos of your wedding, which I then felt compelled to hide from you. That's hardly healthy, is it?"

He closed his eyes and didn't answer.

"If it wasn't for Emer I don't know what I'd have known or believed. She has filled me in about their childhood in

Dublin. Granny Dorgan told me stories too but I can't understand why you shut my mother out, Dad."

"I don't want to remember," he said quietly.

"That's selfish. I need you to remember for me. I'm relying on you to supply the missing details, to create a picture, your picture of my mother for me. What about your courtship? Your wedding? My birth? I only have Emer's version. And what about the happy months spent together in the little flat in Dorset Street? Emer said that you were really happy together in those early days. Mum's death devastated you and it's awesome what you've achieved on your own. I know you've been lonely."

She didn't refer to the fact that her father had been far from celibate down through the years. Why should he have deprived himself of the intimacy and company of other women, anyhow? She didn't expect him to be a martyr. She knew some of his affairs had been serious, some frivolous, but he had kept these women out of her life. For that she was grateful.

"I know you had a tough start, Dad. Emer even brought me once to show me where the little flat was. It became a furniture emporium at one stage, now it's abandoned. Nobody lives or works there." Avril stifled a sob. "The building looked forsaken the day Emer took me there. They're going to pull it down."

"Now you're upset," he said. "That's why I never dwelt on those days, Avril. It was another life. Jackie was the most wonderful person I have ever known. By some miracle she loved me. We created you and you're my blessing."

Avril felt a rush of affection for him.

"We *were* happy together, Jackie and me. We had very little money, some weeks barely enough to make ends meet, but love is a powerful antidote to poverty. Night after night we sat over a one-bar electric fire and she read library books while I studied. She worked in a bakery for a paltry wage. At the end of every week we barely had enough money to buy food, but she put up with it for my sake."

She squeezed his hand again. "Go on, Dad, please."

He took a deep breath, as if to suppress an ache. "After you came along, she had to give up her job, so we lived on a pittance. She wanted me to be free to study, to qualify as a doctor. Jackie had complete faith in me. She suffered deprivation so that I could continue my studies. Your mother was a marvel, never complained, never felt sorry for herself. That wasn't her way. She was funny too, very funny and witty and . . . passionate."

Avril laughed with delight. "Oh, Dad, how wonderful! Tell me more."

He suddenly had an urge to talk, to unburden himself of the years of silence. "She had a great sense of humour although admittedly it was often a bit dark. She had her mother's sense of irony."

"Emer has that too. I think it's an Irish thing."

"Jackie was . . ." he hesitated. It was good to speak her name aloud. "Jackie was everything to me. She calmed me when I was uptight about my studies, caressed me when I was down, made me laugh when I got too serious. She poked fun at my Americanisms and was good-natured when I took off her Irish accent. She sang to me when I was homesick. She had a lovely singing voice, a rich alto. We'd always wanted a piano but of course we'd no room in the flat even if we could have afforded it, which we couldn't. She used to sing and play in Cabra Road with Emer. They both loved those musical evenings." He paused, a far-away, dreamy look in his dark eyes. "Your mother was beautiful inside and out, a good-hearted, fun-loving, compassionate woman."

He caught his breath in this swell of emotion. Avril didn't dare disturb his sudden outpourings.

"One cold November evening, just after dinner, she went out in the dark to buy milk and she never came back." His voice began to quiver. "I left Ireland as soon as I qualified from university. I hated the place from then on. Emer took time off work in the few months after your mother's death to take care of you."

Avril nodded.

"Darling, I'm well aware of how you love Emer. I understand why you do and I'm grateful to her too. When she came to Hawaii for your wedding, she reminded me of your mother – a blonde version, at any rate. I hated to see her as a middle-aged woman."

"But why?"

"My Jackie is young and beautiful, forever young, and I need to keep her so in my mind's eye. What have I now but a few happy memories to keep her alive in my heart?"

Avril rocked, cradling her stomach in her outstretched palms, crooning and softly singing to herself.

Her father, a huge lump in his throat, looked on helplessly.

16

Martin checked in his suitcase at the Aer Lingus desk. Normally he would travel with hand luggage only, but Avril had given him a list of stuff to buy in *Carraig Donn* and The Kilkenny Shop, so he'd had to bring the large case. He was lucky he didn't have to pay the excess weight charge. He knew she wanted the cutlery and the table linen as gifts for his parents and her father – presents to placate them. She was assuming he'd get the job. Avril always expected the best to happen – he loved that about her.

He joined Emer and Maggie in the crowded dining area upstairs. Maggie had driven them to the airport through a downpour. It was obvious she hadn't wanted her friend to be alone when he said goodbye. This wasn't exactly a fond farewell: he was on his way home to the States to tell his wife the bad news.

He had phoned New York a few days earlier to tell Avril her aunt wasn't well and that they should wait before telling her about the pregnancy. When Emer took the phone from him and spoke to her niece, she'd pretended she had a bad chest infection. Martin hadn't enlightened his wife because he knew she'd need someone with her when she heard the news and he wanted that person to be him.

"Cappuccino?" Maggie pushed the frothy drink towards him.

"Thanks, Maggie." He popped two white cubes into the cup. "I should be watching my blood sugar."

"Live dangerously!" Emer offered him a cream cake.

"No, thanks, I'll resist." He made an effort to smile.

"I've to go to the loo," Maggie said tactfully. She stood up and slung her big black leather handbag over her shoulder. "I'm going to get a newspaper. Would you like one for the plane, Martin?"

"An *Irish Times*," he suggested. "Maybe an *Independent* too. Avril will want to read all the Irish news." He took his wallet from his inside jacket pocket.

"Put that away." Maggie waved away his reluctance. "I'll get you some fruit sweets too, shall I? I have to suck during take-off or my ears give me hell."

"Thanks, that would be great."

With a smile, Maggie left.

"She's a wonderful friend," Martin said.

"I'm very lucky."

"What goes around comes around." He admired her tenacity and her gratitude. Even now as she lived a death sentence Emer could appreciate the good things in her life.

"When will you tell Avril?" Emer, avoiding his gaze, stared around at other travellers. The airport was jammed as usual: cranky children, scolding mothers, bawling babies and fraught fathers balancing over-filled trays, climbing over crawling toddlers. A few high-spirited, drunken teenagers emerged from the bar area, singing raucously.

"I'll tell her tonight," Martin said quietly. "No point in postponing it. She'll phone you tomorrow, Emer."

"I'll be ready."

"I'll have to give it to her straight."

"I realise that."

"Avril will want to come over."

"When you get the job?"

"Even if I don't get it, Emer, she'll come. She wouldn't dream of not coming."

"She's obstinate."

"A family trait." He checked his boarding card. "Listen, about the treatment –"

"I don't want it, I told you." She looked away again but not before he saw her grim expression.

"Yes, I know what you said but I have to beg you to reconsider."

Emer took a deep breath and turned back to him. "I see no point in dragging out the inevitable. I know what those treatments can do to you."

"Things have improved vastly since your mother's time," he said softly.

"Have they? Not according to some patients who appeared on *The Late Late Show*. Conditions in the hospitals are scary – scarier than the cancer itself in some cases. Martin, I appreciate what you're trying to do here but I have made up my mind. I would have opted for treatment if . . . if it wasn't so far advanced."

"Well, you know the old adage: doctors differ and –"

"Patients die," she finished for him.

"They don't have to die; that's my point, Emer. You –"

"I trust Noonan."

"I know that but –"

"He's not a bullshitter. He agrees that I left it too late. I should have gone to my GP ages ago. I chose not to, so now I have to accept the consequences."

Martin pursed his lips.

"Go on, argue with me," she prodded gently. "Tell me all the statistics and facts. Tell me that everyone reacts differently; that maybe I do have a chance. Inspire me with the notion of new drugs and wonder cures. Tell me to seek another opinion. Ask me to submit to more tests. Go on – isn't that your job as a doctor?"

"It's my job as your friend."

"I know what Avril will want. She'll think I should go to the States for more medical tests. She'll argue that the best oncologists and researchers are there."

"Yes, and I'll agree with her."

"Naturally you will. Look, Martin, I haven't the energy to argue with you. I promise I will keep my appointment with Noonan tomorrow. I'll take it from there."

"And you'll listen to him?"

"Yes."

"Emer, you will really listen?"

"Yes, I will. I swear."

"OK."

Maggie arrived back with a bundle of papers and two bags of sweets. "Here you go." She handed him a small gift-wrapped parcel. "Some perfume for Avril."

"You're very kind." He felt gauche, tongue-tied, had an overpowering need to get out of there. He stood up suddenly. "Better make tracks."

"I'll see you to the departure gates," Emer offered.

"I'd prefer if you didn't. You sit and finish your coffee." He shook hands with Maggie.

"Give my love to Avril," Maggie whispered.

Martin grabbed Emer and hugged her skinny body. He turned and walked off hurriedly, without a backward glance.

Noelle arrived to spend the night with Emer and was heading up the garden path when Cheryl, from next door, rushed over to speak to her.

"How is she? God help her, isn't it awful?"

"Yes, it is," Noelle said flatly.

"It's tragic. Emer was such an energetic woman. I've always admired her. She was so full of life."

Noelle bristled at the use of the past tense. "She's not dead yet."

"Is her visitor gone back to America?"

"Yes, Cheryl, but he'll probably be back."

The neighbour's eyes opened wider. "Really?"

"Why do you ask?"

Cheryl sniffed. "No reason. I just thought it a bit odd. Old Mrs Kelly down the road told me he was married to Emer's niece, but I knew she must be mistaken."

Noelle felt her heckles rising. "Why?"

"Well, I mean he's . . . he's –"

"Black?" Noelle interrupted.

Cheryl blushed. "Yes – it's not that I'm a racist, but I just couldn't imagine –"

139

"No, I suppose you couldn't."

"I mean I heard he's a doctor and everything but I couldn't visualise how . . . how Emer's niece would marry a . . . a . . ."

"Black man." Noelle felt like punching her in the face. "I think you can call *them* black now, Cheryl. I think *they* prefer to be called black or African American."

"Sorry, I didn't intend to cause offence. I mean, I haven't been living in this neighbourhood for very long. I didn't realise he was a relation. There are so many of them . . . the foreigners, I mean, there are loads of them around here but . . . sorry, I . . . Well, I just presumed he was a client from the library who needed English classes or something. Emer's very good to the n-n-n –"

"Non-Irish nationals?" Noelle snapped.

"Yes exactly, that's what I thought – that he was a non-national, I mean a non-Irish national." She seemed grateful to latch on to this term. "How was I supposed to know he was actually related to Emer? I've never met her family. None of them," she added pointedly.

"Emer's niece last visited here two years ago before you moved in. She used to come here every summer. She didn't come last year because she was married and of course Emer had gone to the States for the wedding the year before."

"Of course." Cheryl lowered her voice. "Does Emer accept this man?"

"Accept him? As what?"

Cheryl clicked her tongue in a very annoying way. "Accept him as her niece's husband, of course. I mean to say it must be awkward."

"Awkward?"

"I personally don't have anything against black people. Look at all the foreigners living in the country now. I mean I think it's wonderful, all the Eastern Europeans. Fred doesn't agree, of course, thinks they're ruining the job market."

"Does he?" If her lazy sod of a husband ever got off his arse to look for a job he might have some cause for complaint, Noelle thought.

"Yeah, says they work for a pittance and that makes it hard for our lads to earn a decent wage."

"That's one way of looking at it."

Cheryl coughed nervously. "But I don't agree with him, naturally. I think it's amazing for Ireland to have all these different nationalities living here."

"Do you?"

"Oh, yes." She paused. "Adds colour and culture and all that. But when it comes to marriage –"

"Are you referring to Emer's niece again now?"

"Indeed."

"I wouldn't worry, Cheryl. They have a great marriage. They're extremely happy. I'll lay a bet that they'll come here to live so that they can care for Emer during her illness."

"Come here? You mean to Dublin?"

"Yes, to Dublin. To Cabra. To this house."

"Oh?" came the strangled response.

"Why not? Emer has loads of room."

"I see."

Noelle was enjoying this. "What is it that's worrying you exactly? Having a black man living next door to you, is that it?"

"No, no, not at all." Cheryl glared. "Of course not. I've no objection to black people. How dare you insinuate that I'm anti anybody? We're all God's creatures. It's just that Emer's niece may have to cope with gossip and censure and . . . lots of people don't like mixed-race marriages."

"Cheryl, this is the twenty-first century. We've moved on. Even in this little island of ours, we've moved on."

"Don't be so flippant. There are issues here. Some people feel that it's better to marry someone from your own ethnic background. It makes sense and I'm not apologising for sharing that view."

"Mixed race? Oh, is that what you're upset about?"

Cheryl bit her lip. "To be candid, yes. I myself don't think it works. Young couples have enough to cope with when they get married. It's my opinion they're better off being married to someone from the same race and background as themselves. It becomes too complicated when –"

Noelle nodded. "You needn't fret about that at all."

"Pardon?"

"You were worried about Emer's niece, Avril, being hitched to a black man. Right?"

"Hitched is hardly the word I'd use but –"

"Worry no more, Cheryl. Avril did marry a man from her race and definitely her background."

"But . . . but –"

"I see you're confused. Well, I'll explain it to you, shall I?" Noelle couldn't keep the acerbity from her voice. "Avril is black too – not as black as her husband of course. There are various shades of black. Maybe the different colours and shades look down on each other too. Who knows? Racism isn't confined to one set of people, as we well know."

"Really, there's no need to be rude. I was merely saying –"

"Cheryl, you're digging yourself in deeper. I know exactly what you were saying and I'm informing you that Emer Dorgan, your lily-white neighbour – no, Emer is more a pale pink colour, isn't she? Well, in any case, she has a gorgeous, clever black niece, a marvellous, talented, highly esteemed black brother-in-law and a hunk of a black nephew-by-marriage who is a distinguished surgeon." Noelle stopped for breath but she didn't give Cheryl time to react. "And even if they had menial jobs or were unemployed – like your Fred – it would make no difference. They are Emer's family and we all love them. How does that grab you?"

Noelle wasn't one bit ashamed of her rising venom. This woman had enraged her. Hadn't Emer enough to contend with without this blatant racism on her doorstep? Choking back more furious words, Noelle turned on her heel and strode purposefully to Emer's front door.

She was trembling with anger. Thirty years before it had been exactly the same for Jackie.

17

Despite Emer's protests, Noelle insisted on going with her to the hospital for her visit to the oncologist the following morning.

"Every relationship should be a reciprocal arrangement," she quoted her husband, Brendan the bastard, who had reciprocated her loyalty with betrayal. The typical scenario – left her for a younger woman who was now expecting his child. That was the worst part and she kept it from her friends because she wouldn't be able to abide their inevitable embarrassment.

When they'd been married, Brendan had convinced her they didn't need or want children and she, reluctantly, had agreed at first. She was young and ambitious and at that time saw children as a possible hindrance and not a blessing, and of course she'd convinced herself that she had loads of time to have a family later. He'd helped her set up the salon – in fact he was the instigator. He had praised her abilities, encouraged her efforts, advised her on everything, especially how to hone her business skills. He was pleased when she made progress, considering her successes his achievement as well as hers. Looking back, Noelle realised that she had played the self-effacing Eliza Doolittle to his self-important Higgins.

Everyone told her how lucky she was to have him. He had showered her with expensive presents: gold watches, designer clothes and a Bentley. She had hated that car with a passion because it was so pretentious, awkward to drive and hard to park. She had sold it the day after they split.

Brendan, according to all her acquaintances, business contacts and friends, had been the model husband. He had worked like a Trojan in his construction company and made handsome profits, employed a housekeeper so Noelle didn't have to bother with domestic duties, brought her on two foreign holidays a year, was generous to a fault.

Her sister Jenny had never liked him. Brendan the paragon was, in reality, a 'philanderer', as Jenny had so succinctly put it. In Noelle's view now, he was a pathetic, middle-aged, over-sexed, over-eager wanker, who thought a baby would bring back his youth. If she ever met him pushing a pram, she'd punch him in his smug mug.

But Emer's illness put everything else into perspective.

In the plush waiting room of the private hospital, Noelle sat staunchly by her friend. The room was tastefully decorated in cream and blue and the elegant windows were draped in royal-blue velvet curtains that Noelle thought particularly nice. A long mahogany table dominated the centre and there were neat piles of magazines and periodicals to distract the patients and their loved ones.

Noelle chatted away about her latest fashion purchases, the new season's styles, the hairdressing business in general and hers in particular, the difficult clients, everything and anything she could think of to take her friend's mind off the purpose of this visit. Finally Emer was called in.

"Good luck. I'm right here." Noelle hugged her hard and walked with her to the door of Mr Noonan's rooms. "Right here," she stressed.

No sooner had Noelle sat down again than her mobile rang. There were no other patients waiting, so she decided to take the call.

"Hello."

"Is that Noelle?"

The nervous voice at the other end alarmed Noelle, who was already up to high doh.

"Who's this?"

"Avril."

"Oh, hi, Avril." How did she get this number?

"I'm sorry to disturb you. I rang Maggie as soon as Martin told me the news and she said you had gone to the hospital with Emer."

It must be the middle of the night in New York. Avril sounded frantic. Noelle made a huge effort to keep her voice steady. "She's just gone in this minute to see the specialist."

Noelle could hear a soft gasp.

"He's one of the finest doctors in Ireland, Avril," Noelle assured her. "Emer's in very good hands."

"How is she?"

Noelle searched for the right words. "Bearing up. She's bearing up."

"I've booked a flight for tomorrow. I'll be in Dublin late tomorrow night."

"Emer will be glad."

"I don't want you to tell her I'm coming."

"I see," Noelle said but she didn't see at all.

"I don't want her to start worrying about me or the flight or picking me up or tidying the house or anything like that."

"Right, right, but listen, I'm free tomorrow night. I can pick you up."

"There's no need. The flight doesn't get in till after eleven. There'll be no shortage of cabs at that hour."

"I'd hate to think of you queuing for a taxi. It wouldn't be right. I'll meet you."

"OK, thanks, Noelle. It's an Aer Lingus flight. Hold on, I can't find the e-mail with the flight number."

"Don't worry. An Aer Lingus flight from New York – how many can there be at that hour?"

"I'm all over the place. Can I text you the number later?"

"Grand."

A slight pause followed. "How does Emer seem to you? Maggie was too choked up to tell me much."

Noelle hesitated.

"Noelle, I'd prefer the truth."

"She looks scared. You may get a shock when you see her. She's lost a lot of weight."

"So Martin said."

"He was great with her. Myself and Maggie are doing our best and Jane in the library has been very understanding."

"Does everyone know?" Avril sounded hurt.

"Only those closest to her." Noelle realised too late how that must sound. "She didn't tell you, Avril, because she didn't know *how* to tell you. That's why Martin's visit was a godsend. She couldn't bear the thought of hurting you. It's very . . . hard."

"I've been crying and crying since Martin told me. I tried to calm myself before phoning you, but now that I hear your voice . . ." A stifled sob followed.

"You can rest easy that we are taking care of her but it will be marvellous for her to have you here." Noelle's voice trembled. "You're family."

"Has she told her brother?"

"Ronan? God, no. At least I don't think so. I very much doubt it."

"But now it's different. She –"

"I'm not certain, Avril. It's been such a long time since they spoke. Maybe you can talk to her?"

"I will. I think she should contact him. I'm sure she should. I'd better let you go, Noelle. I've lots to sort out here."

"You must have."

"There'll be no problem with work or time off or anything like that once I tell my father."

"This news will affect him badly."

"I'm afraid so. Too much unfinished business that he hasn't come to terms with yet. He's great but can be difficult at times. I don't know what I'd do without Martin. He's my rock."

"Mind yourself, Avril. I'll be in Arrivals waiting for you tomorrow night from eleven."

Emer was wobbly when she came out.

This visit was much worse than the previous one for Noelle because this time she was aware of what her friend was going through. She took Emer by the hand and sat her down on the leather sofa. "Well?"

Emer shrugged. "I've agreed to a few more tests."

"That's good."

"Not really," Emer replied despondently. "I'm just going through the motions. I don't hold out any hope myself but if it makes Martin or Maggie or . . . you . . . feel better, then I don't mind."

Noelle squeezed Emer's hand. "You have to try everything."

"He definitely won't be operating. It could do more harm than good."

Noelle didn't like the sound of that. "So what tests are we talking about?"

"Bloods and other stuff. There are some new drugs he wants to try on me. He has to see if I'm a suitable candidate. He's going to confer with a colleague in the States – some guy who's an expert and who's been working on a new medicine. It's all quite confusing and complicated and I hate talking about it."

Noelle stood up. "Let's get the hell out of here. When are you having the tests?"

"Day after tomorrow."

Grand, Noelle thought. Avril would be with her by then.

"It's a nice day. Will we go for a stroll in the Phoenix

Park?" Noelle suggested as they walked to the main entrance of the hospital. "Or we could go out to Malahide for a saunter on the beach. It could be lashing tomorrow. This summer is the wettest I remember."

Emer hadn't noticed the day until that moment: had not seen the early morning sun rising and splashing her bedroom with its soft golden light, hadn't felt the warm rays through the car windscreen. She hadn't put out cake for her robin, either. She was beginning not to notice things, she told herself. It was vital to pay attention: to observe everything, be aware of the world around her. She couldn't afford to waste a precious second.

"Malahide sounds good. First, could you come with me to Marks and Sparks, Noelle? I need new nighties and some underwear. I should stock up for . . ."

Noelle cleared her throat. "I fancy a look into Per Una myself. Feel a new skirt coming on."

"Yeah, I may indulge, too." Emer stuck her hand into the waistband of her navy trousers. "Everything's getting too big. Or rather, I'm getting too small."

Taking her cue from the conversation with Avril, Noelle decided to pursue another line of inquiry as they arrived at the car park. "Is there anyone else you'd like to tell at this stage?"

"Not that I can think of."

"Well, there's no rush anyhow, but people like to be kept in the loop, Emer."

There might be more of a rush than any of them realised, Emer reflected. Jane, at the library, when told the news, had reacted exactly as Emer knew she would. She had burst into tears. How would her other colleagues react?

18

It was almost midnight when Maggie, elegantly swathed in a flowing pink-silk dressing gown, opened the front door of the Cabra Road house and let them in. She hugged Avril in a tight embrace and the younger woman had to fight a compelling urge to cry. This was the first time she had ever entered this house without her aunt having picked her up at the airport. Now she wasn't even waiting at the door. The mugginess of the night added to Avril's pervading sense of doom.

Noëlle carried the suitcases into the hall. "Is she awake?"

"She's having a bath," Maggie whispered. "I told her I'd bring her up a mug of Complan when she was tucked up in bed. She loathes it but she has to have some nourishment. She has the appetite of a bird."

"Let me do it," Avril pleaded.

Emer had difficulty hauling her thin body out of the bath. She felt exhausted. All her bones and muscles ached in spite of the aromatic salts and fresh rose petals that Maggie had scattered in the bath. Emer blew out the scented candle Maggie had left on the windowsill above the toilet, took the clean green towel from the wicker chair and slowly dried herself. Wilting with the heat and her growing lack of energy, she pulled the new soft cotton nightie over her head and eased it over her breasts and belly. Emer hated her body now, hated its fragility.

In the bedroom Maggie had lit the bedside lamp and rolled down the duvet, which she had placed neatly at the end of the bed. Emer slid between the cool sheets and was touched to discover that her friend had splashed her pillow with lavender oil. Its soothing fragrance permeated the air of the bedroom. Emer was rubbing in hand-cream when she heard footsteps on the stairs.

"Thanks, Maggie," she said as the bearer of her Complan entered. "I'm ready for your gruesome concoction now. Hope you added a dash of brandy to it. I'm beginning to get used to this room service." She was lying through her teeth. She hated people waiting on her.

"Emer, it's me!"

Emer's heart thumped as she recognised the mellow tones of her niece. Her mouth fell open in stupefaction. "Oh my God. I must be dreaming."

Avril came into the room, carefully placed the hot steaming mug on a coaster on the bedside table, sat down on the edge of the bed and slumped into the thin outstretched arms of her aunt. Emer, overwhelmed with joy, shifted over to make space and her niece stretched out full length beside her on top of the sheet.

They embraced for a long, long time.

Noelle accepted a glass of spring water from Maggie. The humidity was getting to her and she was parched. "This heat is overbearing. You'd imagine the rain would cool things down but it hasn't. I think we'll have thunder." She gulped down half the iced water.

"Avril looks great." Maggie poured herself tea and cut up an apple tart, a slice of which she passed to Noelle. "What did she say on the drive here?"

"She wants to try all possible treatments. She understands why Emer has refused chemotherapy because Martin had a chat with some expert in New York. Judging from her scan and other tests results, it *is* too late for Emer to bother with it. It would just make her sicker with no real benefit."

"Alternative medicines may help," Maggie said.

"Avril mentioned them too. Diet for one thing. In any case she's ready to take on Emer's care. She had a good cry with me but promised she'd keep it together when she saw Emer. I feel so sorry for her. Emer is her only connection with her mother and now this."

Maggie bit her lip. "I've been thinking . . ."

Noelle munched on a slice of tart. "Mmh?"

"Emer's next tests are tomorrow morning?"

"Yeah, at ten. I offered to go with her but Avril said no – that she was going to hire a car."

Maggie sipped her tea. "Let Avril do it. She needs to feel useful."

"Like the rest of us, Maggie."

"If they don't keep her in hospital, and I doubt they will, what about me taking her to Spain for a week? It would do her good."

Noelle was incredulous. "What about Avril? She won't leave her. I mean the girl has only just arrived."

"Well, naturally I didn't mean straight away. Maybe in a few days or even next week? Avril is here for the long haul, I'm sure. She could come too."

"I think you're nuts." Noelle gulped down the remainder of the water. "This is no time for a holiday. Emer wouldn't dream of it."

Maggie folded her lips in that determined way that irked Noelle. "There's method in my madness, Noelle. I have another idea."

Noelle bristled. Maggie was full of bright ideas suddenly.

Maggie, untroubled by Noelle's unspoken criticism, went on. "You know how Emer always wanted to get this kitchen done up?"

"Well, she's been talking about it for years. Hates the drabness."

"I was wondering how her finances might be."

"She hasn't discussed money with me recently. What's your point, Maggie?"

"If Emer went away on a short holiday, we could arrange for a kitchen company to come in and overhaul this place."

Noelle shook her head. "She's too ill for that. It's a crazy idea. Dealing with painters and renovators is always a nightmare and that's when you're in the full of your health."

"But she'd be away," Maggie persisted.

"I'm quite sure Emer doesn't give two damns about such mundane matters as decorating. Haven't you noticed how worn out she is? How many days does Emer have?

None of us knows, do we?" Noelle's words shocked even herself.

"Hang on, let's think this thing through," Maggie said. "It looks like she'll be spending more time at home now and environment is so important, isn't it? You'd agree with that, Noelle – look how pleased you are with the salon."

"You have a point," Noelle sighed irritably. "But the disturbance would be too much for her. Definitely."

"I have it!" Maggie exclaimed. "Let Avril go to Spain with Emer and leave me out of it. I'll give them the keys to the apartment and any instructions about the air-conditioning and the locks and all that. It would give them a chance to have some private time together."

"The doctors won't let her go."

"They aren't going to rule her life now, Noelle. She made that clear to me. We have to let Emer make her own judgements."

"I do agree with you there. She does need to get some sense of power back. That's one of the worst things about this illness. It's made her feel completely vulnerable and out of control. A little while away would give her space."

Maggie was relieved. She needed Noelle's full support. "A kitchen renovation would also give her a huge lift. The only problem is that it's so hard to get good people at short notice."

Noelle brought her plate and glass to the sink. "That bunch I had in to do up the salon were great and they have a kitchen crew too. I could give them a ring and explain the urgency of the situation."

Maggie beamed. "Do it first thing in the morning and

I'll speak to Avril tonight before I leave. Get her opinion."

"Grand. So, text me early in the morning and I'll get on to them if that's what Avril wants." Noelle took up her handbag. "I won't go up to Emer now. I'm sure it's very emotional up there."

Maggie walked her out to the door. "You think I'm cracked worrying about renovating, don't you? I just need to know I'm doing something."

"I understand. This house means a lot to Emer and it would be nice to have it more comfortable for her, especially as the end approaches. But while she's talked about it a lot, Emer doesn't like surprises. We'll speak to Avril first and take it from there." Noelle linked Maggie in her old chummy way. "Right. I'm sure Avril will be in favour. If I can get the lads in, you book the flights." She took a look around the hallway. "This could do with a lick of paint too. And her bedroom is a bit grubby."

"The whole house? That's a bit too ambitious maybe? Unless we all chipped in. Jesus, Noelle, we can't just take over. Let's deal with the kitchen first. I know Joe would be willing to help out but I'd like him to tackle the garden."

"I'm a dab hand with a paintbrush," Noelle said proudly. "I'll ask Gerald for help too."

"The priest? He'd help?"

"Of course. And he has a few lads from the youth club who'd give a hand. There'll be no shortage of people."

"What about Cheryl next door?"

"We're not asking her." Noelle was adamant.

Maggie accepted that without debate.

"You're good with colours, Maggie, so would you

choose nice bedclothes for Emer's room? And matching curtains? What about the carpet up there? It's very shabby."

"Let's not go too far with our planning, Noelle. Emer's feelings about all this have to be considered."

Noelle ignored her. "I know a bloke who does a great job with wooden floors. Emer would love her floors upstairs sanded like the ones down here, she told me that. This house has great potential. It's old and they used to put fine material into the old houses."

Maggie found herself being drawn in, but she felt they couldn't possibly do all that without Emer's express permission. Besides, it would cost a fortune and who would pay?

"And could you choose a nice soft rug for her bedside? And a few others for around the house. I'll rally the troops and get everything organised. I can get it all under way immediately once I get a deal from the renovation company. If the worst comes to the worst, we could hire a carpenter to do a nixer. Do you know a good plumber, by any chance?"

Maggie had to smile at Noelle's sudden burst of enthusiasm. Nothing suited Noelle more than a new project. She positively glowed once she had something to plan and supervise.

"Try the kitchen company first."

"Rightyo." Noelle pecked her on the cheek. "You pave the way with Avril. It all depends on what she says."

And Emer too, Maggie thought.

19

Avril stroked her aunt's back in large circular movements – exactly what Emer used to do for her when she was a child – role reversal. She helped Emer to sip from the mug and noted how hard it was for her to swallow. She would speak to Martin about muscle relaxants.

"Are you in pain?" Avril asked bluntly as she replaced the mug on the bedside table.

"More discomfort than pain." Emer tried to keep her tone dismissive. "It's not too bad." She didn't admit that her symptoms were unrelenting.

"You've always been a stalwart, Emer."

"I'm not going to lie down under this, but I'm learning to accept and cope with the hand I've been dealt."

Avril went back to the stroking, which seemed to give both of them comfort. "You've got great fortitude. Martin told me how brave you are."

"I'm not brave, darling, but I'm tired of worrying, tired of the discomfort, tired of being scared. I feel so bloody tired all the time."

Avril kissed her forehead. "There are things we can do to alleviate your symptoms. Some natural remedies are fantastic."

"Maggie is all into aromatherapy – no doubt you can smell her efforts here in this room! The lavender can be a bit overpowering, but it does help to calm me."

"What about your diet? You should eat lots of fruit. Berries are particularly good. Dad always told me that."

"Maggie has been buying them for me. I find them easy to swallow and digest, especially with yoghurt."

"I'm a great believer in seeds too. We can make our own vegetable soup and there are lots of fruit and vegetables with anti-oxidant properties."

"I've no objections to eating well. Vitamins may well raise my energy levels. If they work even for a little while, it's small effort and will be worth it."

"I'm going to hire a car first thing in the morning. We'll take a taxi into the Mater Hospital and when you're in having the tests, I'll pick it up and then we're free to do whatever you want, go anywhere you want. I'll need to get an automatic, though. I'd never cope with gears. Bad enough I have to drive on the left."

"I can still drive and my Punto is going strong."

"I want to indulge you, and your Punto is not the most comfortable car, you'd have to agree. Yes, yes, you hate being mollycoddled but you'll have to humour me this time, OK?"

"How long can you stay, darling?"

"Oh, Emer, I'm not going anywhere."

"Did Martin get the job? Are you moving here permanently?"

Avril stopped stroking and put her arms around Emer's shoulders, cradling her. "There'll be no news for Martin for a while yet. But one way or the other, I'm staying with you."

"I won't hear of it."

"Look, we had decided on this move before I knew you were sick. I wanted to settle in Dublin and that's why Martin agreed to do the Bon Secours interview. So don't for a moment think this is some act of heroic generosity on my part. We're family, that's all, and I'm here."

Suddenly Emer felt as if the fog in her mind was beginning to clear and a huge burden of solitude had been lifted from her. The arrival of her niece had changed everything.

Avril lay back down and began to stroke Emer's forehead gently. "I'm going to make this as comfortable as I can for you, Emer."

Emer thought of how her mother had died – painfully yet peacefully at the end. But the end is so final: the emptiness and loneliness that follows when a loved one's life is extinguished. The warmth, the love, the humanity is gone. And yet, in a way, it was this nothingness that Emer yearned for: no more pain to be endured, no more fear, no more insufferable fatigue. Obliteration beckoned and it didn't seem that bad. A vacuity of silence and rest might be welcome. A peaceful blank was what Emer longed for when the time came, but she dreaded the grief, the hurt and the loneliness that Avril would have to endure.

Emer closed her eyes. "Do you believe in an afterlife?" she asked.

Avril stiffened.

"Do you, sweetheart?"

Avril mused for a moment. "Actually, I do."

"How do you visualise it?"

"I don't see it as an actual physical space – not heaven or hell or any place we can imagine." Avril's tone was calm. "But I believe there is a spirit world, a home we return to where we feel totally accepted."

"You consider us then more as spiritual beings who have a physical existence?"

"Exactly. And this physical, human world is temporary, whereas our spiritual life is eternal."

"That's a comforting philosophy, Avril."

"And I believe my mother's spirit is looking down on me and on you. I believe we'll all be together somewhere in the great beyond, not physically together, not together as we experience it now but some other kind of deep association. I believe you'll be with her and your parents and everyone you have ever loved. And some day I'll be there too. I do believe that, Emer."

"I don't."

"I know you don't." Avril playfully pinched her aunt's nose. "You're an agnostic! But you do believe in a kind of immortality?"

"I believe we don't really die as long as we live on in other people's hearts – if we're lucky enough, that is, to have been loved. And I believe in the immortality of art, music, literature and sculpture. Artists never die, do they? As long as we're reading poetry and books, as long as we visit galleries and go to theatres and listen to music, we keep the souls of the creators alive. I often feel as if I knew Shakespeare or Joyce or Kavanagh better than I know my neighbours – know in a deep way, that is."

161

"I guess so."

"It's about attachments, links we feel with others, whether they are dead or alive. Writers share their innermost feelings. How many of us really do that?"

"We exist on fluff: inane conversations, empty sentences, half-baked ideas and second-hand emotions."

"Well put!"

"Not my words. Yours."

"When did I say that?"

"I can't remember when but I remember the words. I thought they were clever and true."

"Well, I'm glad I said them."

"You've always showed me the way, Emer."

"I'm pleased."

"Then there's music too," Avril continued. "What was Beethoven feeling when he composed his fifth symphony? What emotions does he draw out in us?"

"Powerful," Emer butted in. "Music is a potent force and it doesn't have to be classical music either."

"No, I love jazz and Gospel."

"I'm still into the good old 60s and 70s. 'While My Guitar Gently Weeps' – did you ever hear a nicer song title?"

"That's the reason you write poetry, isn't it? To connect?"

"Oh, I nearly forgot to tell you. A local publisher has just contacted me to tell me he's going to publish my stuff. He had it for nearly a year and I'd given up hope, but then out of the blue –"

"Gee, that's excellent! When is it coming out? When?" Avril clapped her hands.

"Now, don't get carried away. It won't be a mighty tome. It's a small book."

"You'll be in print, that's what matters. All of us who pick up the book will hear your voice again and again." Avril hugged her aunt. "Your little piece of immortality?"

"It will be out for Christmas, he said. *Red Poinsettias*, I'm calling it."

"I'm over the moon. Wait till I tell Martin and Dad! It's really great news." Avril paused. "You'll have something else to look forward to as well." With her free right hand, Avril stroked her tummy. "Honey chile," she lilted exaggeratedly, "allow me to introduce you to your Grand-aunt Emer."

Emer gasped.

Avril went on talking to her tiny bump. "She is the greatest aunt anybody ever had. In fact she is the greatest mother anyone ever had and if I manage to be half as good as she has been, you will be one lucky little kid."

"Oh, a baby, Avril! A baby!" She drew her niece's face down towards her own and kissed her two cheeks tenderly. "I'm so happy for you, darling. I'm so, so happy for you and Martin. You're all right?"

"Never felt better."

"How long are you gone?"

"I have five months to go. ETA is early November."

"Scorpio like Jackie," Emer whispered.

"I never thought of that. How cool!"

November held a special significance for Emer. It was the month of her sister's birth, the month of the Holy Souls as her Catholic upbringing had instilled in her, and it was also the month of Jackie's death. That hadn't occurred to Avril either.

"It's the best news ever." Emer's gladness spilled out into the room.

"It's something for us all to look forward to," Avril agreed.

"Your dad must be chuffed."

"Delighted about the baby, but he's angry with me now. Angry that I want to live here and raise our child in Ireland."

"He has good reason. He wants to be near his grandchild."

"He's welcome to visit any time. He knows that but –"

"He doesn't like Ireland."

"We'll work it out. Emer . . . I want you to see the baby, I need that." Avril stared soulfully into her aunt's face. "You can hang on. You can do that for me, can't you?"

Emer kissed her cheek again. "I can definitely try."

"And you'll have your book too. You must keep up your strength and your spirits, Emer. We have two beautiful productions in the pipeline. You promise me you will be there for them?"

Emer held her niece close, closed her eyes and tried to pray for the first time in years.

"Emer?"

"Yes, darling?"

"What about your brother?"

Emer's body grew rigid. "What about him?"

"You should phone him."

Silence.

"Emer?"

A tiny sigh escaped from Emer's lips and would have been imperceptible if Avril hadn't been lying so close.

"Emer?"

"*Shh*, darling. We'll see."

"I'm going to sing to the baby the song you used to sing to me. Remember?" Avril started to hum: "*Just a song at twilight . . .*"

Emer well remembered the old sentimental song she used to croon to her niece when she was a baby in the months she came to live with them in Cabra Road. She graphically recalled those horrible winter months following the hit-and-run that robbed them of a wonderful sister, daughter and mother and robbed her brother-in-law, Sam, of a wife. And her brother Ronan had compounded the tragedy with his cruel aloofness.

Winter killed, November numbed, she recited mentally her own poem. Perhaps the coming winter would provide the restorative.

20

"They think a few days away would buck you up," Avril explained, the following morning as she poured Emer another coffee. "Maggie offered the apartment."

"That's thoughtful of her but I don't feel up to a plane journey."

"OK." Avril wasn't going to push it.

"July there would be unbearably hot." Emer slid the breakfast tray over in the big double bed and stretched out her legs. "I want to remember the good times in Spain."

"*Red Poinsettias*?"

Emer nodded absent-mindedly.

"You look miles away, Emer."

"You don't mind if we don't go abroad?"

"Whatever you want is fine by me."

"I don't know what Noonan and his team will say today about the laser treatment. I may go ahead with it and as I don't know the dates, I'd prefer to stay closer to home. A short break in Ireland, maybe?"

"We could go to Kerry or Galway? Kenmare is nice."

Emer was lost in thought.

"It's entirely up to you," said Avril. "I'll pick up the car this morning and I'll be used to it in a few days. A trip down the country will be great practice for me to get used to Irish driving and –"

"You'll never get used to Irish drivers!"

"Ah, they're worse in New York! Especially the cabbies."

Emer smiled at the memory of jumping out of the way of the notorious Big Apple yellow cabs. "But they do provide great entertainment!"

"Yeah, the ones who know where they're supposed to be going. A lot of cabbies are new arrivals and haven't a clue."

"I know where I'd love to go," Emer spoke her thoughts aloud, not listening to her niece. She was in her own world and seemed to be addressing her words to herself. "There's a fabulous place I visited with my very first serious boyfriend, Ben." She laughed.

The unexpected sound of laughter in the room was lovely. Avril was madly curious about Emer's romantic past and had always wondered why her aunt had never married. As a young girl she used to make up stories of heartbreak or she concocted tragic dramas of unrequited love with all its pining solitude. Now she was too used to Emer's pragmatism and realistic approach to life to consider either of those scenarios likely.

"Ben? Dad said he was convinced you'd marry him, that you and this guy were quite an item."

"Your father got on well with him. They watched football together in the pub. We actually did discuss marriage but in the end we agreed to go our separate ways."

"Pity." Avril silently willed her aunt to continue.

"Young love hardly ever lasts."

"Oh, Emer, don't say that!"

"Ah, that's just cynical old me prattling away, pay no attention! You'll be all right, sweetie. Martin worships you."

"He has every reason to! What about this Adonis of yours? I want to hear everything – all the juicy details!"

"It was nothing you'd find exciting. Your generation would take it for granted: you form intimate relationships at a much younger age than we did, you start work earlier – part-time work at any rate, you stay on later in college and most of you have seen the world by the time you settle down. My little story would be tame by your standards."

"I wasn't exactly dripping in boyfriends in High School, Emer. Dad wrapped me up in cotton wool; any poor guy who wanted to date me had to be vetted first. His ideas on child rearing were Victorian and Grandma Jones was as bad. And when did I travel the world?" Avril pouted.

"True, you weren't as free as a lot of young people. Your father was just trying to protect you."

"Go on! Tell me about this fabulous place. Describe your romantic adventures – I love to hear you talk of times past."

Emer had to smile at her niece's childlike curiosity.

"We had a wonderful secret weekend away. We were young and feckless and out for a good time. I lied to my mum because she'd have freaked out."

"You lied to Granny Dorgan? I'm shocked."

"I had to – she'd have forbidden me to go. Ireland in the seventies didn't sanction dirty weekends for nice girls!"

"'Dirty weekends'? That's a horrible expression."

"Exactly. And it summed up the views of holy Catholics who considered extramarital sex as worse than murder. Sex? The word wasn't even spoken aloud."

"The Church's influence, I suppose?"

"The Church, yes, the ultimate power and most people fell for its strict teachings. Certainly my parents did. So, to get away for a weekend, this guy and I lied to both our families. I told Maggie of course. We had to have our girlie chats about it. It was a daring escapade. Sounds like the Middle Ages, doesn't it? We even pretended we were married so that the hotel would give us a double room, although I think the receptionist was suspicious. Honestly, those times were unbelievably prudish."

"*You* weren't, obviously!"

"I was in love," Emer said dreamily. "Or maybe it was lust. A real erotic adventure."

"Stop teasing me!"

"I'm serious, Avril. That guy brought out a side in me that nobody ever had before." She grinned impishly. "Or since – unfortunately." She lay back on the pillows and closed her eyes. For a moment her face cleared of all anguish and pain.

"Where did you go with him?"

Her eyes still closed, Emer pictured those walks in the driving rain, the way she skidded and squelched in her light sling-back sandals through sodden fields in the late afternoon, the fish and chip dinners in the greasy take-away. They had practically no cash and what they had they'd spent on the hotel and the train and bus fare.

"Was it very romantic, Emer?"

"Very."

There had been moments of great happiness and passion: nights of burning kisses in a warm bed with her inexpert but ardent lover, as the rain pelted down the windowpanes. His caresses had melted away her chaste fears and doubts and his tenderness had moved her. She could still conjure up the feeling of his hard flesh against her clinging softness, the tingling touch of his lips on her velvet skin, the . . .

"Emer?"

She opened her eyes. Her niece was sitting on the bed, a bemused expression on her face.

"Where did you go with him?"

"Where else but the wild west? And it was wild – wild and free and beautiful, sensual, loving and gentle and –"

"My God, you wrote about it, didn't you? The poem blew me away."

"Did it? Good!"

"My aunt the vamp! Where did all this fun and frolicking take place?"

"Clifden." Emer stretched slowly and sensuously and made a purring little sound.

"In Connemara?"

"Passion in the Twelve Bens. Now, that's another possible title for my book, don't you think?"

"You're incorrigible!"

"I hope so. Will you say that about me when I'm gone? That I was incorrigible?"

"Among other things!" Avril kissed her aunt on the top of her head and jumped off the bed. "Will I check out

Clifden on the Net and make a reservation somewhere?"

"No, let me." Emer sat up slowly. "I'll get the number from Directory Enquiries. I know the hotel I want."

And most likely the room number, Avril thought as she went to the bedroom door. "I'll run your bath. Wait till Noonan sees you this morning. You have a glow about you!"

"He'll put it down to the new medication," Emer said.

"Probably." Avril winked. "But we'll know better."

21

Maggie opened Emer's hall door with her spare key and let Joe and Noelle in ahead of her. "All quiet on the Western Front?" she asked.

"Yup," Noelle shouted back as she made her way down the hall to the kitchen.

Once she knew they were genuinely up for the job, Emer was delighted with their plans. The house had really been getting her down. But some things she was concerned about. She'd left a list of the things she did not want them to throw out. There were some things she loved, likes her mother's crockery – even if it was chipped and cracked.

"I'd better find that list she said she'd leave in the kitchen press," said Noelle. "We'd better follow instructions, or there will be blue murder."

"OK," Maggie shouted back. "You take a look and I'll show Joe out to the back garden and let him see what's in store for him."

Joe Walsh groaned inwardly. Although he'd willingly agreed to help sort out the garden, he was suffering from a fierce hangover. For his boss's retirement do the night before, the whole section from the department had turned out in force – even retired people had turned up to pay tribute to Ron Maher. He'd been a terrific assistant secretary and would be missed. Rumours were rife as to who would replace him. Joe had no interest in that particular promotion, although some of his colleagues had encouraged him to apply.

Now, here he was, about to take on physical exertion when what he sorely needed was some sound shut-eye, but he wanted to do this for Maggie. His wife, who had been completely demoralised by Emer's diagnosis, had cheered up from the moment she and Noelle had hatched this renovation plan. Privately he thought that Emer must have agreed to it for their sake. Anything he could do to keep the momentum going was a small price to pay.

"Christ on a bike!" he bellowed when his wife opened the back door and he surveyed the scene before him. Garden, did she say? This was a jungle of Jurassic Park proportions. Grass, or what had once passed for grass, had gone mad, grown upwards and outwards, weaving in and out and creeping over stones and rocks and everything in sight. The supposed flowerbeds were completely overgrown and gone to seed and down the centre of the erstwhile lawn the straggly reeds had entirely covered the path.

"Jee-sus!"

His horrified astonishment made Maggie smile but she scurried off when she heard the kitchen crew arrive at the front door. She wanted to be in on Noelle's plans before they started to rip out all the presses.

Noelle, in deep cahoots with the kitchen company supervisor, turned to Maggie and handed her a large sheet of printed drawings.

Maggie was amazed. "Brilliant, Noelle. These plans are spot-on."

"This is Christy. He's the owner of the company; he drew up all the plans."

Maggie shook hands with the moustachioed, red-haired barrel of a man who stood before her. His ruddy complexion and cheery expression reminded her instantly of her local butcher.

"Christy's a draftsman by profession," Noelle explained. "He took in all my ideas and my advice, it goes without saying."

Then why bother saying it? Maggie was peeved by Noelle's imperiousness.

"So, they're going to make a start tomorrow."

Noelle seemed to think this was also a compliment to herself and maybe it was. This company had, after all, renovated her salon. Maybe the speedy agreement was down to Noelle's persuasive charms. On the other hand, Maggie earnestly hoped their instant availability wasn't down to a bad track record.

Christy took one last look around, surveying the scene. Then, nodding his goodbyes to the two women, he bowed ceremoniously and left.

"So, how about a cuppa?" Maggie switched on the kettle. She glanced out of the window and saw Joe on his mobile phone. She wondered what he was up to because he had a guilty expression on his now florid face and he was gesticulating madly as if he were giving directions.

"Christy was great coming to the rescue like that, wasn't he? We were damned lucky to get him." Noelle went to the fridge to get milk. "After our tea-break, I suggest we go to DID and make sure the electrical goods measure up and will be ready to be delivered by the end of the week. We have to get everything installed before they get back from Clifden. Avril left us a blank cheque. Nice for some! We could pick up some smaller items as well. That kettle has seen better days and a new microwave wouldn't go amiss."

"OK," Maggie agreed, "and then we can go into Clerys to get some nice kitchen accessories. Is their sale still on? What's our budget?"

"Avril told me not to worry about costs. She isn't short of a few bob so we could also have a look at curtains. We'll have to buy ready-made as we're in a rush. I've a few ideas too about rugs and stuff."

Maggie was sure she had. Noelle seemed to have forgotten that she had appointed Maggie to choose rugs and fabrics because she was 'good with colours'. They sat listening to Marion Finucane on the radio as they drank their tea and Noelle glanced at a medical magazine that Avril had left on the table. Maggie was glad of the few minutes' respite from Noelle's incessant 'plans'.

All too soon, Noelle jumped up and grabbed Maggie's cup. "C'mere till I tell ya!" she said as if they'd just been talking, while she emptied the teapot down the sink plughole. "That bloke can come this Thursday to sand and polish the floors upstairs."

Maggie had wanted another cup of tea but of course Noelle hadn't thought to ask. And Joe hadn't even been offered one. She'd better take him out a cup of coffee and a pint of water before he died of drought.

"Floors too, Noelle? I don't know. We're spending Avril's money. We'd better not get too carried away."

"Avril has plenty of readies. She'll be inheriting this lot, so it's an investment for her." Noelle thumped her playfully.

Maggie rubbed her arm, annoyed by Noelle's insensitivity. A knock at the front door prevented her from complaining as Noelle went off to answer it.

Father Gerald Moore, out of his clerical garb, wearing blue dungarees and white T-shirt, stood in the porch armed with old cloths and rags and a load of paintbrushes. Behind him, lined up in the front garden, were four young people carrying tins of paint, turpentine, sandpaper and rollers.

He kissed his niece. "Good morning, Noelle. All present and correct and ready for action. Allow me to introduce some of the folk group."

One tall auburn-haired boy came forward and shook Noelle's hand. "I'm Stephen."

"Yes," Gerald said proudly. "This is Stephen and he'll be in charge. He's the leader of the choir."

"Hope it won't be like *Lord of the Flies*!" Maggie remarked as she came forward to welcome Noelle's uncle.

"What, my dear?" Gerald kissed Maggie on the cheek, apparently unfamiliar with Golding's classic. He turned to his niece: "We got the colours you asked for: Apple White for the bedroom, Sunseed for the kitchen and dining-room and Eyre Square for the hall. Isn't that what you wrote out for me?" He checked a scrunched-up piece of paper that he pulled from the front pocket of the dungarees. "Oh, and here's the receipt."

Maggie was raging. Noelle hadn't consulted her about colours at all. What the hell was Eyre Square when it wasn't the centre of Galway? It could be any damned colour because Noelle could be very dramatic when it came to décor. She knew Sunseed was a nice creamy pale yellow and it wasn't too strong but less insipid than Magnolia. White in the bedroom would be fine but still, it would have been nice to have been consulted. She'd swing for Noelle one of these days.

Gerald pointed down the garden to the street outside. "Is it all right that I parked there? I don't think we're in anyone's way. You have to be careful these days what with all the new regulations and penalty points and so forth."

"Maybe we can move it around to the back lane?" Maggie suggested. "I'll ask Joe to do it."

"Grand, grand." Gerald beamed. "I borrowed the minibus from the Parish Centre as the old folk's club won't be needing it this weekend. A brainwave, eh?"

"Ger, you're a treasure!" Noelle was about to link him indoors when a horn hooted loudly and they all turned to see a gigantic truck pulling up on the road outside.

"Yis'll have to move the van!" the driver, harassed and hot, shouted.

"What the hell . . . sorry, Ger!" Noelle exclaimed.

"Hold it!" Joe ran up the hall, puffing and panting. "They're the lads with the rotavator."

"What lads?" Noelle asked with a frown.

177

"Horticultural students from the Botanic Gardens and they're here to give me a hand. Don't worry, they're not charging the earth – just digging it!" Joe laughed. "I'd never be able to tame that jungle by myself."

"It's huge job," Maggie intervened on behalf of her husband, "and we're short on time."

"Well, OK," Noelle said grudgingly, "but you might have told me about it, Joe. We must work as a team."

Maggie, who had also been in the dark about her husband's sudden arrangements, could have kissed him there on the spot. Teamwork, my arse, she thought. It depended on whose game plan they were following.

It was halfway through the afternoon and the sun came out amid the showers. Joe and the lads from the Botanic Gardens had stripped to the waist. The garden was beginning to take shape. The new soil had been raked in smoothly but was turning muddy.

Maggie brought out a tray of cold drinks for them. "God bless the work! Janey, you've made fantastic progress out here. Are you going to plant new grass seed?"

"I've ordered a rollout lawn. Faster and less hassle in this rain." Joe gulped down a full pint of the chilled fruit juice. He belched loudly. "I needed that. No seeding. I thought it would be better to have a lawn laid, as it would look much nicer when Emer sees it. We're going to put in some new shrubs too." He pointed to a heap of hacked branches on the patio area. "Those were past the point of rescue, I'm afraid."

This time Maggie was shocked. "Noelle will have a fit."

"Isn't she spending money like water in there?" Joe gestured to the house.

He had a point. Noelle had zoomed through the department stores like a mad thing: bought four sets of new curtains for the bedrooms, blinds for the kitchen, rugs for everywhere and new bedclothes for Emer's room and the spare room that Avril was in.

"Well, you can argue the toss with her," Maggie emphasised. "I'm staying out of it."

Joe shrugged. "Noelle doesn't faze me."

"She's a control freak," Maggie said.

Joe collected the empty glasses from the lads and came back to where his wife was standing with the tray. "Controlling things is her way of coping since Brendan Geraghty left her."

"You reckon?"

"I saw him yesterday in town, Maggie."

"Brendan?"

"Mmh. He was having lunch in Toddy's with his new partner."

"Did he see you?"

"He called me over to show off his new little son. They've called him Nicholas after her father."

Maggie was struck dumb.

Joe put his arm around his wife. "There's no need to say anything to Noelle about the baby."

"Of course I won't say anything. That news would finish her."

"I got the impression that she already knows," he said.

Maggie gasped. "She never said a word about it. Not a word and she's usually so forthcoming with her news – good or bad. I suppose she's too upset to discuss it."

"I always thought she didn't want kids."

"Joe, it's different when her ex-husband produces a son and heir when her childbearing years are gone. He's way too old to start fatherhood. He's fifty-four."

"What about Paul McCartney and Sting and all those rocker dads?"

"You could hardly include Brendan Geraghty in that league – a rocker? Never met such a stick in the mud. I feel for Noelle, though."

"So go easy on her." He slapped her bottom playfully and went back to planting the shrubbery.

Noelle had just hung the lilac-coloured curtains in the front bedroom when she stepped off the chair that Maggie was holding steady for her. "Good colour, aren't they?"

"They're lovely," Maggie had to admit. "Lucky the paint dried so fast."

"Yes." Noelle ran her finger over the sill. "The open windows did the trick. This was a great day all in all. It was like one of those makeover programmes on TV, wasn't it? Ger promised the young people a trip to the mountains tomorrow." Noelle looked up at her handiwork with delight. The curtains, cleverly hung, framed the windows elegantly. "Ger has great energy for his age and he loves kids but he told me he's been warned to be careful – never to be with one of them on his own. Sick, isn't it? Every priest is considered a potential paedophile. The priesthood suits Gerald – he's a born minister of God – but celibacy has its huge drawbacks. It's shame he couldn't have had children of his own."

Maggie heard the catch in Noelle's voice. A ring at the front door gave her a little shock. This would be the man to roll out the lawn and she didn't want Noelle to know about that particular development yet.

"Who could that be? A nosy neighbour I'll bet wondering about all the comings and goings, maybe that one Cheryl from next door? Maggie, did you notice she's keeping well out of the way these days? I had words with her."

"Did you?"

Another ring at the door, this time more insistent.

"I'll get it, Noelle. You unpack the rug."

The man who stood on the doorstep looked no more like a gardener than Maggie looked like a nun. He had dark hair streaked with grey, a clean-shaven tanned face and piercing green eyes. She flushed as he scrutinised her. "You the man to lay the lawn?"

"Not the lawn."

His twinkling eyes disconcerted her. He stepped back and glanced up at the hall door to check the number. "I'm looking for Emer Dorgan," he went on, staring at her in an impish way.

Maggie stood, hands on hips, and stared back. "I'm sorry, she's not here at the moment."

He smiled again. "Maggie, isn't it? You haven't a clue who I am, have you? I didn't think I'd changed that much. You haven't!"

Maggie peered closer, squinting without her glasses, then hurled herself at the visitor and squashed him in a bear hug. "Ben Fogarty! As I live and breathe. Ben Fogarty! Is it really you?"

He grinned. "Last time I checked!"

"Come in, come in."

Clearly relieved with this reception he followed her into the hallway.

"Watch the paint cans. As you see we're up to our ears

decorating here. Noelle's upstairs hanging curtains and generally bossing us about. You remember Noelle?"

"The hairdresser?"

"A salon owner now – quite the entrepreneur."

Ben edged his way in around the paint-spattered ladder. "So, what's all this activity about?"

"It's a surprise for Emer. She's away for a week."

"I haven't been in touch for a long time. I thought it would be easier to come in person. I took a chance I'd find her here since it's Saturday and I thought she wouldn't be at work. It never struck me she'd be away. I should have phoned."

Typical man, Maggie thought.

"I'm home now and thought I'd look her up. It'll be nice to renew old friendships." He glanced up the hallway.

"You're home," Maggie said, her thoughts racing. "On holidays?"

"No, for good, I've retired back here. My son is working in London in the City and since my marriage broke up I didn't see much point in staying on in Sydney. I'd planned to retire here when the time was right. My mother is still alive so I'm glad to be back to keep an eye on her. She's not getting any younger."

Maggie couldn't take her eyes off him.

"What's the news, Maggie? You have a daughter if I'm not mistaken."

"Yes, she's leaving school next year. Hasn't a notion what she'll do yet but she's not bad at languages. An Arts degree doesn't tie them down into one area so they're freer to make choices. They're all into their autonomy these days, fair play to them. And your son is in London, isn't that great – in the City, you said? And your mother is still in the land of the living? You're lucky. Emer and myself have both lost our parents – ah, sure you know about Emer's father and sister, Jackie. Didn't she die when you were . . . you were around. So here you are back again after all these years. Retired, did you say?"

"Free as a breeze!"

"Well for some!"

"Is Emer free?"

"Free?"

"I mean, is she involved?"

Maggie pretended not to understand. They were still standing in Emer's hall surrounded by pots and buckets and paint-stained rags and here was Emer's long-lost boyfriend obviously very keen to meet her again. It was surreal.

"Involved romantically," he whispered with not the slightest hint of a blush.

He had a damned nerve!

"The last time I was in touch with Emer – we had a chat on the telephone one Christmas – she told me she was single and perfectly happy to be so – but that was years ago, so I was wondering."

"I wouldn't know," Maggie interrupted a bit defensively and realised how feeble that sounded. If he remembered anything at all, he'd know that Emer and she were confidantes. Did he fancy his chances? Imagined she'd still be interested in him? Men – they were clueless.

"Is she away on business?" he pursued.

"No, on holiday with her niece who's back from New York," Maggie explained. "She's staying with Emer for the moment."

"Avril?"

Maggie was impressed that he remembered.

He leaned up against the wall "And Emer? How is she keeping?"

"Oh Ben, you don't know. How could you?" She abruptly took him by the arm. "Come into the sitting-room and we can have a drink. I'll call Noelle to come downstairs. Joe, my other half, too. He's gardening in the back. I'd like us all to have a talk."

"Sounds serious," he said cautiously.

Maggie looked at him squarely in the eye. "It is."

22

For Emer, the approach to Clifden had changed beyond recognition in the years since her first visit in the 1970s. New housing estates, holiday villages and apartments had sprung up everywhere. She'd been dismayed to discover that the Atlantic Coast Hotel had closed down. The place where she and Ben Fogarty had shared two glorious nights had gone forever.

But one sight cheered her as they drove in from the Dublin Road: standing out in all its unpretentious glory was the steeple of the church on the hill overlooking the town. This spire was Clifden's hallmark in her mind.

Avril had gone on the net and booked two rooms in the Station House Hotel. They arrived at about six in the evening after a leisurely drive. Avril had to break up the journey several times because she knew her aunt became very uncomfortable if she had to sit in the one position for too long. They'd stopped twice for coffees and for a light lunch en route and now Emer needed a rest before they decided where to have dinner.

Emer was totally agog at what she saw. The hotel was a masterpiece in planning, located on the original site of the former railway station. She wondered how long it had been since the last steam train departed from Clifden. The Station House Platform and Engine House had been brilliantly restored.

Emer, through the windscreen of Avril's rented Focus, peered with growing admiration. "Look at the old brick!" she said.

Avril manoeuvred into a tight car space in front of the bar. "And the wood looks like oak. It's beautifully done. In one way I feel I'm stepping back in time and in another way it's ultra modern."

The women took it all in. The courtyard on three sides of the hotel housed designer boutiques, a bar, a hairdressing salon, a beauty clinic, a jewellery shop, an antiques shop among others, and the buildings kept the appearance and atmosphere of the former railway station. Old signs aimed at passengers and advertisements for Craven A added an authentic air of bygone days.

Avril turned off the engine, undid her seatbelt, got out and hurried around to open the passenger door. Emer eased herself out of the car.

Avril took their bags from the boot. "We'll have a nice few days here, Emer. Recharge the batteries."

The large tiled foyer was welcoming. A well-trained, well-groomed, friendly receptionist booked them in and gave them their keys. They had adjacent rooms on the third floor.

Avril insisted on carrying both bags from the lift.

Emer opened the door to 312 and was pleased to have a large airy room. "This is nice, functional but not fussy."

She checked out the bathroom. "The shower is OK but I prefer the ones you can detach from the wall. I like the water to reach all my bits."

"You might be better having a relaxing bath. The bathtub is big enough anyhow. Martin loves a big bath. I'm right next door so you go for a nap and I'll call you for dinner. Eight o'clock, the receptionist said. OK? I'll book the restaurant downstairs."

"Wouldn't you prefer to eat in the town? I'm sure you're anxious to see everything."

"I'll go for a ramble when you're having your rest. We can explore together tomorrow. All right?"

"Great." Emer could barely keep her eyes open. The double bed had her name on it. "Enjoy your stroll and I'll see you at eight. Are you dressing up?"

"I'll wear the black dress – it's elegant and still fits." She stared down at her tiny bump. "I'll have to think about bigger clothes soon."

Emer stripped to her underwear and crawled between the sheets. The bed was surprisingly comfortable – springy and soft and welcoming. Her bones ached from the long drive.

She was making an effort not to complain. She knew from experience that sickness alienated people. No one wanted to hear the minutiae of anyone else's illness.

Avril was expecting her first child and this should be a time of great excitement for her. She was starting out on a whole new life with a bright new future. That was how it should be. Emer was coming to the end of hers and she had to let herself experience it in her own way.

She'd arranged with Mr Noonan to have the laser

treatment the day after they got back from Connemara. If it eased her swallow that would be a massive relief. Nothing she did now would prolong her life but she'd make certain that her last months or weeks would be as pain-free as possible.

She wanted to enjoy her remaining time and she wanted to leave her family and friends with good memories. Whatever it took to keep her up and moving and apparently well for as long as possible, that's what she'd do. She owed it to Avril. Maggie was desperately upset and Emer blamed herself for this: she'd confided too much. She was able to keep Noelle at a safer distance.

Emer took a muscle relaxant – a prescription Martin had organised through a contact in Dublin – and closed her eyes. They burned in their sockets. Her body was no longer her own. It seemed a separate entity, one she no longer identified with, one she no longer liked.

The sounds of children playing came from a room down the corridor. A little girl was laughing loudly, and an adult, presumably the mother, was hushing her but the child carried on laughing despite all pleas for silence. An overpowering sadness enveloped Emer.

She thought about her mother and her father and times past. She thought about Jackie and how awful it was that she never saw her daughter grow up. She would have been a grandmother soon.

And Ronan? She would make one last-ditch effort to patch things up. She didn't want any loose ends. She'd phone him when she got home. He was her brother and he had a right to know of her illness. If he chose not to visit her – that was fine.

Words from a Neil Diamond song reverberated in her head like a drum. "*I am, I said to no one there.*" But what am I? What the hell am I? I think, therefore I am. Bloody brilliant, Descartes. Now, Will, it's your go. Remind me about the infinity of reason. "Yeah, what a piece of work!" She scolded herself for the self-important lofty questions that more and more infiltrated her efforts to explain herself to herself. Words, words, words, with all their inadequacies didn't alter the stark reality.

A salty tear trickled down her face onto the pristine pillow. She let it fall and then another and another. Pain twisted in her gut but she saluted it. Pain was real. It was a friend, a constant, and a version of what she was now.

When Emer was alone she could give in to her darker thoughts. She allowed herself to wallow. It was necessary and it wasn't hurting anyone. She thought about the coming days and weeks and prayed to some vague spirit somewhere, some munificent presence. She prayed for courage. She focused on the word. Cour-age. Cour-age. Over and over she repeated the mantra. Courage. Courage. Give me courage. Soon, she drifted into a light sleep.

23

The shrill ringing of the telephone on the bedside table woke Emer just before eight o'clock the following morning. Grumpily, she leaned over and fumbled for the receiver. Must be Avril, calling her for breakfast, she guessed. She could have done with more sleep but clearly Avril had to check on her. Her niece was on the alert all the time now.

"Hello," she muttered, uncurling the phone wire and flopping back on the pillows. She stifled a big yawn.

"Emer, sorry, did I wake you?"

"Maggie!"

"Yup, it's me."

"Is everything OK?"

"Of course."

Emer sat up drowsily. "A bit early for a call," she complained. "Are you sure everything's all right?"

"Everything's fine. I just couldn't wait any longer to phone you. Wait till you hear what happened! I tried to phone you last night to tell you but you didn't answer your mobile. Then I texted you."

"I had the phone off. We were in the dining room from eight and then we had a few drinks in the bar, which is why I'm suffering now. I thought I'd get a lie-in."

"This news couldn't wait a moment longer. I'm bursting to tell you."

"What?" Emer tried to sound enthusiastic.

"You had a caller. You'll never guess who! Not in a million years, not in a zillion, will you be able to hazard a guess because even I was dumbfounded and –"

"Ronan? Was it Ronan?"

"No . . . oh, I'm sorry, Emer. That never occurred to me. God, I'm thick. I feel like a right twerp now."

"It's just that I was thinking about him and I wondered if, you know, it might be . . . it doesn't matter. So, who was it?"

"I feel awful, Emer. I'm so sorry."

"Will you stop apologising? There's no reason for my brother to have called out of the blue. He's not a mind reader or a psychic, is he? Tell me, go on. Who called?"

"Ben Fogarty." Maggie, who had been waiting all night to give this thrilling news, now felt it was irrelevant, trivial.

"Ben Fogarty?" Emer croaked.

"Yes, he called yesterday."

"Ben Fogarty?" Emer repeated, in a daze.

"Yes, sleepy-head!"

"He telephoned me?"

"No, he didn't telephone. He called in person."

"You mean he visited me?"

"Yes! Are you awake at all?"

Emer shuffled onto her side. Her back was hurting like

hell. Every day brought new pains and aches. "Wait till I get my head around this. Ben Fogarty called to my house to see me?"

"Yes, yes, yes!" Maggie screamed with delight.

"How do you know?"

"Know what?"

"That he called to my house?" Emer couldn't piece it all together. Her brain was fuzzy from last night's over-imbibing. "Were you there?"

"Yeah, it was lucky that I happened to be there at the time. Noelle and Joe were there too. We were up to our oxters in paint and –"

"How is it going? The spruce up?"

"Great. We're enjoying it immensely, Emer. I hope you approve when you see the changes."

"I know I will. You and Noelle have great taste. I'm looking forward to the change and I really appreciate what you're doing. I'm blessed having such good pals."

"You've been so good to us, Emer. We're the ones who are blessed."

Emer heard the tremor in Maggie's voice. "So, how did he look?"

"Who? Ben? Oh, yeah, he looked fine. More than fine, actually, gorgeous. He's still a hunk, Emer."

"Good for him!"

"He wants to see you."

"When there are pink blackbirds flying!"

"He's home in Ireland for good. He's retired, said that he'd made enough money, that there were more important things in life than work. He wants to catch up on time lost."

Emer hoped it would keep fine for him. That's what she herself had planned.

"I think he still holds a torch for you, Emer, because –"

"He shouldn't be holding torches at his age – he's liable to get burnt! What did you tell him?"

"That you were in Clifden for a week's holiday with Avril. He remembered all about her. He mumbled something about Clifden too and the weekend you spent there. He's lovely. Still as friendly as ever and full of chat. He would genuinely like to see you, Emer."

"That's not what I meant. Did you tell him I was sick?"

Maggie hesitated.

"Did you?"

"I had to, Emer, I had to. He's on his way down."

"Down? Down where?" Panic rose in Emer's throat.

"To Clifden."

"*What*?"

"To see you. He's on his way by now, I expect. He said he'd set out early before the morning traffic."

Emer shot out of the bed, her head woozy. She reeled a bit and her sight went blurry. She clung onto the bedpost "He's on his way here? Are you mad, Maggie? I can't see him. I don't want to see him. Jesus H Christ, you're insane!"

"He's a nice fella, Emer. He always was. You two were very close at one time and –"

"At one time yes, but not for three decades. He's a stranger, a foreigner. He's a ruddy ghost. What were you thinking of? Well, obviously you weren't thinking at all. Jesus wept! This is bizarre! It's crazy. Are you mad,

Maggie? Yes, you are, you are mad. I don't want to see him, I definitely don't. What would we have to say to each other after all this time? This is the pits."

"I was only trying to help. I thought you'd like to see him. It's a compliment that he wants to see you again. I made a mistake obviously."

"Yes, this time you did, Maggie."

"I'd better go." There was a catch in Maggie's voice. "Don't see him if you don't want to. Avril can keep him at bay if that's what you want."

Emer was contrite now. The last person in the world she wanted to offend was Maggie. She'd hate to be guilty of ingratitude. She wanted to say that she didn't feel well at all, that she had slept badly and that the new medication was making her nauseous but it would sound like a pathetic excuse, a cry for pity.

"I really do have to go, Emer. I'm dropping Holly into Tesco this morning. She's staying over at a friend's tonight and her bag's too heavy to take on the bus. I'll talk to you later."

Emer managed a small bowl of cereal and a yoghurt for breakfast. The dining room was almost empty by the time she and Avril came down. The waitresses were attentive, hurrying to finish their morning chores. Stragglers at breakfast were never popular.

Her niece dipped a sausage into a runny, yellow egg yoke. "I think it's serendipity! And we were only talking about him the other day. Wait till I tell Martin this. Ben Fogarty! It's like a fairy tale."

"A horror story, you mean. I don't know why you're

going on and on about it. I'm not going to see him." Emer stirred a spoon of sugar into her coffee. "I've no intention."

"Why ever not?"

"I'm not seeing him. That's all."

"But why?" persisted Avril.

"You know why."

"I don't."

"Yes, Avril you do. And if you don't, you're blind."

"Because you're ill?"

"For one thing and Ben Fogarty is a complete stranger at this stage. We've spent a lifetime apart and people change."

"Not fundamentally," Avril argued. She spread her toast with blackberry jam, carefully covering every corner. The action reminded her of Granny Dorgan who used to bring her blackberry-picking on fruit farms near Swords in the summer and afterwards they'd hurry home to make jam in the big cosy kitchen.

"I'd have nothing to say to him." Emer picked at her fingernails.

"You don't know that."

"I do."

"You don't have to spend a long time with him then, do you? Just meet for a coffee or something. Play it by ear."

"No."

"You're acting up big-time."

"I'm entitled."

"You're not entitled to be a pain in the butt."

"Thanks."

"Don't go pretending you're all hurt and insulted."

"I couldn't be bothered arguing."

"Fair enough. I'll meet him at reception and organise something."

"No."

"Yes, Emer. You'll regret it if you don't."

"You'll regret it if you keep badgering me," Emer warned. "I'm not going to meet up with Ben Fogarty today, tonight, tomorrow or any other time."

"The poor man is getting up at cockcrow, battling traffic and unfamiliar roads, driving all the way down here on his own from Dublin, expecting to meet you. You'll have to meet him – you're not that callous. He must want to relive your past here together!"

"What planet are you living on? I am not here to rekindle some long-dead romance, Avril. You've lost whatever wit you had to begin with, that's all I can say. I am here for a few days' rest and you can't have forgotten why. I am dying, Avril. *Dying*."

"We're all dying."

"Don't be flippant. It doesn't suit you."

"You're not dead yet." Avril met her aunt's glare with a wink.

"Listen very carefully, I'm not saying this again, Avril. I am *not* going to see him. It's my decision and it's final. End of conversation."

Avril's eyes narrowed, just as her father's did every time he was challenged. She stuffed her mouth with a big chunk of brown bread. Despite all arguments and protests, Avril was not to be deterred. Right after breakfast, she was going to make an appointment for her aunt with the hairdresser next door. Then she'd persuade

Emer to wear the new jeans and white shirt she'd bought before their trip and she would help her apply her make up. With a leather belt accentuating her waist, she'd look casual but chic.

Although she didn't realise this, Emer remained a very attractive woman. The illness had not destroyed her beautiful face. She was thinner, true, more gaunt and strained-looking, but her wonderful blue eyes still had a haunting quality. She was bound to captivate Ben Fogarty all over again. This hint of romance could do more for her aunt than all the medicines and treatments in the world.

"I never knew you were a bully," Emer said. "And Maggie is as bad." She sipped her coffee slowly, a scowl on her lips but Avril thought she caught a faint trace of a smile playing around her aunt's eyes.

24

Ben politely stood up as Emer left him to go to the ladies' room. They were in the Abbeyglen Castle, one of their old haunts on their visit all those years before. After lunch, they went out to the reception area for coffees. The open fire and cosy couches and the antique furniture gave the place a homely atmosphere. Ben gazed out at the swimming pool and beautifully manicured sloped gardens. The helicopter pad catered for the wealthy clientele. He sat down again, glanced through the hotel brochure and sipped his cappuccino, trying to get his thoughts together.

Emer had appeared calm at first, if a bit distant. Maybe she was self-conscious but there certainly had been no shortage of conversation since he'd picked her up at her hotel. They'd asked polite questions, had the customary chat of two friends who had not seen one another in years.

He'd told her about his mother in the family home in Swords and his sister in Wexford with her husband and three grown-up children. He'd waxed lyrical about his son in London who'd secured a well-paid job with great prospects. They'd talked about Ben's work and his life in Australia.

She'd spoken about her job in the library. She told him all about Maggie and their holidays in Spain, about Noelle and her marriage break-up and her new business. She discussed Avril and Martin's marriage and the pregnancy and their plans to settle in Ireland, everything but the elephant in the corner which had reached mammoth proportions. She hadn't referred to her illness at all. He didn't think it his right to ask.

Ben tried to assess if he had done the right thing coming down to Clifden to see her. Had he been too presumptuous, too naïve? Had he upset her? Emer was very ill and his visit might serve as a bleak reminder of how things used to be.

Emer wobbled as she emerged from the toilet cubicle. Lately that had been the way and she wasn't sure if it was the medication that was causing it. She'd ask Noonan about it. Maybe indulging in the second glass of Chianti at lunch had been a mistake?

She steadied herself at the wash-hand basin and soaped her hands. Seeing him again had unnerved her. He didn't seem different at all. It was surprising how well they still got on. There was a slight tension but that was only natural. There was no hint of pity in the way he looked at her. She was enjoying his company. He was a very sexy man and, Avril was right, she still had a pulse!

Emer examined herself in the mirror and combed out her hair – she'd never liked the 'just done' look – and rummaged for her make-up bag. Might as well have a quick fix.

"Sorry to keep you waiting." Emer sat down opposite him and plonked her handbag on the carpet beside her chair. She stirred her cappuccino, watching the bubbles foam and then evaporate.

While she was much thinner than he remembered, what struck him was how she had maintained her beautiful blonde hair. It was shorter now but just as glossy and full as it ever had been.

"Would you like a short walk on the beach?" he asked.

"OK."

"Maybe you'd prefer a drive? I must say the roads have been totally overhauled since I was last here."

"EU funding," she remarked. "Have you noticed other changes?"

"Here?"

"No, in Dublin."

"It's certainly more frenzied than I remember although traffic is a lot slower! The people have got quicker, rushing about and fussing and of course it's become more cosmopolitan with all the different nationalities. There's a buzz about the place but I think it's lost some of its old appeal. The shops are the same shops you see in London, Rome, Paris or wherever. It's not the Dublin I remember."

Emer agreed. "We've lost our slow pace of life and a large part of our identity. There's much more crime now too."

"Murders seem to be an everyday occurrence judging by the news."

"Also a lot of petty crime and the loopholes in the law are scandalous – into court and out on the street on the same day. The revolving door, they call it."

"Sydney is a lot more laid back. I had a good life there, a healthy life. Why didn't I stay, you may well ask, but that's not the question, really. It's rather why I stayed so long – I'd only intended to work there for a few years. My brother, Liam – you met him, didn't you? He had the company up and running by the time I went out to help. Then I met Sarah and the rest is history! Life runs away from us." He noticed her wry smile. "I can't believe I said that."

"Let's go for that spin while the rain holds off. The drive up the Sky Road is wonderful. Great views."

He made for the desk to pay the bill. "Would you like me to book for dinner here tonight?"

Gourmet food would be wasted on her, she thought. "I think I'd prefer to stay nearer to our hotel. Avril and I had planned on going to EJ Kings in the square."

"EJ Kings. We ate there on our last night that weekend." He smiled over at her. "Remember?"

"Yes." She blushed. "Yes, I do."

The road meandered up and up, high above sea level, unveiling impressive views of the unruffled ocean below. The dark and pale greens and rusty browns of the land merged miraculously with the iridescent blues of the sea. Flashy yellows and deep purples of gorse and heather spattered the hillsides.

"Awesome," Ben enthused. "Australia is a fantastic country with its varied landscapes and climate but a sunny day in Ireland beats all. The colours are . . ."

"Like a prism?" she suggested.

"Yeah!" He grinned boyishly.

His accent hadn't changed but he had developed a slight twang and he definitely had the Aussie lilt. If he'd said *fantastic* once, he'd said it fifty times today. It was engaging. He hadn't lost his looks, either. Maggie was right about that. Although his hair was greying at the temples and it had receded slightly, it was still full and wavy. His handsome face was tanned and windswept and his green eyes twinkled.

"I did a lot of outdoor activities over there, especially water sports," he told her, as he negotiated a sharp bend. "Everyone does. Diving is my favourite sport so I intend to continue it here and I might join a sub aqua club . . ."

He flushed.

"Ben, it's all right." She put a hand on his knee, which jolted him. "You are allowed to talk about the future."

His shoulders hunched over the steering wheel. "I don't know what to say."

"Pull in here." She pointed to a viewing lay-by at the side of the road. Two other cars and a coach were already parked there, their owners happily snapping photographs of the expansive sea views below and beyond to the horizon. A small group of tourists was walking seaward down a grassy trail, excitedly gesticulating and jabbering in German or Dutch – she couldn't properly make out which language.

He parked beside the tour coach, on the crest of the hill. She lowered the passenger window further and breathed in the fresh sea air.

He played with the keys in the ignition. It was up to her.

"Let's get this out into the open," she began.

"You don't have to. It's none of my business and I don't expect –"

"I know you don't, Ben. I want to tell you. The past few months have been really difficult for me – and for others. I'm not underestimating how hard it is for Avril, in particular, but also for my friends. We're all walking on eggshells trying not to upset each other."

"I know how distressed Maggie is."

Emer turned to look at him. Her eyes were moist. "At first I didn't want to see you –"

"I can imagine!"

She placed a finger on his lips to hush him. "Let me say this while I have the guts." She took a deep breath. "My pride took over. I thought I didn't want to see you because I look so different, I feel so different –"

"You don't, Emer," he protested.

"Yes, I do, Ben. Let's be honest?"

"I am being honest. You look wonderful to me. You're thinner but that's all. When I thought about you through all these years, what I carried in my mind's eye was the gentleness of your eyes. I realise that sounds sickeningly smaltzy and I remember how you hate that kind of talk, but I mean what I say." He took her right hand, gently turned it and kissed the wrist.

An ancient giddy sensation in the pit of her stomach kicked in. She hadn't expected this. Maybe it was the heat of the day or the idyllic setting or their close proximity in the car or the two glasses of wine, but whatever it was Emer felt hugely attracted to this man. Ben leaned forward and kissed her on the lips, a soft, delicate kiss.

He took her in his arms and the gentle pressure of his lips on hers, the robust feel of his arms around her and the tenderness of the moment encouraged her to respond in full.

Her mind whirled as he prolonged the kiss, his lips urged her lips apart, but it was a gentle prodding, an exploration. Emer slumped and melted under his touch. Fire burned in her belly, burned and whirled and consumed. Her heart soared and her body ached, a splendid, yearning, burning ache she had feared she'd never experience again.

25

A mixture of brassiness and shyness, he'd once called her. That afternoon Emer lay apprehensive, trembling in her whiter than white pants and bra between the virginally white, crisp hotel sheets. She wished she had indulged in a spray-on tan before this adventure, but in her wildest dreams she couldn't have imagined this episode. The darkness would help to camouflage her pallid skin. She watched him draw the curtains, casting out the snooping sun.

He had stripped to his boxers – a navy-blue pair that hugged his neat bum. His body was nicely tanned and his hairy, muscular chest brought back memories of bygone clammy nights of Connemara copulation. Her toes tingled and she wanted to giggle. She hoped it wasn't an attack of pins and needles as that would hardly be a turn-on!

What was going on with her? She was dying, for God's sake, riddled with cancer, and here she was at four in the afternoon about to let this hunk of a man into bed with her, not having seen him for over half of her life. Jesus, was she going mad like the others who had encouraged this visit? Was there an epidemic of craziness? Or had the disease already fried her brain?

He smiled reassuringly as he slipped into bed beside her. Before she knew it, he had wriggled out of his underpants and thrown them on the floor.

"Ben," she laughed into his shoulder. "I'm not sure about this."

"You're not?' He looked offended.

"It's not that I don't want to or anything – I do, I really do – but I think it's a bit sudden –"

"Sudden?" He inhaled loudly and sat bolt upright. Then he exhaled just as loudly as he stared incredulously at her. "Sudden? I've waited for this moment for more than thirty years. Do you realise that, Ms Dorgan? I've crossed lands and oceans, countries and counties to be here today. Thirty damned years and millions of miles and she says it's a bit *sudden*!"

Emer chuckled.

Then he laughed loudly, squeezing her shoulder.

"To be honest, this is not really me," she confessed. "I feel shy."

"You were once a seductress!"

"Only with you," she insisted.

"Well, that's good for the ego anyhow!"

"Seriously, it's been a very long time for me," she admitted.

"Me too!"

"Really?" She scrutinised his face.

"Cross my heart. Sarah and I hadn't made love for years before we split. She was never well and –"

"I don't think I should be hearing this," Emer said guardedly.

"You're right."

"I'm just not comfortable talking about your wife."

"Ex-wife," he corrected her. "But you are right, Emer. In any case, my relationship with Sarah has nothing to do with us."

Emer wasn't sure if the moment was spoiled now.

"We were good together, weren't we?" It was more of a statement than a question. "We seemed to fit – mentally and spiritually certainly but also . . ." He paused. "Also physically. We were really great together. That's the way I remember it, anyhow."

"I remember it too," she whispered.

"I never had a lover quite like you," he went on, lying close to her but not touching and staring up at the ceiling.

"Ditto." She coughed. "I wrote about it."

"What? You wrote about our . . . ?"

"Lovemaking. Yes, I wrote a poem."

"That I have to see."

"You will some day. It's going to be published."

"You've got to be kidding!"

"I'm not. Don't worry, you're not mentioned by name. It's about a man and a woman and . . . it's quite sensuous, really. It could be any man or woman of course."

"But it's us?" He seemed pleased.

"Mmh, it's us back then. '*The way we were!*'" she sang softly.

He hooted loudly and she hushed him, terrified that Avril might be next door, having come back early from her shopping expedition. Then he whooped and his body shook with laughter and delight. "You're some tulip! I always used to say that, didn't I? Emer Dorgan the poet! Who'd have thought it, eh, that I'd end up in a sexy poem in a book? Bloody mad, that is! Far out!" He laughed again, unable to hide his glee.

She looked at him longingly. "Ben?"

He turned cautiously to her and took her in his arms and he continued to chortle as she clung to him. The laughter turned to hugs and the hugs to kisses. This time she was the one who opened her mouth and pushed her tongue between his teeth. She traced the contours of his lips and tongue with her tongue, sipping and licking.

He lay back and gently tugged her on top of him and she straddled him. She hid a gasp as she felt his erection.

He knew she couldn't possibly bear his weight – she was so thin. He looked up at her, clad in a little lacy white bra that pushed up her breasts, giving her an exaggerated cleavage. He reached up and cupped her breasts.

"You're lovely," he said.

Desire drove away any feelings of guilt or shame or embarrassment. "Make love to me," she whispered, unfastening the bra and flinging it away.

He pulled her head down to his and kissed her again, a slow lingering kiss. Emer stifled a gasp as he eased her onto her side and swiftly and expertly pulled down her panties. She couldn't yet believe that this was actually happening.

"Ben," she whispered into his ear as she leaned over and snuggled into his neck. "I don't know if I can manage this."

"I can!"

She hiccoughed and giggled and hiccoughed again. What was in that blasted wine? She was behaving like a schoolgirl after her first pint.

"Go easy, will you?" she whispered. "I feel a bit stiff."

"I'm stiff too, thankfully!"

He stroked her back and playfully slid his hands down to her buttocks, lower and lower, fingers tracing feather-light circles on her sensitive skin. She squealed with pleasure. She slid on top of him again. His hard penis pushed against her. She moved slightly sideways to give his hand access and he deftly slipped his searching fingers between her legs and stroked her clitoris. She was wet with excitement.

"Now, now," she begged.

He watched her as she slept, her hair tossed on the pillow and her cheeks glowing, her breathing slightly laboured. He was near to tears. The frailty of her, the vulnerability was heartbreaking. This was the moment he'd waited for through all the years. He'd hoped for it, prayed for it, envisaged it, dreamt about it.

But he'd never imagined this.

He'd considered naturally that she might be unavailable. He'd even dealt with the probability that she mightn't want to see him. In all his conjectures he'd never thought that she might be ill. It had simply never occurred to him. When he'd thought of Emer he'd always remembered her as lively, energetic, bubbly, funny. She'd had such enthusiasm for life. She'd been lusty and loving, sexy and sentimental – a great girlfriend, a great girl.

Today she had shown some spark of her former desire

and feistiness and humour and he'd done his utmost to make it a good afternoon for them both. He'd tried his best to please her physically too, to excite her and bring her to climax. He'd been patient and considerate, stroking her, whispering words of love, encouraging her to let go. She'd made a marathon effort to react and respond as he wanted.

However, it was not to be. Their lovemaking, although sensitive and sweet, lacked the ardour and passion it once possessed because it had been tinged with a silent sadness. A tacit acknowledgement hung in the air that nothing could or would ever be the same for them again.

26

Emer awoke to a darkened room and it took a few seconds for her eyes to adjust and to register where she was and what a stupendous event had occurred.

She stretched out her legs under the crumpled sheet, which had twisted under her body during their lovemaking. Fingers and hands had been busy fondling, stroking and touching. Ooh, it had been fantastic, as Ben had kept repeating: "Bloody fantastic!" Over and over he'd murmured words of love, sweet words, dirty words, words of encouragement, praise and flattery and all the time she'd responded and kissed and stroked him and cried out as they'd risen higher and higher to a pitch of excitement she hadn't experienced in years.

She was sore and her body still smarted from their love antics but she felt well – better than well – alive. Her flesh tingled, her blood rushed and her heart sang out in celebration.

"Mmh," she mumbled sleepily and reached for him. She wanted to make love again. "Ben?"

He wasn't there.

Emer stretched over and flicked on the bedside lamp. She was alone. The empty space beside her mocked her lustful desire. Hopefully he was in the bathroom and not yet dressed. She could inveigle him back to bed.

The duvet cover was neatly folded on the chair. She didn't remember doing that – Ben must have. Odd. The action seemed highly incongruous given their strenuous hours of sexual athletics.

Emer shrugged. Maybe he was a neatness fanatic? God, was he one of those fastidious men who'd pick up after her and drive her nuts? He hadn't struck her like that and she didn't remember that about him from the past but then you never really knew, did you? They'd only been reunited for a few hours. Was he like that character in *As Good As It Gets* – the Jack Nicholson character who had that illness – obsessive compulsive disorder? That would be downright spooky. Was he punctiliously showering now, cleaning himself of her bodily fluids?

No sound of splashing water emanated from the bathroom. No manly singing in the shower.

Emer got up and wasn't surprised to find herself unsteady on her feet. The giddiness amused her because this time she understood the cause. She had no one to blame but herself and she didn't blame herself one bit. She felt worthy of congratulation not censure.

Too much activity, Ms Dorgan, she imagined Mr Noonan berating her. You've had far too much overexertion for a woman in your condition.

Naked and feeling wonderfully liberated and unself-conscious, she padded over the soft carpet. She tapped on the bathroom door. "You in there, lover?"

No answer.

"Ben?" Emer tentatively pushed the door open.

The bathroom was vacant. Disappointment hit hard. He must have gone out for cigars. He'd badly wanted a smoke, so he had told her as they lay panting and sated. Maybe he went for a newspaper? He'd mentioned that he'd been scouring the property pages since his return, in his search for a new house.

She went back to the bedside table and looked at her watch. Seven p.m. Blast it! She'd been asleep for at least two hours. She was due to meet Avril for dinner at eight o'clock. It didn't give her much time to get ready. And she had no appetite – for food at any rate. Ben had agreed to join them for dinner in EJ Kings.

No more nookie for now.

She'd have a quick shower to freshen up and shake herself out of this sluggishness. She sniffed her body and was pleased to find she was redolent of him: she smelled of male, that musky, moist man-smell that comforted and thrilled her at the same time. God, it had been such a long time. She'd almost forgotten the taste and smell of sex.

She threw on her dressing gown and got her shower cap although it seemed a pointless exercise, as Ben had messed up her hair, not that she was complaining. She rummaged in her toilet bag and took out the new body lotion that Maggie had bought for her. Then she noticed a big purple bruise on her inner thigh. "The price of passion," she said aloud and headed for the bathroom.

She didn't notice the scribbled note left on the coffee table by the window.

The phone rang and rang. Avril was starting to worry.

This was the third time she'd rung Emer in the last two hours. They couldn't still be out, could they? Had they gone for a longer drive than they'd intended?

It was seven-thirty now and she hadn't set eyes on her aunt since midday when Ben had picked her up at reception. They'd mentioned a short drive but a short drive wouldn't keep them out until this hour. She knew Emer had wanted to go to Carraroe at some point but it was a fair distance away, and sitting in the car for too long wouldn't do her any good. Would Ben have been so foolish?

Emer would be exhausted if she overdid it. Avril admonished herself for worrying unduly but at the same time she felt an enormous sense of responsibility for her aunt's welfare. She'd try the phone once more.

"Hi Avril. What? Oh, I was in the shower. Sorry I didn't hear the phone. No, we came back earlier. Oh, did you? I must have been asleep. Tired? Oh yeah, well, I am a bit, yes. We didn't stay out too long. We came back around four, I suppose. I was in bed. No, no, he slipped out for a while."

He'd slipped in for a while too!

"No, I'm absolutely fine. The bed did me good."

Well, that was certainly true.

"OK. Great, Avril. Knock in fifteen minutes and I'll be ready. What are you wearing tonight? Oh yeah, the blue suits you. See you in a while."

Emer hung up. She sat on the bed in the damp towel and began to rub in the body lotion. A gorgeous aroma of rose permeated the room. As she replaced the cap on the bottle, she saw the white unlined page out of the corner of her eye. It was a scrawl written on the pad provided, with the hotel logo, name and address.

Cautiously she went over to the table and picked it up. She recognised the handwriting. Her heart sank as she read the words.

Dear Emer,

This was the most wonderful day I've had for a long, long time. It was a pleasure and a privilege to see you again. I thoroughly enjoyed every minute and I hope you did too.

A privilege? Why the formality?

I decided not to take up your kind invitation to dinner. I hope you understand. The time we spent alone together was very special and I don't think it would be possible to prolong the happiness we shared this afternoon. Please give my best to Avril. Enjoy the rest of your holiday in Connemara.

So, he had gone. Where? Back to Dublin?

You have been in my heart all my life and you will continue to be.

Love,

Ben.

There was no mention of seeing her again, no information given about his whereabouts or his plans, nothing but this . . . this contrived, stilted crap. Had she been so taken in by his charm? What had he been playing at? Why had he left her like this? They'd been so close, so intimate, so in tune with one another this afternoon.

Or had they? Had she imagined their affinity? Had she satisfied some need deep within her that bore no resemblance to what he was feeling?

Emer read and reread the note, each time becoming more disillusioned and angrier with herself. Then she tore it up in little pieces and tossed the scraps into the waste paper bin.

27

Maggie pressed the red disconnect button on her mobile phone and ended the call. Disgusted, she fell back into the plush pink-suede cushions of her sofa.

Joe, as usual, had his head stuck in the sports section of the *Irish Times*. Saturday's coverage was of biblical importance to him. He was on the alert for his wife's signal: she would nudge him, want to tell him all about the call and he'd 'mmh' and 'ah' in the right places to placate her. He had it down to a fine art at this stage. He scratched the back of his neck; the label of his new T-shirt was annoying. He waited, grateful for this unusual respite, as he wanted to read on about the upcoming All Ireland Final.

Maggie was uncharacteristically silent. "You OK, sweetie?" He absent-mindedly stroked her knee and kept on reading. "Was that Emer?"

"No. It was Ben Fogarty."

He looked up from the newspaper. "What did he want?"

She wagged her head from side to side, her face taut and her brow furrowed. "He wanted to explain why he wouldn't be seeing Emer again."

"Oh?"

"He doesn't give a damn about anyone but himself." She peered critically at her husband. "You need a haircut, do you know that?"

"I like my hair this length." Defensively he ran his hand through his greying curls. "Why the criticism of Ben Fogarty? You thought he was God's gift."

She glared at the mobile phone.

"What exactly did he say?"

Maggie sprang up from the couch, defiance blazing from her dark eyes. "Some mumbo jumbo about what a fabulous afternoon they'd spent together and how deeply affected he was by Emer's illness. He wittered on about how lovely she was and how brave and how he'd always admired her and always would."

"That's nice, isn't it?"

"In the next breath he was telling me why he couldn't see her again. He couldn't face it, he said, it was too harrowing. Ben's full of crap, a charmer on the outside, but when the shit hits the fan he can't handle it. Didn't he do the same thing on his wife? Obviously he has a history of bolting when sickness enters the picture. He's a creep."

"How do you really feel?" he joked, then instantly regretted it. This was no time for teasing – he could see by her expression that she was in no mood for levity. "Calm down." He patted the cushion beside him. "Come on, sit down and we'll talk this through." He was racking his brain for something suitable to say to soothe her. If she flared up again, he'd lose patience. He wanted to avoid a row at all costs.

"I feel awful," she confessed.

"Why should you?" He put his arm around her in that territorial way she loved. "You've done nothing wrong."

"I persuaded Emer. She didn't want to see him. Her gut instinct told her not to and her gut instinct was right. I bullied her into seeing the bollix, mistakenly thinking it might give her a boost."

"Maybe it did."

"Fat chance."

"Have you spoken to her since?"

"No." She shuddered. "I should have kept my big trap shut; I should have known better."

"It's not your fault. It's not anybody's fault. Ben Fogarty went on an impulse to see his former girlfriend. They had a good time – isn't that what he said? Now he feels he can't go on seeing her and that's all there is to it, Maggie."

"Emer must be feeling rejected."

"How do you know? You're not a mind reader, are you?" Maggie could be a right pain when she started analysing things.

"I know how she felt about Ben and how self-conscious she is about her illness and her appearance. Now she has to deal with this rebuff on top of everything else. I know exactly how she's feeling."

"I'm sorry, love, but you do *not*. Emer is her own person and a very strong one. She agreed to meet Ben and it had nothing to do with your powers of persuasion, believe me."

Maggie always grossly overrated her influence over other people and their behaviour; consequently she suffered from an inordinate sense of responsibility. She felt guilty about working when Holly was small; guilty about missing her father's eightieth and what turned out to be last birthday party because they were on holiday in Cornwall; guilty about the one Christmas they went abroad and 'abandoned' her mother who went quite happily to spend Christmas with her sister in Longford; guilty about birthdays forgotten, missed parties, burnt dinners. When guilt was handed out Maggie was first in the queue. "Stop beating yourself up about it."

"I pestered her. Avril did too." She groaned. "I put Avril up to it, convincing her it would do Emer good. She only agreed to see Ben to get me off her back."

Joe continued in his placid voice. "Maggie, you're wrong. Emer met Ben Fogarty because she wanted to. No doubt she was curious. He doesn't want to see her again. So what? Maybe she doesn't want to see him either? There was no possibility of a relationship. Emer is probably glad that they met, had a good time, caught up with each other and now she's most likely relieved that he's moved on."

"I wish I could believe that, Joe."

"Ben has confessed something that you don't seem to be able to admit."

"What's that supposed to mean?"

"Ben Fogarty is the first person to declare that he can't handle the fact that Emer is dying."

Maggie folded her lips tightly together. The tears stung her eyes but she obstinately held them back.

"You mightn't like what he just said on the phone, Maggie, but I think he has guts. He had the temerity to confess that he couldn't handle it. You see that as a flaw; I don't. The man had the courage to tell the truth."

"Brutally."

"Granted, but this truth is brutal. Emer is dying and there's not a damn thing we can do about it. None of us can, darling, not even you." He drew her to him and kissed her forehead.

"I know she's . . . dying." Maggie gulped down the word. "But we can't just ignore her. I know it's tough looking at her suffering, watching her trying to swallow, to digest the tiny bits of food she puts in her mouth, and trying to keep up a false pretence that she's doing all right. I see how breathless she's become, how drained, how exhausted after the slightest effort, how difficult she finds climbing stairs. I witness her painstakingly putting on her make-up, dyeing her hair, choosing new outfits in her new tiny size. She does this more for us than for herself. I know how hard it is for her to watch her own decline. She's getting weaker day by day. Don't you think I realise this? That I feel it?"

What Maggie didn't see was how hard she had been to live with during the last few months. Her mood swings were more volatile than ever. She snapped at him for the slightest thing, she lost the head with Holly three times a day. She shouted at her daughter for the slightest misdemeanour. Holly and he knew precisely how agitated she was. He didn't say any of this; he merely massaged her neck in an effort to get her to relax.

"Being upset is no excuse, finding it hard is no reason

to bale out. Dying is hard. Living is bloody hard too. Nobody told us it was going to be easy. If every time we found something difficult we ran away, where the hell would we end up? No wonder the world's gone mad. There is more selfishness now than ever before. The old and the sick are abandoned, some are forsaken by family, ignored by society, untidy problems brushed under the carpet. Ben Fogarty's attitude is a symptom of universal selfishness! We can't act like he does; we have to stick together, Joe."

He squeezed her shoulder. "Not everyone is as honourable as you."

"It's not about honour. It's about friendship. We're going to see this through – no matter how hard it is. It's not about us anyway – it's about Emer. He didn't get it, did he? It's not about him or us or Avril or anyone else – it's about Emer."

He hugged her to him for a brief moment and then stood up. "I'll pour us a drink. Do you fancy a nice bottle of Pinot Grigio? There's a bottle in the fridge. Tonight we'll send out for a takeaway. Holly is staying over in Alison's house so there's no need to cook; we'll just chill out together – the three of us."

"Three?"

"The pair of us and the Pinot! How's that?"

"Thanks, Joe."

There would be no more sports results for him today, he thought.

"Joe?"

"Mmh?"

"Do you think Emer will like the house in Cabra Road? Do you think she'll be happy with the new décor?"

"She'll love it. Sure you and Noelle know her well and know her taste and, from what you say, she often talked about what she'd like to do with the place."

"Are you sure? You're not just saying that to make me feel better?"

"No – she'll really like it. In any case, she'll be thrilled because she'll see it for what it is: an act of love."

Maggie managed a smile, a little one, and Joe, planting a kiss on the tip of her nose, went off to get the wine. Once again he'd deflected trouble. He was bone-weary. This whole business was wearying.

28

The sea was calm when the two women got out of the car and surveyed the scene before them. The birds twittered loudly as if some celestial row was in progress, the breeze blew softly from the sea and the sun smiled kindly. This is what Avril had dreamed of, this is what she'd spoken about to her father when he'd scoffed and told her she was being ridiculous.

The views of the Atlantic from Renvyle House were truly staggering as the changing seasons reflect the differing moods of these waters: mild and benevolent in sunshine, but savage and warring in wintry weather, and indeed sometimes in summer – as recent weeks proved. Emer reflected on how many Irish fishermen had, over the centuries, given their lives to the sea; the waters around this island gave and took away life arbitrarily it seemed to her. Some deep primeval passion raged in her heart as she watched the waves roll.

After a brief stroll in the gardens and over the tiny

manmade bridge, they ambled down to the lake to throw a few pieces of bread they'd saved from breakfast to the assembled ducks. Avril saw that her aunt was trying to hide her fatigue behind a mask of forced smiles.

Some hikers, puffing and panting from a brisk hill climb, saluted and the women waved back their hellos. Another guest who was loading the boot of his Mercedes with scuba-diving gear looked over.

"Lovely afternoon," he shouted to them.

"Yes," Avril called. "Enjoy your dive."

The peace was momentarily interrupted by the distant sound of gunshots. Clay pigeon shooting was taking place further afield.

Martin would be all on for the golf if he were with them. She wouldn't have minded a game of tennis, she thought sadly. She and Emer used to play quite a lot in the old days in Charleville Lawn Tennis Club in Phibsborough. As a teenager Avril had spent many an enjoyable afternoon there when her aunt worked in Phibsborough Library nearby and Avril had made some nice friends. She must try looking them up when she got back to Dublin.

Emer, standing beside her with a vacant expression, was fidgety as she scattered pieces of bread on the lapping water and the ducks, so tame they ventured right up on the bank, comically quacked their gratitude.

"Coffee time," Avril announced and led the way through the solid wooden door with its big black cast-iron latches, into the tiny porch where anglers had left their tackle and big wellington boots. An assortment of umbrellas lined one wall, because of the long weeks of wind and rain they were experiencing this year.

Cosily ensconced in comfortable couches beside a small peat fire, the two women sipped their coffees in silence. The unmistakable smell of burning turf was synonymous with Ireland, bringing Avril back to former happier times when she'd travelled as a child with her aunt and her granny "down the country" for summer vacations. Granny Dorgan was a true Dub but she loved the peace and tranquillity of the countryside for her annual summer holiday.

A young couple wandered in, chatting and laughing, swimming gear and wet towels under their arms. The girl's curly wet tresses framed her face and her healthy glow emanated happiness.

Avril thought the hotel was very quaint and wondered if they should have booked to stay here instead but then Emer had specifically wanted to stay in Clifden. She hadn't uttered a word about Ben Fogarty's visit, not a word, and Avril was determined not to quiz her about it.

"You look a bit tired." Avril finally broke the silence, pouring her aunt another cup of coffee. "Are you sure you're all right to stay here for dinner? We can cancel and head back to our hotel, if you'd prefer."

Emer put her cup down on the wooden table. "I'll be fine, darling. I just needed a little rest."

Even if it were manna from the heavens it wouldn't do any good for Emer.

"Did you notice that young couple?" Emer asked suddenly. "I'll bet they're on honeymoon."

"Certainly in love," Avril agreed.

"Yeats spent part of his honeymoon here, you know."

"The poet? WB Yeats? Are you kidding me?"

"Some connection with Gogarty, I believe."

"I'll Google it," Avril said.

After a few moments Emer nodded off in her armchair. The soft rise and fall of her chest exuded innocence. Her low breathing was barely audible, her vulnerability heart-rending.

Avril was determined to avoid long drives, big meals in restaurants, excitement of any kind for the next couple of days.

They'd be leaving Connemara in two days' time and Avril would be relieved. She'd been worried since they'd left Dublin. The responsibility of looking after her aunt was scarier than she'd anticipated. She'd had no real clue how sick Emer was – or at least how far her sickness had advanced. It was only when she saw her out of her own environment that the illness was so forcibly irrefutable. Each day Emer lost some of her sparkle.

Her aunt began to snore softly. Avril's cell phone rang and she hurried outside to take the call. Martin's number came up.

"Hi, honey," Avril shouted excitedly into the phone. A crackling noise was her response. "Martin, I can't hear you. Martin, can *you* hear me? Sorry, sorry, what did you say? This is a very bad connection." More crackling noises but she made out a few words: Cabra, job, already here. "You're here? In Dublin? You got the job? Oh, Martin, that's wonderful. I'm absolutely delighted, honey. I'm fine, really. I am. Emer? Oh she's . . . Martin, I missed you so much. You've no idea."

Avril eavesdropped on the pair at the next table who were talking very loudly and had apparently been playing croquet and lawn bowls that afternoon. The woman was sulking, petty and quarrelsome about scores or something, and Avril felt pity for the morose husband who was clearly used to being harangued.

Emer studied the menu. For the sake of her niece, she had to choose something she knew she could swallow and that she could pretend she was enjoying. In reality Emer dreaded every meal and, because of her cocktail of tablets, she had no appetite whatever. Avril, by contrast, was eating for two and was starving.

"I'm having the crabmeat for starters," she said enthusiastically. "It sounds delicious – lemon and chive mayonnaise, scrumptious!"

Emer couldn't help but smile at this burst of exuberance. "I'll have the vegetable soup."

"I'll settle on fish for my main course. The scallops or the turbot, oh, but what about the cod? It's impossible to decide! What are you having, Emer?"

"Crêpes – the vegetarian option. Why not try the scallops? I can assure you, you won't be getting them in Cabra Road. Now, what about the wine?" She consulted the wine list.

"None for me, thanks." Avril patted her tummy.

Emer had every intention of ordering a nice Merlot and liquids were easier for her now, so if that included sedation by alcohol she was signing up for it.

A piano player took his seat and started a medley: nice easy listening, middle-of-the-road pieces, swing, and jazz and some pop.

"Ha!" Avril cried. "He's playing your song now, at least one of them. He timed it well. A nice touch, hasn't he?"

The familiar opening chords of 'Lady Madonna' tinkled around the dining room.

"Tell me all about the phone call. Martin is ensconced in Cabra Road, and he'll be waiting for us on Saturday? I hope the bed in the back room will be big enough for the two of you."

"Three of us."

"OK, two and a half of you," Emer conceded with a grin. "Isn't it great he got the job? Of course I had no doubt that he would. They're lucky to have him. He'll be a terrific asset to the hospital. Aren't you thrilled?"

"I am," Avril confessed. "I've missed him like hell."

Emer watched her niece tuck enthusiastically into her food. She was thankful that Martin had got the job in Dublin; it would make things easier for all of them.

What good was she to Avril? Nothing but a hindrance and a liability and a worry. Martin's arrival was the answer to a prayer. Emer, in fact, had recently tried to pray – unsuccessfully, but she had tried.

They went into the long glass conservatory for their after-dinner coffees. It was past nine o'clock and the sun was setting. It filled the glassy enclosure with a beautiful orange-red luminescence and Emer, poised elegantly on a wicker chair by the window, seemed to take on a translucent air, an ethereal gentle radiance. Although the wine had given her cheeks a glow, she was almost waif-like in her frailty.

Avril knew she could do nothing to help. Maggie had said the exact same thing and so had Noelle. It was horrible to feel such powerlessness. But Martin would be around from now on and he would do his best to keep Emer from too much pain and discomfort. Also, the procedure next week would help her swallow. Martin said it would.

She couldn't wait to feel the strong arms of her husband around her. And she missed her dad. Although he was often a pain in the rear, although he could be arrogant and bristly and full of his own importance at times, he was her father. She'd phone him tonight and tell him she loved him.

Emer didn't order coffee. She was sipping and savouring a third glass of wine from the bottle of Merlot. Its red richness, aromatic bouquet and velvety texture had tranquillised her considerably. She felt content in the comfort of her niece's company.

29

The week after Emer had the procedure done dragged by but, after initially suffering pain down her throat and soreness in her trachea, her swallow improved greatly which made eating easier. She'd even attempted some diced chicken, but the truth was she hadn't enjoyed it. The vegetarian diet suited her better. She had begun to like the bean feast Avril prepared every second day, and the vegetable lasagne and all the other pasta dishes Martin prepared. Emer also managed quite well to masticate quiches and omelettes, but soup was now her favourite food and Maggie and Noelle had each made huge cauldrons. Maggie was experimenting today with wild mushrooms, she'd told her earlier on the phone.

Noelle had created some delicious desserts and insisted it was no bother trying out new ideas with jellies and sponges and cream and puréed fruit. She loved messing about in Emer's new kitchen.

They were all extremely kind but Emer wanted to get

up as soon as possible and get her life back to some semblance of normality. Martin had told her he was sending for some new medication that might help to restore some of her energy. Noelle had got some herbalist client of hers to make up potions.

Emer, more than anything, wanted to do a few mornings' work again in the library and she'd ask Mr Noonan what he thought. If he was against that, maybe she could do some work from home? She could continue to make lesson plans for Deborah Dixon. It was important to keep her brain active at least. What she needed was a laptop, then she could work in bed if needs be. She'd ask Joe about getting her one as he had connections.

The sedation in the hospital had exacerbated Emer's already depleted energy, which is why she'd spent these few days in bed but the hours were endless and she was bored. Although Martin had fitted an extension to the aerial in her bedroom and she was able to watch her new flatscreen TV, she was on the verge of going mad. How many daytime programmes could a body watch before reaching vegetative state? She knew it was easier for Avril and Martin when she was upstairs, as it gave them a chance to be alone together and enjoy the newly decorated house.

Never had Emer been so pleased than the previous Saturday when she and Avril had walked through the front door. Exhausted from the car journey and from trying to keep up her spirits for Avril, who was eagerly waiting to see her husband, Emer's breath was taken away when she stepped into the hallway.

Her old, shabby house had been transformed She'd exploded into silly laughter when Maggie, Joe and Noelle jumped out from the kitchen with a celebratory bottle of champagne and dragged her into the beautifully restored room with its warm wood presses, stainless-steel fittings and fixtures and newly tiled floor.

"Oh my God!" Emer had squealed in rapture.

"Come quick, Emer, wait till you see the garden! It's like Eden out here!" Noelle had shouted from the back door. "New bushes, new flowers – even new feckin' grass – the Chelsea Flower Show pales in comparison. Joe installed some solar lights. Look, aren't they the business?"

Emer had spotted the knowing glances that passed between Maggie and Joe. She wondered what that was about.

"We did upstairs too," Noelle had continued happily after an astonished Emer had viewed the garden. "We painted and washed and scrubbed and put up new curtains and the floors are sanded – no more threadbare carpets."

Maggie flinched but it was obvious that Noelle was unaware of any unintended insult.

"Your room is gorgeous," Noelle went on. "Come up now and see it with me."

Emer had linked her friend upstairs. She'd felt a girlish excitement at seeing everything so fresh and bright. Her room with its new creamy-white walls and lilac bedclothes and curtains and pine floor was tasteful, elegant and peaceful.

"Sensational!" She hugged Noelle.

When she turned around she saw Martin on the landing embracing his wife, Avril weeping softly into his shoulder.

He came over to Emer and kissed her tenderly on both cheeks. "Thanks for bringing her back to me."

"Welcome home, Dory," Maggie called out as she climbed the stairs, holding the drinks. "We missed you." She handed Emer a glass. "Cheers!"

"This is the happiest homecoming ever." Emer looked at each of them in turn. "Thanks. All of you. I never thought it would turn out so perfect. It's just the way I always wanted the house to be. The amount of work you've done is unbelievable. I absolutely love it."

Joe, his arm territorially around Maggie, felt his wife stiffen as she watched Emer walk around surveying the scene. The expression of joy on Emer's face couldn't hide the underlying pain and exhaustion. In the week since she'd been away, Emer had noticeably deteriorated.

Martin took control. "Enough excitement for one night, everyone; we have to let these ladies get some sleep."

"Ah no," Emer protested, "let's have another drink downstairs. We've loads to catch up on and –"

"Not on my watch," Martin said firmly as he took the champagne flute from her hands "My wife needs her beauty sleep, you know, whatever about you lot of brazen black-guards and boozers!"

"I am tired," Avril admitted. "We can celebrate some other time."

Gratefully, Emer acquiesced.

That was a week before. Now it was time to get up and get on with it, whatever *it* was. She heard the sounds of muffled shrieks and creaking bedsprings from the room next door. They were at it again, that pair of lovebirds.

Considering Avril was now over six months pregnant, Emer had to admire her energy and zest for the pleasures of the flesh. Granted, Martin was one amazing specimen, a handsome man with a lovely smile, warm eyes and a well-toned body.

Much more importantly from Emer's point of view, he was sincere, loving, good-humoured and generous. He would make a terrific father.

The way the young couple were attracted to each other, the way they beamed and openly showed their affection reminded Emer of her sister's love for her husband and his for her. Jackie and Sam had been the same: fondling, laughing, kissing and cuddling all the time. It had been heartening to see then and it was heartening now.

Emer had never experienced such love and she wasn't sure she would have been capable of it. What must it take to entrust yourself wholly to another human being? What confidence and faith are required to expose yourself fully, to bare your soul to another person, to risk everything? She certainly had never met anyone who had inspired that devotion in her. Her recent fling with Ben, pleasurable as it had been, was just that – a fling. There had been no possibility of a commitment and therefore no real challenge.

Emer's thoughts raced round and round in her brain: thoughts about her parents and their marriage, thoughts about Jackie and Sam, about Martin and Avril, about Maggie and Joe and other couples she often admired and sometimes envied. Wouldn't it be easier to get through life on the arm of someone who truly loved you? Would it be easier to get through death?

Emer finally fell into a restless doze and had weird

dreams: Jackie was running up a hill, calling Emer to hurry up and follow, but her feet were stuck in the muddy grass.

"Wait! Wait!" Emer begged.

Jackie laughed and ran on, her long black hair blowing wildly in the breeze, her skirts billowing. She ran on, higher and higher, up and away and disappeared over a hill. Emer was unable to budge.

Other bizarre images took over. Her father, singing merrily, was frying onions in a sizzling pan in the new kitchen, delighted with the gleaming pots and pans and all the other accoutrements. The door was flung open and Emer's mother burst in from Bingo, displaying a set of grotesque china she'd just won which she clattered down on the kitchen table, ruining the new surface. Her father's face changed and he frowned fiercely. Emer tried to shout a warning at her mother but no sound came out of her mouth. She was dumb and paralysed.

Ronan appeared out of nowhere, attired in a beautiful dress suit, a white carnation in the lapel of the jet-black jacket, and came over to Emer, smiling.

"It's going to be OK, Emu. Don't worry about a thing." He handed her a carnation. "For you."

"Thanks, Ronan."

"You're welcome," he replied graciously with a little bow.

"You're welcome!" roared her father but his smirk increased menacingly.

"You're welcome," her mother mimicked mockingly. "You're welcome. You're welcome."

They leered, baring teeth and making hissing sounds. Ronan joined in, grinning and sneering. They had changed. No longer her loving parents and brother, they were strangers, hideous sinister strangers who had stormed her home.

"You're welcome, my dear!" They hooted with vicious laughter. "You're more than welcome!" It became a chant, a screech, an eerie incantation. "Welcome! Welcome!"

The images went blurry and dimmed and finally faded away like watery snowflakes on burning soil, and Emer awoke, hot and sticky and trembling. She lay there for a few moments more, listening to her own irregular breathing.

There were no more sounds from next door. Avril must be taking the GP's advice and having an afternoon nap. Presently she heard the drone of the lawnmower from the back garden. Martin said he enjoyed this chore every Saturday but she was sure he must be fibbing.

"It will be OK, Emu," she spoke aloud to herself.

Shaken, she hoisted herself up in the bed and leaned over to the bedside table. Nervously she lifted the receiver. Her fingers dialled automatically – the numbers were engraved on her brain even after such a long time.

Della's crisp and supercilious tones on an answering machine:

We're sorry but we're unavailable to take your call at present. Please leave your name and your number after the beep and we'll get back to you as soon as possible. Thank you.

Emer hesitated. Then, raising her voice in as cheerful a tone as she could muster, she said:

Hi, Ronan. It's Emer. Phone me when you get a chance. I'd love a chat. Hope all is well with you.

30

The hazy September morning was balmy and scents of newly watered lavender wafted through the open kitchen window. Avril was preparing lunch. She searched for the egg slicer, not yet familiar with this bright new kitchen with its sundry presses, drawers, nooks and crannies. Some of the gadgets that she needed she'd found among the various culinary utensils in the large new cupboard beside the pull-out food larder. The kitchen was a masterpiece of design and space and light. It was such a pity that her aunt would never enjoy it to the full.

"I hadn't cooked much before you came to stay," Emer had explained almost by way of apology. "I just didn't have the interest."

"But you need nourishment," Avril had remonstrated gently. "We agreed you must keep up your strength."

Emer joined her niece at about twelve noon. She was walking with difficulty, the pain gnawing, but she straightened up when she saw Avril at the sink.

"Good morning. I'm preparing a mixed salad for lunch. It's nice and light. Noelle dropped in some delicious brown bread she made."

"Noelle made bread? I can't believe it. She's turning into a domestic goddess these days. When did she call?"

"About ten o'clock. She was in a rush, said something about a crisis in the salon."

"Hope it's nothing serious."

"I'm sure it's not, Emer. Noelle is a bit of a drama queen."

Avril took a J-cloth and polished the black marble worktop. It looked superb but was hard to keep clean; the slightest smudge showed up. "How are you today? Has the new medication helped at all?"

"I'm doing OK, love." She came over and patted her niece's swelling belly. "How about you two?"

Avril chopped some fresh parsley and added it to the bowl of cooked sliced potatoes, onion and mayonnaise. "I felt a big kick in bed last night but it had stopped by the time I woke Martin, so he wasn't impressed. Will I cut up some cucumber?"

"If you like. To tell you the truth, I don't have much of an appetite."

Avril had realised that.

"I'll try some, to please you." Emer ambled back to the kitchen table and sat down. She stroked the wood lovingly. "I'm glad they didn't throw this out. My mother got it as a wedding present from her mother and she cherished it. I'm thrilled it came up so well." The table had been stripped, sanded and polished. It had been restored to its former antique oak glory and Emer shuddered when she remembered the gruesome nightmare.

"Maggie wouldn't have let them throw that out," Avril said. "I still can't believe what a good job they did here, and in the rest of the house. Look out at the lovely sun, Emer. It's so nice to see it even for an hour, especially after the last week of rain. Weren't we lucky to have had any fine weather at all in Connemara? I never remember a summer this rainy."

"It's been bad all over Europe. Global warming."

"Probably," Avril agreed. "Maggie phoned to say she'd call in tomorrow after town. She asked if you needed anything in Marks – underwear or toiletries or whatever." Avril brought over a small plate of assorted salads. She knew a big pile of food would disgust Emer. "I'll make a stew for dinner. I got some nice gigot chops from the butcher's, lovely and lean. I'll cut up the meat into bite-sized pieces or I can take it out of yours – you don't have to worry about it, if you want to stick to your near-vegetarian regime. You'll get the nourishment from the meat's juices. Will I throw in some celery? You used to love celery."

"You're very kind. Did you get the fruit cake in the Spar?"

"Yeah, we can have some after lunch."

"It's not for us. Avril."

"Oh?"

Emer lifted her fork and moved pieces of lettuce around the plate.

"Are you expecting a visitor?" Avril joined her at the table.

"Yes," Emer answered enigmatically. "I hope so."

Avril glanced out of the window at her husband who was busily weeding around the shrubs. His muscular hairless chest glistened. Shirtless, he looked sinewy, sensuous and strong. Desire flickered in her abdomen. How many hours before they could go to bed? Being pregnant had made her more sexually charged than ever.

She still marvelled at her feelings of love and lust for this man. He was passionate, exciting, spontaneous. He didn't know he was handsome, didn't realise the powerful effect he had on her, maybe that was what made him so desirable. The baby lurched in her tummy. New life flickered in her body and her heart sang and yet she felt guilty for these feelings of happiness. Guilty because of Emer. Scared that the feelings wouldn't last.

Martin seemed to have settled in well at the hospital although he didn't talk much about his job. It had been very different in New York when she had worked with him at the clinic. Their nights had always been full of chat about patients and procedures and funny incidents that happened during the day. She missed that kind of communication and yet she knew he was sparing her feelings, because her life was now given over to the care of her aunt. There is only so much sickness any of us can cope with.

She wondered was Martin happy with the move to Dublin. She hoped with all her heart that they would be able to settle. In the end Martin had signed the contract for only six months, with an option to extend. It was early days, much too early for them to make a life-changing decision, he'd said. In her heart she agreed with him and she often wondered about how she'd feel when Emer was no longer with them. Would she still want to live in Ireland? And what about Martin's mum and dad? They'd never interfere but they must want their grandchild to grow up near them. Her dad missed them. She'd have to stop hassling herself. Her first concerns now must be for Emer.

It had taken Maggie's husband, Joe Walsh, the best part of the full week in July to get the garden in order. Once the gardeners had finished on the first day, he had more planting, weeding, raking, and pruning to do. It had been a marathon job but worth every backbreaking minute when Joe had seen Emer's joy.

Martin was more than pleased to keep up the job. The flowerbeds looked splendid, and even the straggly mimosa had been rescued and had thrived. He had just finished plucking away some of the spreading ivy which threatened to run amok and strangle the nearby magnolia. Despite the welts on his hands from the shears and the backache from hours of stooping, he felt good, proud of his labours. He was rewarded with magnificent scents: rosemary and lavender beside the patio had been a wonderful idea. He'd planted other herbs in pots just outside the back door: thyme, parsley, bay leaves and mint. Avril loved to cook with herbs. He breathed in contentedly. There was nothing like the smell of freshly mown grass. He loved gardening and had been deprived of the pleasure in New York. Tending balcony plants hardly qualified.

Emer would never tend her beloved garden again. Mr Noonan had advised complete rest, shaken his head when she'd begged permission to go out into the garden to help. Martin had no wish to contradict her specialist, Emer was his wife's aunt and he had no right to meddle, but he couldn't see the harm in letting her help a little – nothing strenuous and under his strict supervision. Maybe he'd ask her to water the window boxes this evening when the sun went down. After lunch he'd bring her out here and have her sit on her favourite seat beneath the apple tree. She could work on her new laptop and write some poetry if she was inspired.

The next door's back-bedroom curtain was drawn hastily and he spotted Cheryl quickly jumping out of sight. Stapleton the Snake, that's what Avril had nicknamed her because of her unfriendliness and reported backbiting.

He'd tried to greet her on numerous occasions as he returned from work but she'd always beaten a hasty retreat indoors. Emer merely told them that Cheryl kept herself to herself but that was not the impression he'd got. It seemed that she had been more in touch with Emer before he and Avril had moved in.

There was a nice couple, the McDonnells, both university professors, on the other side of the street, but they were away on holidays for the whole summer with her family in Clare. They'd be back at the end of the week before college started. Their adult children had long flown the coop. They had a key to Emer's house and were good neighbours by all accounts.

He hadn't formally met any of the other residents of the street since they'd moved in two months previously. Peculiar, as Avril had always told him about how friendly the Irish were. Of course, neighbourhoods changed dramatically when everyone was out at work all day. Granny Dorgan's generation had been stay-at-home mothers and there would have been a lot more socialising when Avril visited on holidays here as a child.

Emer's closest friends had been gracious and pleasant and warmly received him. He wouldn't jump to conclusions but the lack of welcome on the street was not encouraging.

Time would tell.

Emer wiped her chin with a napkin. She was drooling again – how frustrating and irritating. She'd eaten as much as she could manage.

"Delicious! Thank you, Avril."

The lunch had barely been touched.

"I like working with food, I've discovered. In New York I didn't have the time. We got in late from the clinic every evening and I must confess we ate a lot of convenience dinners. Here, let me." She took the plate from her aunt and placed it and her own in the new built-in dishwasher.

"What about Martin's lunch?"

"He'll eat after his shower. He's sweating after the garden work."

"Such a way for him to have to spend his Saturdays! We can get a gardener, I told you that, Avril."

"Martin enjoys it. He loves being out in the air."

"I hope you've done the right thing." Emer's forehead creased.

"What do you mean?"

"Coming back here. I'm not sure it was wise."

"We both wanted to. That job in the Bons is right up his alley and I should be able to pick up a nursing job once the baby is weaned –"

"Weaned? The poor little mite hasn't been born yet. Next thing you'll be signing the child up for college."

Avril laughed. "What I meant was there's no hurry for me to find work."

"No, you've a full-time job nursing me."

"Stop, Emer."

"I know why you're here, Avril. It's because of me, because of this damned cancer. I don't want to be a burden. I've always dreaded that. Please don't feel obliged –"

"Listen, mad aunt of mine, we've been through all this. It's a privilege to be here with you. In any case Martin applied for the Bons job long before we knew about your illness. He wanted a new experience."

"I just wish this hadn't happened. I always wanted a swift end, a sudden heart attack or something, but we don't have control over these things. I used to say that if I became seriously ill I'd swallow a bottle of vodka and a handful of tablets but when it happens it's –"

"Emer, don't talk like that. How would I have felt if you'd had a heart attack and I'd no chance to see you again? To enjoy our women's chats and to have a laugh, to tell you all about our lives and Martin's crazy extended family and about how things were in New York. Besides, I need you to help me through this pregnancy."

"I'm no use to you, Avril. I was never pregnant."

"You can listen to my moans and make sympathetic noises."

"You never moan."

"That's not what Martin thinks!"

"You must be bored stiff here without your job and your friends. Looking after a sick woman is not exactly riveting. You need to get out more. You don't have to baby-sit me. You'll have enough minding to do in the years to come."

"I'm not one bit bored, I can assure you. You and Martin are all I need at the moment and if I do feel like getting out, there are loads of things for me to do. Yesterday I met a woman in the supermarket and she invited me to join a gospel choir."

"That's a brilliant idea."

"I may give it a whirl, so that's quite enough of your objections and arguments. All right? It's our pleasure to be here with you. We would have visited you this summer, anyhow. You are not to feel anything but what we feel – genuine happiness at sharing this special time together." She crossed the kitchen, hugged her aunt tightly and was still shocked by the feebleness of the bird-like body.

"Poor Martin! He married a fool," said Emer. "Oh, here he comes now, your handsome husband. Did you have a nice shower?"

Martin leaned over and kissed Emer on the forehead. "I sure did. I'm famished. Have you two eaten?"

"We did." Emer stood up stiffly from the table. "If you don't mind, Avril, I'd like to have a little nap."

Avril's spirits sank. Her aunt was only up an hour at this stage. She must be feeling dreadful. Martin thought better of his brainwave of Emer going out to sit in the garden under the apple tree. She looked pale and ready to collapse. "You go on up, Emer," he advised. "A siesta is a good idea."

"I'll nip up ahead and open your bedroom windows." Avril led the way out of the kitchen. "The more air in the room, the better."

Emer hesitated at the kitchen door. "Martin, would you do me a favour?"

"Sure."

"Would you cut that fruit cake on the counter? Cut it into tiny pieces, crumble it."

"Are you still peckish?" he asked.

"No, would you put it out in the garden and leave some on the window-sill?"

"In the garden?" he queried. "You want the cake outside?"

She nodded.

He raised a quizzical eyebrow.

"It's for a friend," she explained. "A flying friend."

"Noelle on a broomstick?"

Emer smiled. "It's for my robin. I've neglected him lately. I hope he's still around."

"I've seen no sign of a robin," Martin said. "Maybe the garden renovation drove him away."

Emer nodded ruefully.

Martin polished off a large salad, a small ham and cheese quiche and half a batch loaf. He joined his wife in a cup of tea. "Did you check on her?"

"She's snoozing away," Avril said, pouring him another cup of his favourite brew. "It's not a bad idea, actually."

"What?" Martin said absent-mindedly, his eye flicking over *The Lancet*.

"Bed." She ogled him but he didn't seem to notice.

"You must be tired, honey. Go on up for a rest." He turned the pages to an article on micro-surgery.

Avril kicked off her sandals and ran her right foot up and down his bare leg. "I'm not tired at all."

He looked up and smiled. "You're not?"

"No," she drawled, then licked her lips seductively.

Martin was up out of his chair like a shot. He lifted his wife in his arms and carried her up the stairs, kissing her neck as he went.

"I am so damned randy." She giggled into his chest. "I can't get enough of you."

"On fire with desire?" He kicked open their bedroom door, which was on the far side of the landing, opposite Emer's room. He pretended to pant. He made loud grunting sounds.

"Stop, you nutter! We don't want to wake Emer."

"OK, then, you'll have to hush up yourself. No shrieking in ecstasy when I bring you to the pinnacle of pleasure!"

"Get me between the sheets and we'll see who screams first!" Avril felt happy. Horny and happy – an intoxicating combination. It was great to be with Martin again, to kiss him and stroke him and make leisurely love. Having his strong body under hers was the best aphrodisiac ever. Making love was life. Life had to be lived.

31

One Tuesday morning, Emer more alert than she'd been in weeks, pushed the breakfast tray down the bed and hoisted herself up on the new firm non-allergenic pillows Noelle had bought. Her body ached but her mind was crystal clear, the drugs no longer muddying her brain.

She opened her laptop, waited for it to boot up and then created a new file. She went to *Format* and chose the *single line spacing* option. She'd stick with the tried and trusted *Times* font – it was less distracting than some of the others.

Spelling Rules, she typed in carefully. First, she'd tackle plurals. She'd simplify the rules, give examples and set exercises. This was a new avenue for her to enjoy and explore. She began with simple plurals: *add s*. Now, she'd think up a list of humorous nouns for Deborah, words that would entertain the child: anaconda, bumboat, cockatoo, dunderhead, escapade, freckle, gum-boil. Emer racked her brain for a funny *h* word. Hook-worm?

Hogshead? The child was all into sounds so Emer wanted to appeal to her fondness for alliteration. Hollyhock. Yeah, good one for assonance as well. She giggled as she typed it in and shifted up further in the bed to get more comfortable. Once the child had mastered the spellings she could make up sentences with the words, a task Debbie enjoyed.

Avril popped her head round the door. "Did I hear laughter?"

Emer flushed. "Silly, I'm just being silly."

"Nothing wrong with that." Avril peered down at the small screen. "Working on a new poem?"

"Not at all. What poem would include such a miscellaneous mishmash?"

"Well, I can't see without my lenses and I haven't put them in yet. I'm giving my eyes a rest."

"Mmh," Emer murmured but she wasn't listening, the job in hand absorbed her. "I'm going to print out some revision exercises for Deborah Dixon. Maybe you could post them to her mother?"

"Has she e-mail?"

Emer stopped typing and stared up at her niece. "Now we're sucking diesel! I could e-mail her two or three times a week. It would keep up her practice and it would give me something worthwhile to do with my time. Deborah was always telling me about her computer games. Her dad gave her his iMac because he was investing in a new one. E-mail is the answer."

"Can you ring her mother now?"

"There's no hurry. I want to finish this list first. Can you think of a funny noun beginning with *J*?"

Avril lifted the breakfast tray. "What do you mean by funny?"

"Nothing sophisticated, nothing sardonic, just a comical word that would engage a ten-year-old who loves sounds."

"Jamboree? Juggler? Juggernaut? That kind of thing?"

"Juggernaut, yeah, that's good." Emer typed it. "A jolly jellyfish journeying home from a jamboree, jumped on a juggernaut and juggled his . . ."

"Jellies?" Avril suggested, getting into the swing of the madness.

"Juggled his jellies, I like it." She typed the sentence and grinned. "Sounds crude and lewd but the kid won't be aware of that. Deborah loves making up silly sentences. I gave her a few Edward Lear poems that amused her. 'The Dong with a Luminous Nose.' Remember that? I taught you that when you were a tiny tot. Maybe I shouldn't be fostering her sense of the absurd."

"Ah, if kids can enjoy themselves when they're learning, there's no harm, and the quicker we all develop an appreciation of the absurd the better."

Emer didn't respond. She was engrossed in her alphabetical list. Avril was happy that her aunt had found a mission.

Noelle stood rooted, hands on hips, frowning at her manager. "You're *what*?" She knew her voice was sharp but she could do nothing to mask her disgust.

"I'm leaving," Anita answered icily, "and I'm giving you two weeks' notice as my contract demands. It's normal procedure."

"Procedure?" Noelle echoed in disbelief. "How can

you talk about contracts and demands? I thought we were friends."

"We were never friends, Noelle." It was after 10 p.m., the salon had been closed for over an hour and she wanted to get away. She had a date. They stayed open until nine on Thursdays to facilitate late-night shoppers and her day had been quite long enough. "We had a business arrangement."

Noelle was stumped. She took a seat beside her employee, in a daze of disbelief, and tried to steady her voice. "Why do you want to leave?"

"I need a change," Anita replied, examining her nail polish.

Fury bubbled up in Noelle but she managed to camouflage it. "A change? Why?"

Anita stood up abruptly, went to the reception desk, rummaged underneath it and dragged out a flashy red handbag. She searched inside and drew out a matching vanity bag. Instead of coming back to Noelle, she took a seat behind the desk and this gave her an aura of authority, which annoyed Noelle even more.

"Have you got another job?"

Anita Dunne gaped at her boss from under her perfectly applied false lashes. "Of course."

"Where?"

"In the city centre." Anita started to file her nails, a gesture of indifference guaranteed to provoke. "A large salon. I'm going to run it."

"More money, is that it?"

"I will be earning more. That's not, however, why I'm leaving here."

"If you have something to say, Anita, I'd rather hear it. Were you unhappy here?"

Anita nodded.

"Why?"

"Oh, you know, this and that."

Infuriating. "Was it the other girls or the clients or what?"

"No, the girls are great – the ones who stay, that is. Have you noticed how many have left in the last six months, Noelle? Never a good sign of management, when there's such a big turnover of staff."

Noelle actually hadn't noticed anything amiss, had accepted the girls coming and going as part of the new breed of employees. The young changed jobs as often they changed their underwear and didn't seem to need security of tenure.

"I'm extremely overworked. I don't feel appreciated if you must know."

"Appreciated?"

"Yes, it's not nice to feel taken for granted."

Taken for granted. Brendan's parting words to her. Good God, did these people need constant reassurance and ego-massaging?

"I can see by your face that you haven't a clue what I'm talking about." Anita put away the vanity case and clicked her handbag shut. "So, there we are. I'll lock up, shall I? I'll place an ad in tomorrow's paper. Or would you prefer to word it yourself?"

"I'd prefer you to tell me what happened here. I don't understand what the hell is up with you?" Noelle's voice rose to a squeak.

"Alright, I'll tell you. You don't know the meaning of

time, you're always late for appointments, you've kept me waiting on numerous occasions. In fact, you're never here. You expect me to take care of everything, every little detail. I'm stuck in this salon most nights till after eight."

"You're my manager, Anita. That's what I pay you for and –"

"You said it! I'm the *manager* not the owner. It's your business not mine but I'm the one with the headaches, the tension and the niggling worries and ongoing battles that take place on a daily basis without your even knowing. You're losing clients because they like to get to know their stylists and none of the junior staff stay long enough for that. Linda may leave too. She's not happy."

"Linda has been with me nearly as long as you have," Noelle blustered. "She's very loyal and trustworthy. She has her own list of clients. She's popular."

"Exactly. She's always booked up and I can't take the rest of the regulars myself. How long is it since you actually took a scissors in your hands?"

"You have the devil of a cheek to address me like this. Enough is enough!"

"Yes, enough is enough."

Noelle sat open-mouthed.

"No job is worth this amount of hassle." Anita took her jacket from the coat rack and buttoned it up. "So, that's it."

"But . . . but why didn't you talk to me before now?"

"I tried."

"When?" Noelle challenged her. "When?"

"Every time you condescended to put in an appearance here."

"I'm here every day," Noelle protested.

"Sure, you breeze in for an hour in the morning, you come in with lists of questions and instructions and demands and then you breeze out again. I tried to talk to you on numerous occasions. You're too busy, always too busy."

Noelle spluttered with anger. "I am busy. I have to deal with the suppliers and the advertising agency and the recruitment agency. You have no conception or idea what it takes to run a business –"

"Well, that beats bloody all!" Anita stormed to the door. "Lock up, won't you?" She turned, waved cheekily and closed the door behind her.

32

At the top of the busy Whitworth Road on Dublin's north side, afternoon traffic chugged by and late September light streamed in the long windows of The Porterhouse pub. Maggie sat in stony silence as Noelle, who was on high doh, gesticulated madly and ranted and raved at the top of her voice. Maggie did her utmost not to interrupt the hysterical tale of woe, but she was embarrassed by the stares of two businessmen at the next table.

"She accused me of neglecting my own business." Noelle's apoplectic tone rose to fever pitch as she furiously stirred her coffee. "She hasn't a clue, not a damned clue how hard I work."

Noelle crossed her arms, a look of petulance on her face. Even now, Noelle could not see how abysmally she had treated her manager. For months Maggie had tried to warn her that she was spending far too much time away from the salon and that it wasn't fair on the staff. Emer apparently had said the same but their advice had fallen on deaf ears.

"You'll find it hard to replace Anita," Maggie said cautiously. "She was a Trojan worker."

"We can all be replaced," Noelle snapped. "I'll probably offer the job to Linda. She deserves the promotion and she's very respectful and knows her place. Anita got too big for her boots, that's par for the course in this profession, but it's the treachery that gets me."

"That's a harsh interpretation." Maggie nodded sympathetically at the two men who got up from the nearby table and stared hard at Noelle as they left.

She didn't notice, she was so caught up in her caustic account. "Bit the hand that fed her, that's what the bitch did. She had no gratitude, took all my kindness for granted."

"Anita obviously doesn't see it like that."

"I was a good employer, Maggie. I paid her well. I know I expected a lot from her, trusted her with my business, gave her extra responsibility – but wasn't that good for her? Didn't that give her experience? She should be thanking me – not walking out."

Maggie checked her watch.

"She said I was never there, that I didn't know the meaning of time, was always late for appointments, kept her waiting on numerous occasions. I kept *her* waiting!"

Maggie knew better than to argue, but facts were facts. Noelle was notorious for being late, had been all her life from the time they were in school. She didn't see anything wrong with keeping people waiting, saw her time as more important than anyone else's.

"I'd better go back. I told Linda I'd meet her at three."

"It's a quarter past now," Maggie pointed out.

"God, is it? Oh well, she's plenty of clients to keep her

occupied until I arrive." Noelle stood up and slipped on her brown suede jacket. "Will you give my apologies to Emer? Explain that I won't be able to call over until I get this mess sorted out."

"Emer realises you have a business to run. She'll understand."

"But be sure to tell her all about it, won't you, Maggie?"

Did it still not occur to Noelle that Emer might have more pressing matters on her mind?

In fact, later that afternoon, Emer did want to know the whole story. Avril had served coffee out in the garden, before heading off for her prenatal hospital visit. Then she was going to a gospel choir rehearsal.

Maggie poured more coffee. "I'll have to give this stuff up or I'll go into overdrive. Joe blames coffee for my sleep problems."

"Tell me all the juicy details about Noelle." Emer nodded encouragingly.

Maggie was amazed. "Does it not seem trivial to you?"

"Not at all, I find it diverting."

Emer was glad to hear about other people's problems, their amusing anecdotes, their difficulties or their triumphs, good news or bad news, everything and anything to focus on – other than herself. Cancer had turned out to be a self-absorbed mistress who demanded far too much attention. She smiled and sighed and groaned at various intervals during Maggie's blow-by-blow account.

"She's her own worst enemy," Emer finally said. "She doesn't learn from experience. She finds it hard to see anyone else's point of view."

"And she never listens to advice." Maggie shook her head in frustration.

"The thing is that she's a good person, really well-intentioned and generous, full of life and exuberance, but she lacks self-awareness. Possibly we all do."

"When you're running a business, people skills are vital." People skills. Emer hated that expression.

Maggie moved her chair towards the kitchen door, out of the breeze. "Are you sure you're comfortable enough out here? It's a bit chilly. I don't want you to catch cold."

"It's warm for the end of September. I love being out in the fresh air. The garden is so beautiful, thanks to Joe and Martin's efforts. Oh, did I tell you? My little friend is back. He probably never went away although I think the extensive work out here disturbed him, but I spotted him when I got up this morning."

"The robin?"

"Yeah, he looked a bit forlorn. Maggie, would you be able to get some –"

"Fruit cake?"

"Yes, please. Avril will think me insane if I ask her again. I intended to go to the shops today but my energy levels dropped completely. Sometimes I get a bit light-headed so I didn't risk going out on my own. There's no rush of course, only when you've time."

"I can make time."

"Go on, say it. I'm an idiot."

"No, you're not. It's great that he didn't leave. It shows there's a kind of connection, a mutual . . ."

"Reciprocity," Emer supplied. "My little robin is a sign of the cosmic harmony all around us."

"Do you think that birds have souls?"

"I believe all living creatures have," Emer said simply. "That's probably sacrilege, is it?"

"Who cares? It's a nice thought."

Emer moved a little and flinched, a gesture she thought imperceptible.

"How is the new medication working? Is the pain still bad?"

Emer closed her eyes. "It's bearable. I cut down on the dose as often I can although Martin doesn't approve. It tends to make me a bit nauseous but it's not too bad. I've come to like milk again and that helps to settle my stomach and I'm sleeping much better." She said nothing about the horrifying nightmares. "Now, that's enough about me. How is Holly doing back at school? Is she finding sixth year hard?"

"Don't start me! She's out every other night. She refuses to give up the job in Tesco and she's working Thursday nights and all weekend. The school specifically asked that they wouldn't work during their final year, but sure you may as well talk to the wall! She has a new pal, Neasa Boland, whom I don't like the sound of at all although I haven't met her yet. She's a few years older and knocks around with a gang from college. As far as I can see, all they do is party."

"They're young."

"And foolish," Maggie went on. "They drink too much and money seems to be no problem. Holly is easily led, Emer. She thinks it's cool to be in with the Uni crowd but she's naïve in many ways. I think they're into pot and everything. How do I know what they're at? It could be cocaine for all I know. Apparently it's the new drug of choice."

"It's worrying."

"When I tell her she has to settle down to study she just argues and tells me I don't 'get' her. I get her all right. She says she doesn't take drugs and only has a few pints – a few pints at sixteen! She thinks I'm out of touch, but the fact is that if she falls behind in her studies, she'll have to repeat the Leaving Cert next year. That would be a complete waste. Honest to God, I feel sorry for her teachers. She's not putting in the effort. It's a shame because she's academically bright but has no work ethic whatever."

"What does Joe say about it?"

"Tells me I'm being too fussy. He's convinced she'll cop on soon and get down to it."

Emer sat up and shifted her weight into a more comfortable position. Her back was sore. "I'd be tempted to lay off her, too. Remember we hated being told what to do. Trust her, Maggie. She was always a good student. She might be falling off a bit now but she'll peak later. And, as a wise woman once said, there's no substitute for brains."

"I hope you're right." Maggie stood up and took the coffee cups. "Right, let's go in. Are you going for a nap before dinner?"

"No, I think I'll read in the front room. I'll stay up as long as I can. Some days are better than others: I hate spending too much time in bed. I'm pacing myself but the longer I stay out of the bedroom, the more connected I feel to what's going on around me."

"That's important. You seem peaceful today, serene almost. I've just come from Noelle who is traumatising about nothing and here you are – you're a marvel, Emer."

"Lately I've sensed a new mood in myself. I'm not sure

when or how it started, but I've begun to feel different, more accepting or something. In the first few months I was terrified, baffled, questioned why I got sick. I was angry that it happened to me but not any longer."

"Really?"

"I've stopped fighting it. I want to reserve my energy for other things besides anger. I need to enjoy these last few weeks or months or whatever time I have left. Avril's presence here and her pregnancy have made things much easier – put things into perspective. I feel now that everything's right, that the timing is right."

"I can never see your illness like that and I must tell you that I am angry, angry and upset, and I don't understand – and never will – why bad things happen to good people."

"I'm sorry you're in so much pain."

"It's *your* pain that's the issue here. How can you say that the timing's right?"

"'*There is special providence in the fall of a sparrow.*'"

"The bleedin' Bard again?" Maggie groaned. "OK, let's get you in. Where's your book? In the front room?"

"Yeah, so is my laptop and I'd like to get some more work done. I want to send some stuff to Deborah tonight."

"How's that working out?"

"The kid loves it and it makes her feel very important to be getting e-mails. It's like a game to her and that's the way learning should be."

Maggie linked her pal up the back step. "How's Avril? I thought she seemed tired when I came in. She has a lot on her plate."

"Meaning me?"

"That came out wrong. I've offended you."

"I'm not that touchy. Avril's monthly checks are going fine. Soon she'll have fortnightly visits. Everything's in order, they say. Martin was like a kid when they got the scan photo. He's as proud as Punch and he's getting on well in the hospital too. He's very busy, naturally, and the job is demanding but he's working with a nice team. He says his colleagues are helpful and friendly and he gets in the odd game of golf, so I think he's OK with the move here."

Maggie helped her to the kitchen table and sat her down. Emer was quite stiff.

"Now, I'll peel a few potatoes for the dinner and that'll give Avril a start. Then I'll be off. I want to supervise Holly's homework for a change, see what she's up to. She needs to make a study plan and I can help her with that if she'll let me."

Emer watched her rinse the cups in the sink. "I rang Ronan."

"What?" Maggie swung around. "When?"

"Two weeks ago."

"Why didn't you tell me?"

"Nothing to tell."

Maggie came over and scrutinised Emer's face. "What did he say?"

"I wasn't talking to him."

"Della?"

"She wasn't there, either. I left a message on their answering machine. No reply; not yet, anyhow."

"Maybe they're away."

"I'm not ringing again, Maggie. It's up to him now."

33

January 2008

It was after 3 a.m. in the spare bedroom and their herbal teas had long gone cold. Ronan, still dressed in trousers and shirt, lay lengthways on the bed, his head and shoulders supported by the folded pillows, thoroughly riveted by Avril's unfolding narrative. He enjoyed hearing about the different parts of Emer's life, from the individual perspectives of herself, her niece and her friends. Avril was a faithful reporter of all she'd heard, seen and learnt.

The nippy morning air went unnoticed by them. He had listened in rapt attention up to this point. Now he felt compelled to interrupt.

"That's what Maggie told you? That Emer had rung and left a message on my answering machine. By my reckoning then she must have telephoned me in early September."

"Yes, I think so." Avril hesitated. "She never told me she made the call."

She must have been too disappointed, he surmised,

when she'd got no response. "That was almost four months before she died. Four months, dear God, I could have come to her. I could have shared the last weeks of her life." Emotion choked him. "I could have made my peace with my sister, helped you out with her nursing. I could have . . ." He buried his head in his hands.

"You didn't know," Avril murmured. "Don't blame yourself."

Ronan's ashen face turned even greyer. "She must have deleted the message." His lips creased into a hard thin line. "And she did it out of spite. She's manipulative, that's what she is and always was. Twisted, my wife is twisted."

Avril was startled by his sudden venomous outburst.

"Della always hated Emer," he explained.

"But why?"

Ronan shrugged. "It's difficult to say. I think she was jealous of Emer's openness. Della was 'circumspect' as my father once described her. She was reserved, stiff. From the beginning she resented Emer's outgoing nature, her confidence, her unreserved personality and her honesty. Emer had no time for snobbery and materialism of any kind and she didn't suffer fools. They often argued. Looking back on it now, I believe Della felt inadequate. The rift was a long time in the making before the big bust-up."

"I never understood any of it," Avril confessed. "Emer never spoke to me about the row and my father avoided the subject too. All my life I've wondered about it and why everyone shied away from discussing it."

Ronan was lost in thought.

"I shouldn't have listened to her," he said after a few moments. "I've put too much *meas* on what Della said.

My mother warned me about that, but I thought Della so wise, so clever. She wasn't clever at all, though, just selfish and controlling and I didn't see it." He paused, leaned over to where his heavy jacket was thrown on the end of the bed and took the starched white handkerchief from the breast pocket. He loudly blew his nose. "I've been such a fool."

The bedroom door creaked open and Martin tiptoed in, dressed in pyjama bottoms, his muscled chest bare. "Avril," he whispered angrily, "are you mad? It's nearly four o'clock in the morning." He shivered. "It's freezing in here. This is crazy sitting here in the cold night air. It will soon be time for Grace's feed. You've had no sleep in almost twenty-four hours."

Ronan jumped up. "I've kept her up. I wanted to hear about Emer."

His contrite face softened Martin's approach. "My wife has to get some sleep. Tomorrow will be another long harrowing day with the removal and constant visitors. She must sleep."

"Of course." Ronan nodded furiously. "I apologise." He looked at Avril with sheepish eyes.

Avril stood up from her bedside chair and calmly but firmly ushered her husband to the door. "Stop worrying, Martin. I'm having a nice chat with Ronan and as we all know it's long overdue. There's no point in my going to bed now. I'll feed Grace at five-thirty as usual. Then I'll sleep until eleven or so if you would go to the funeral parlour in the morning and check on the final arrangements." Avril patted her husband's arm. "Maggie said she'd go with you and she's already ordered the flowers. I'll speak to Gloria tomorrow as well."

"Gloria?" Martin didn't know any Gloria.

"The lead singer with the Gospel choir," Avril explained. "They're singing the funeral mass and they said they'd do some of the old Latin hymns at the removal." Avril looked over at her uncle. "Emer liked them. The *Tantum Ergo* and others."

"We grew up on those hymns. I could go with you to the funeral home in the morning," Ronan offered, wanting to be of some help.

"What about Grace's ten o'clock feed? She's always starving by mid-morning." Martin was in a mood, that was obvious, and it occurred to Avril that he felt left out. She'd been talking to her uncle now for over three hours. Her husband must have been lying in bed all this time, angry and upset and fretting about the time.

"Noelle is coming over early and she can feed Grace. I've already expressed more than enough milk. It's all right, Martin. I'll get my rest and tomorrow will work out fine. The neighbours are looking after the food and everyone will muck in."

He took her hands in his. "I'm only thinking of you."

She went up on tiptoe and kissed his forehead. "I know, sweetie. Go back to bed. Get some sleep and stop worrying."

Ronan looked on in envy. Such tenderness had long been missing from his life. Where had he and Della gone wrong? When had the rot begun to set in?

Martin caressed his wife lovingly, rubbing her back in gentle circular movements. "Please don't stay up much later, darling."

"This is important," she whispered urgently.

Ronan heard and his heartbeat quickened.

"I know." Martin pecked her on the lips and left the room.

Downstairs they continued their chat by the gas fire in the sitting room. "It's more comfortable here." Avril handed her uncle a steaming cup of cocoa. "We should have come downstairs ages ago and then Martin wouldn't have been disturbed." She laughed and then reddened. "I'm kind of high, I think. I've been crying and crying for days, for weeks and, to be honest, I think I have no more tears. Now, here I am with you and I'm actually laughing."

It wasn't laughter, it was hysteria, Ronan realised. His niece was suffering from sleep deprivation and severe emotional distress. She was overwrought, overtired and now she was talking to a long-estranged uncle. She must be confused. He certainly was. Such extremes of emotion would bewilder anyone.

"What would Emer think if she could see us now?"

"Maybe she can," Avril replied cautiously. "If she can, I think she will be pleased." She moved closer on the couch and linked her uncle. "This family has been at war for far too long. It's time for a truce."

Ronan squeezed her hand. "You're a beautiful person, Avril, non-judgmental, kind, warm. You remind me of Jackie. You're so like her."

"Except I'm black." Avril stared at him. "Was that the problem – was that what caused the division – my father's race? Was that what your wife objected to?"

He flushed. "It's not that simple and –"

"It is," Avril insisted quietly. "It is that simple."

"Della didn't approve of the marriage but I don't think she had anything against your father *per se*. She thought that Jackie would be censured, ostracised. She worried that people would be hostile –"

"And you?" Avril challenged him. "What did you feel?"

"You don't understand what Ireland was like back then. We had very few . . . coloured people –"

"Coloured," Avril echoed with a nod.

Ronan gulped hard. "I don't know how to describe the fear –"

She waved away his explanation. "I've been subjected to hostility, racism, misunderstanding all my life, Ronan – in America as well as here. Ireland doesn't hold the monopoly on racism and bigotry. Fear, you said, but fear is founded on ignorance. People must be educated. One in three non-Irish-nationals experiences harassment – that's the latest statistic today – today, not thirty years ago. How many of these immigrants are black? The Poles are more acceptable – is that it? They're great workers. The Filipino nurses are welcomed with open arms. But black? My husband – an expert in his medical field, a man who has devoted his life to the sick – was spat at in the street the other day – the two women who roared abuse at him presumed he was living off the State. Racism – I could write a book on it. It all boils down to the 'them' and 'us' syndrome – that's where it's at, Ronan. Them and us. I guess it was the fact that a black man loved a white woman – your sister – that was the real *problem*, wasn't it? That a black man had the audacity to love her and –"

"Avril, if you –" Ronan started to protest but Avril wasn't having any of it.

"They loved each other. They were really happy together – did you know that? Did your wife not understand? They were deeply in love. Dad told me. Emer told me. Gran told me she had never seen such devotion between two people. They were happy – poor but happy. They had nothing and they had everything; those were Emer's words."

Ronan blushed.

"I was born and they were ecstatic – that's the exact word Dad used. They were in love and living very happily until the night of that terrible accident –"

"Accident!" he exclaimed. "It was not an –"

Avril sucked in her breath, then recoiled from him in horror. "What are you saying?"

Awful awareness struck Ronan dumb. This girl had no clue of what had really happened. Nobody had told her that her mother had been brutally slain – murdered by mistake. The police had never admitted this but Ronan knew – he knew then and he knew now. Jackie's death was viewed by Della and – he now had to admit, by himself – as some sort of punishment, a kind of nemesis. When Della had voiced this opinion, Emer had flown into a rage; one cruel word had borrowed another and it was too late for either to redress or apologise. Each woman had remained intractable and he had sided with Della. The prior rancour and bitterness bubbled up into a frenzied row and then a vacuum of silent anger and recrimination.

Jackie's poor crushed body had been found dressed in her husband's bloodstained overcoat. Samuel Jones had been the intended target – the victim of a racist attack. His brother-in-law knew too, Ronan was sure. He must have suffered inordinate guilt. Emer had also known, he was convinced, but couldn't admit it. She certainly hadn't confided anything of this to Avril, he now realised.

She shook his arm. "What are you saying?" she wheezed frantically. "Ronan, tell me. What do you mean?"

Ronan hesitated, aware that the answer to that question would change everything for the young woman before him. Was she strong enough to bear the truth?

"Tell me, Ronan!"

Ronan sighed deeply. "It was probably a racist attack, Avril. We all knew that."

"But –"

"The police called it a hit-and-run because there were no witnesses to contradict them. In fact, they turned a blind eye. Nobody wanted to admit it. But Emer knew it, your father knew it and I did too. Your father knew the probable perpetrators – they were a violent bunch of louts who had been harassing him all along. And, you see, your mother . . . your mother was wearing your father's coat that night to keep out the cold . . . those monsters must have thought it was him."

Ronan saw the shock register on Avril's face. He felt terrible doing this to her.

"Emer hated the fact that I blamed your father for Jackie's death. I hated him for marrying her. I resented Emer too, could never understand why she was so supportive of their marriage. To be truthful, I was too narrow-minded and bigoted to understand. I was stupid and blind. I'm so sorry for everything, especially for not being part of Emer's life – and yours."

"I'm . . . I'm . . ." She gulped. "I'm hearing the words now and I don't want to believe you. I don't want to but

I do. In my gut I know it's true. No wonder he wouldn't talk about her – my dad. He couldn't tell me. He couldn't bring himself to tell me."

Ronan nodded.

"He said she died instantly . . . but was that true? Was it?"

"Let's hope so," he said quietly.

Avril rocked in her seat. "My mother didn't suffer. She was killed instantly." She kept rocking. "She didn't suffer. She was killed instantly." Over and over she crooned the words to herself, as the glowing coals of the gas fire cast shimmering shapes and shadows on the walls.

Ronan sipped his cocoa to calm his jangling nerves. He put his arm around his niece again and she stopped rocking. They huddled close together on the long couch staring into the fire.

In the moments of silence that followed each was lost in thought. Finally Ronan took her cup from her and put it on the table.

"Can you finish Emer's story, Avril? Would that upset you too much? I'd like you to tell me about her final weeks – if you feel up to it, I mean. I don't want to cause you any more suffering."

Avril stared hard at the flickering flames. "I'd like to," she whispered. "I like talking about Emer. It keeps her alive and warm and here with us, not cold and lonely in the back room." She snuggled back in his arms. "It's good that you're here, Ronan. It's right. And I'm glad you told me. I'm sad and I'm glad all at the same time. It's better to know the truth." She felt strangely safe with him now as she stared down at the hands that held her – the same hands as Emer's: long tapering fingers and short palms. The telling of Emer's story had worked magic, had brought them together. Her daughter, Grace, would know this man, her uncle, Avril was determined. And she would get to know his children, her Irish cousins, even if from a distance.

"When you've finished the story and you go back to bed, I'll sit with Emer. I'll stay with her till morning. I'd like to, if that's all right with you."

Her silence was consent.

34

November 2007

November came in gently, the weather still unseasonably mild. Avril's pregnancy was progressing nicely, with no complications. She'd kept her weight at a healthy level, much to her doctor's delight, and her blood tests were perfect. The baby's head engaged early so there was no possibility of a breach birth. The drawback was the constant pressure on her bladder, lower backache and the desperate urges to pee.

Emer managed a half-day's shopping with her niece and enjoyed every moment of the experience. Choosing baby clothes was a wonderful adventure these days with the vast ranges and styles to choose from. Emer remembered the limited choices available when Avril was born. It certainly was a different Dublin.

Avril had decided she didn't want to know the sex of the baby in advance so they stuck to lemon, green, brown and white colours. Others would buy the 'blue for a boy' or 'pink for a girl' outfits, Emer promised her. Avril spotted a gorgeous little red babygro that would be perfect for Christmas and Emer duly admired it. She tried to sound enthusiastic but inside she was unsettled – there was no way she'd be with them at Christmas, she feared.

They also purchased some blankets, sheets, and other baby accoutrements: bottle warmer, changing mat, car seat, crib and a multicoloured mobile of butterflies to hang over it. Mothercare was an Aladdin's Cave.

Emer's present would be a beautiful state-of-the-art pram that they'd ordered from Clerys and a handcrafted pinewood cot for when the child was old enough to sleep in it. She would give them a generous gift of money too when the time came.

One morning's shopping wiped her out.

The next day, Mr Noonan, as expected, scolded her for overextending herself. He was still doing regular blood tests and altering her dosage of the various concoctions and medication.

"I have to congratulate you on your resolve, Emer, but I can't fudge the issue: the cancer is spreading at a faster pace. All I can do is try to slow its progress."

"I realise that, Mr Noonan."

"You'll have to play your part too. You can't be overtaxing yourself, racing around the town."

"I know," she agreed, "but it did me good. Buying baby stuff was terrific. It's lovely to have something to look forward to and what's more important than a birth?"

He nodded.

"Avril needs me and I like to be needed. I won't always be able to help her and I won't be with her for much longer."

Mr Noonan came out from behind his desk and pulled up a chair beside hers as if he were meeting a friend for a jolly chat. There was no way of saying this but bluntly.

"Have you got your affairs in order?"

"Of course."

She had made her will years before and she hadn't had to change it in the intervening time, but those words coming from his lips, albeit spoken gently, were ominous.

Emer knew she was dying day by day, minute by minute, but sometimes she was able to stop thinking about it altogether. She engrossed herself in the lives of others. Sometimes she even succeeded in forgetting that her body was a time bomb.

Emer had grown to like Mr Noonan more and more with each visit. Her initial impressions of his aloofness and coldness had been wrong – of course she had been in shock that day five months before and not in a position to make character judgements. She could hardly believe that five months had passed since that fateful June morning when she'd first walked into his rooms.

"I'm nearing my allotted time span."

"I'm sorry, Emer. You should still keep up the medication and when the pain becomes worse – and it will – then we'll talk about hospitalisation."

"I want to die in my own home, Mr Noonan."

"Have you discussed that with your niece?"

"She'll want that too."

"It may not be feasible or practicable. You'll need morphine and the dosage will have to be monitored."

"I'm going to enquire about hospice nursing at home."

"That's a possibility and your niece's husband is a

doctor, of course, that does make a difference. However, you may have to reconsider. We have more facilities here in the unit. Leave your decision open for the moment, will you?"

He was kind but not too soft with her, truthful and always honest. She appreciated his professionalism and his humanity. His staff could not have been better. Emer had no complaints with her hospital experiences although she knew others were not as lucky.

There were still some horror stories doing the rounds about patients who had been wrongly diagnosed and others who had died while awaiting treatment. Emer knew people like her – with private medical insurance – were privileged. This was wrong and it appalled her. In former times she would have fought their fight but now her depleting energy wouldn't permit that.

"The best I can do is to look after myself for as long as possible and be there for Avril and her baby. I won't be a bother to anyone, if I can help it."

"There's no need to say that, Emer. I know you well at this stage."

"Yes, I think you do – better than anyone else, maybe."

Mr Noonan shook hands with her and she left.

The weather broke on the sixteenth of November and a storm blew up quickly and without warning. The rain bashed against her bedroom window and the sky darkened, thunder clouds looming menacingly. Emer came downstairs to find Avril furiously scrubbing the kitchen cupboards. The marble counter top was littered with packets and bottles and tins of food.

"What are you up to, darling?"

"I was restless, got a sudden burst of energy." Avril continued to wipe the shelves of a top press. She was standing on a chair and precariously leaning into the enclosed space.

"Avril, get down. Do you want to fall?"

Her niece didn't turn around. "I'm fine. I'm just finishing this one. Do you know there's still some dust left in here from the carpenter? Maybe it's wood shavings. Just one more swipe and it will be done."

Emer went over and gripped the back of the chair to steady it as Avril got down. "You are pure mad!" she admonished her niece. "If Martin saw you, he'd be raging."

"It's no big deal. Would you like a coffee?"

"I'll get them," Emer said. "You sit down."

She noticed her niece wiggle on the hard kitchen chair. "Would you prefer to go inside to the couch? You look very uncomfortable."

"I can't remember what comfortable feels like." She wriggled again. "I'm like a beached whale that's swallowed a coiled spring."

Avril's stomach contracted in a long spasm. "*Gee! Ouch!* That hurt!" she scolded her tummy.

As she spooned the instant coffee into the mugs, Emer scrutinised her niece. She put some chocolate biscuits on a plate. "Have you started, do you think?"

"Started what?"

"Labour." She poured Avril's coffee and brought it to her. "You may have started labour."

Avril was startled. "I'm not due for another ten days."

"Nobody told Bonzo that!"

Another long piercing pain drew a groan and a few muttered curses. "I think you may be right, Emer. Gad!"

"Start your breathing exercises. Short small pants, that's it." Avril went to the phone in the hall. "I'm phoning Martin." She left the kitchen door ajar so she could keep an eye on her charge.

"*Ow, ouch*! This is goddamn painful. I'm only after getting over the last one and another bloody pain comes."

It amused Emer the way Avril spoke with a mixture of Americanisms and Irish idioms. The hospital receptionist told Emer to hold on and Martin was paged and soon came on the line.

"Martin, hi, I'm fine thanks. It's about Avril, I think she has started. Yes, honestly. I feel you should get here as soon as possible. I know first babies usually take their time arriving but," she lowered her voice, "this time it might be different. Her contractions are coming every three or four minutes as far as I can make out. They came on fast and furious. Of course, I don't honestly know when they started – I'm not long up out of bed." Emer twiddled with the telephone cord. "Can you get away? Great, we'll see you soon, then. Luckily, she has her bag packed for weeks past. I'll have her ready at the door for you.

"Thanks, Martin, now take it easy in the car. You know what the traffic is like and the rain always slows things up. I wish I could go into the hospital with her and save you calling over here. I could call an ambulance and you could meet us. . . . All right, I know it's not on, I haven't . . . you're right."

Emer went back to the kitchen where Avril was huffing

and puffing. "I'm scared, Emer." She was very flushed in the face.

"Don't be. Martin's on his way," Emer announced, her heart swelling with emotion.

"I guess this is it," Avril muttered between pants. "It's time."

"Yes, love." Emer hugged her niece. "Everything in its own time."

Maggie put the remains of the delicious sherry trifle back in the fridge. "Did you enjoy it? Good, there's plenty left for tomorrow. I can see you're worried, Emer. Martin will phone the minute there's any news."

"But they went in hours ago, hours ago. I really thought she was going to drop the baby here in the kitchen!"

"You're gas, do you know that? It's not that bloody easy to *drop* them, I can assure you. Sure I was eighteen hours with Holly. Eighteen hours – I'll never forget it. Neither will Joe! I'll never let him."

Emer glanced at the clock on the cooker again.

"Let's look at *EastEnders*, will we?" Maggie gently pulled her friend up from her chair, linked her into the sitting room and again noticed how slow and stiff Emer was; she walked now like an old woman and it broke Maggie's heart. She took the remote control and flicked on BBC One. She wanted to get Emer's mind off the hospital. "OK, Dory? Make yourself comfortable, pile up the cushions. It's starting."

Emer hated *EastEnders:* too many hassles and fights and depressing storylines. It lacked the humour and humanity of *Coronation Street*.

The phone rang and Maggie jumped up and ran out to the hall. Emer followed awkwardly after her. Her back was acting up again. She felt decrepit.

"Yeah, she's here, hang on!" Maggie handed the phone to Emer.

"Oh, Martin, thank God! That's great! Congratulations! A beautiful baby girl!" Emer put her hand over the receiver. "Maggie, it's a girl. It's a girl!" She spoke again to her nephew-in-law. "And Avril? She's OK? I'm sure she's exhausted, God love her. Give her all my love, will you?" Emer's eyes filled up. "And the baby – what weight was she?" ("Seven pounds nine ounces," she relayed to Maggie.) "That's big for a first, isn't it? I'm sure you're as proud as anything. Well done to all three of you. Maggie is standing here beside me and she says congrats too. We'll open a bottle and when you come home you can wet the baby's head with us! Take your time. Would you prefer to stay there tonight with Avril and the baby? . . . Ah, sure Avril will need her sleep. And the baby too must be worn out – it's an ordeal for the little mite. Isn't it wonderful – you have a baby daughter. Doesn't the word sound lovely – your daughter? . . . Yes, yes, she's my grandniece. Martin, I'm so pleased for you both. Tell Avril I'll be there in the evening for the permitted hour come hell or high water."

Maggie mouthed at her and made gestures.

Emer giggled. "Maggie's here. She was wondering what name you finally decided on? . . . Are you sure? That's nice of you both. I'll see you later. Don't rush back and give your two girls my love." She hung up.

Maggie had opened the whiskey bottle and poured each of them a drink when Emer joined her. "Well, what name?"

Emer beamed. "They're going to let me choose."

"Have you any ideas?"

"Loads. I'll have to see her first to see if the name suits but I'd love them to call her after Jackie. No, not Jacqueline – her second name."

"Which is?"

"Grace. How would that sound? Grace Liston. It has a certain ring to it, don't you think?"

"It's lovely." Maggie raised her glass. "Here's to baby Liston, hopefully Grace."

Emer felt every bone and muscle in her body ache. She had barely enough energy to turn in the bed. She leaned over and switched off the bedside lamp. In the darkness, her thoughts swirled. November sixteenth. It would soon be Jackie's anniversary. The month of the Holy Souls, the 'faithful departed'. The month to remember the dead. But now it was also the month of Grace's birth.

Maggie had stayed until the proud father returned. They had a drink with him and after Maggie had helped Emer to undress and get into bed, she had left in a taxi.

The rain had finally stopped, Emer realised. Things always seemed better after the rain.

35

The baby slept placidly in her grandaunt's arms. She was a pretty infant, perfect and petite, with a neat head full of glistening dark curls. Her moth-soft eyelids fluttered gently, her breathing barely audible.

"Magic!" Emer lightly ran her lips over the baby's forehead. "Her skin's amazingly soft, Avril. She's a beauty."

Avril grinned proudly from the bed. "Martin is behaving like a complete idiot since she arrived: running around like a headless chicken, checking her every two minutes when she's here with me and when she's taken to the nursery he's drawn there like a magnet, badgering the nurses with inane questions and queries and demands. They have the patience of saints. He's rung his mother in Philadelphia twice since last night. She's wildly excited. And his dad, of course – this is their first grandchild too."

Emer was mesmerised by the sleeping bundle in her arms. The baby's body, though small, was strong and sturdy. Each tiny movement of her fingers or twitch of her mouth fascinated Emer. This teeny person was just starting out on life's journey while she was . . . Emer remained transfixed, staring down at the baby, but she'd heard the catch in Avril's voice at the mention of Martin's parents.

"I presume you've been talking to your own dad." Emer continued to admire the new arrival and avoided looking directly at her niece.

"Martin phoned him last night just after he phoned you but he got no answer." Avril reached to her bedside locker for tissues. "Must have been at a conference or something, but he knows I'm in hospital because Martin left a message on his answering machine."

Emer continued to cuddle the baby.

"I expect he's busy." Avril wiped sweat from her chest and neck, tore off her cardigan and threw it on a spare chair. "Why are hospitals always so infernally hot?" She tossed the used tissue into the waste-bag hung on her bed.

"Well, we can't let this little one get cold, can we, sweetheart?" Emer gently stroked the velvet cheek. "Why don't you close your eyes, Avril, and have a nap? I'll be here to watch her."

"Where's Martin? Has he gone for coffee?"

"He got a text message and he went out to make a call."

"Must be the hospital. He had to defer some of his surgery but another specialist is taking over his urgent cases, which leaves him a bit freer for a day or two. Then he'll take a week off when the baby and I come home."

"You'll need help and you'll need rest. Now, lie back and close your eyes for a while."

Avril did as she was told but her mind refused to

switch off. Eyes still shut, she whispered to her aunt: "Have you come up with a name for her?"

"Yes. Don't feel you have to use it though. She's your daughter. It should really be you or Martin who chooses, or both of you."

"We wanted you to pick her name, Emer." Avril opened her eyes and sat up again, she was too restless to doze. "We discussed it and we both felt you were the one to name her."

"All right then, what about Grace? I've always liked that name. Looking at her now, she's so serene, isn't she? I think it suits her."

"It's a lovely name," Avril agreed. "Mum's middle name. Yes, that's a great idea and it does suit her. What do you think, Daddy? Grace?"

Emer half turned to see Martin coming back into the room, with a gigantic teddy bear in one arm and a magnificent bouquet of red roses in the other.

"You big softie!" Avril laughed. "Look what your Silly Billy of a daddy bought for you, Grace! You'll be smothered!"

"Grace." Martin rolled the name around his mouth to test it. "Grace, yes, you're our little emblem of calm, our good-luck charm. It's a wonderful name, Emer. The teddy is for you, Avril, by the way, not for the baby."

"Ah, gee, Martin!" Avril took the huge bear and snuggled into it. She buried her face in the soft brown fur. "Are you going to spoil me?"

"What's a daddy to do but spoil his only daughter when she has just given birth?"

Avril, startled by the deep familiar voice, looked up in

astonishment. Emer whipped around in her chair and Martin burst out laughing at the stupefied reactions of the two women as Samuel Jones, looking tall and handsome, and resplendent in an immaculate grey suit, strode into his daughter's private room. He kissed Emer on the cheek and gently took the sleeping infant in his arms and cradled her. "Hi there, little one. I'm your Granddad Sam."

The first few days after Avril came home with Grace were marvellous, days full of joy and laughter. New life was a wondrous thing and it made its presence deeply felt in the house which had experienced such sadness in recent times.

There was a constant stream of well-wishers who all wanted to hold the baby. Grace was the centre of attraction and brought smiles to everyone's face. Members of the gospel choir were regular visitors and brought handmade knitted caps and coats and bootees. One girl, Alice, a talented mezzo-soprano, had crocheted a magnificent christening robe. Emer was glad that Avril had made such lovely friends in the short time since she'd settled in Cabra Road.

Maggie got broody when she first saw Grace. She fell in love with the soulful dark eyes. Noelle came on the second day with a beautiful outfit but she didn't stay long. Emer wondered if seeing the baby had upset her but Maggie assured her that that was not the case. It seemed Noelle was now doing her fair share in the salon, spending her working hours there and looking after her staff, as well as her clients.

Maggie was very occupied with her work as a consultant. She was training staff in a large department store and giving lectures on human resources, staffing, and conflict management in various firms throughout the city. The winter months were her busiest time but she wasn't complaining – because work, in many ways, kept her sane, kept her from fretting too much about Emer.

The two friends explained their heavy work schedules and why they couldn't spend more time with her and Emer assured them she understood. They had to carry on with their lives. She certainly didn't expect everything to come to a standstill for her. Privately she was glad that their visits had become less frequent. It was too difficult for all of them to keep up an act.

Besides, life was busy for Emer too. She had got a sudden burst of energy, from where she wasn't sure. Baby Grace had transformed the house, dominating time and schedules and conversations. Everywhere she looked there was a conglomeration of baby stuff: nappies, changing mat, bottles, blankets, a baby bath, cardigans, babygros, furry toys, a pram, a buggy. Everything she saw and heard delighted Emer.

Martin, as arranged, had a week's leave from work and took to fatherhood like a major general. He made endless lists: Grace's feeding times, Grace's nappy changing, Grace's sleeping hours, shopping expeditions for extra things for Grace. He recorded everything about her: when she slept, when she peed, when she did a poo, when she burped, even when she yawned. Avril just laughed at her husband's temporary insanity. It was a military campaign. But none of them could deny that Martin was best at consoling the baby when she cried. She nestled into his shoulder and seemed to become an extension of his body.

He was able to *read* when she was hungry or tired or wet. It just came naturally to him, which was just as well as Avril was exhausted for a few days after the birth.

Martin made her rest as much as possible because breastfeeding was tiring. She expressed two bottles a day and they used these for the night feeds. Avril was feeling vulnerable and weepy and Emer suspected her niece might have been suffering from the 'third day blues'. She was glad that Sam was with his daughter at this crucial time.

They'd put Sam up in the spare room, the peach one at the back of the house, once long ago inhabited by Ronan, and he mucked in with all the chores when Martin allowed him: nappy-changing, winding and burping. He insisted on washing Grace's clothes by hand, in a very mild soap powder. He was as pernickety about Grace as Martin was.

Sam was forever staring into the baby's pram, crooning and smiling and singing softly in his deep bass voice. It amused Emer to see him so enamoured of the child and it reminded her of how he was with Avril when she was small.

The first week of Grace's life passed with all this love and activity and fun. The neighbours had all been in except for Cheryl and her husband. Emer was conscious of the snub. Avril noticed but didn't say anything. She understood clearly.

The time for Sam's departure finally came and the night before his flight back to New York he asked Emer if they could have a private tête-à-tête. He persuaded Avril and Martin to go out for a meal and convinced Martin that Grace would survive without them for a few hours. Martin reluctantly agreed and eventually Avril did too, because she knew her father needed some time alone with her aunt.

Emer stretched out on the long sofa and Sam fixed an extra cushion behind her back and threw a rug over her knees. He lit the gas fire and Emer felt its warm glow fill the room. Lately she'd been feeling the cold. The baby was asleep in a carrycot on the floor beside them.

Sam brought over a side table and set a glass of whiskey on it for her. "This will do you good," he said. He poured a glass of red wine for himself and settled down in one of the armchairs. He took a sip from his glass. "Merlot, my favourite, it's nice and full-bodied. How's the whiskey? If they could see us drinking on duty, they wouldn't be too impressed, would they?"

Emer didn't want to waste their time alone in idle pleasantries so she got straight to the point. "I know you're worried about Avril living here, Sam. Don't worry, I doubt very much if they'll settle here after . . . I doubt if they'll settle here for good."

"I don't want to interfere in Avril's life," he stated. "She must have told you how uneasy I was by their move here. I acted petulantly and I regret having upset her. In her absence, I've had time to reflect and reconsider. It's up to them where they want to live."

"But Dublin wouldn't be your choice," she prompted.

"Quite frankly, it wouldn't. You know how I feel about the place."

"I know how hard this was for you – coming back to

Ireland. I'm so glad you did come, Sam. It's important to Avril." Emer hoisted herself up against the cushions and winced before she could mask it.

"You're in pain," he said quietly. "You usually do a great job of hiding it, I've seen that in the last few days, but I wish you wouldn't when you're with me. Emer, I'm so damned sorry this thing has happened to you. It's not fair. You don't deserve it."

"Nobody deserves sickness." She sipped her drink, her swallow tightening.

"You're right. Nobody does. I see cancer every day in my practice. Sometimes I can do something, sometimes I can't. It's awful when I can't."

"Mr Noonan feels the same. He's a wonderful doctor and a good person. So are you, Sam. Jackie was lucky to have met you."

Sam grunted.

"I envied her the way you loved her."

"More fool you, Emer. My love for Jackie was what killed her."

"It was *not*." Horrified, Emer put down the whiskey on the coaster he'd positioned near her. She stared hard at him. "It certainly was not. I never want you to say that again. Never think it again. Do you hear me, Sam?"

He took a sip of wine and stared into the fire. "Why not say it? It's the truth."

"No, it is not. Love didn't kill Jackie. It was hate, hate and malice and stupid blind bigotry."

"She was wearing my heavy army coat, Emer. That night, she was wearing my coat. Why on earth did I let her use the cursed thing?"

"You wanted her to be warm, Sam. You loved her, you wanted to protect her."

"But I didn't protect her, did I?" Sam jumped up from his chair. He went over to his granddaughter and gently pulled her blankets up around her exposed shoulders. "Those louts thought she was me. That car was meant for me." He turned back to Emer, his eyes flashing. "They killed Jackie, they murdered her, mowed her down in cold blood but that bit *was* an accident. It was an accident of mistaken identity. They meant to hurt me."

Emer nodded. "I know. I've always known."

"I'm sorry, Emer. I never said that to you before. All these years and I never said sorry. I couldn't."

He came back to his armchair and pulled it closer to the sofa. He sat down, a grim expression on his determined face, and took her hand and gripped it. The thinness of her fingers and the limpness of her touch moved him. "I'm saying it now. I am truly sorry for having caused you and your family so much pain."

"Sam, please. None of it was your fault."

"I took her away from you. I stole your sister. I caused your poor mother agony, torment. I often felt she became ill because of her grief."

"That's not true, Sam."

"Your family was split. I caused such suffering. And I deprived Avril of a mother's love." He started to shake. He was a big man, strong and muscular, and it was horrendous to see him sitting there helpless, castigating himself for something that happened thirty years before. "Your brother despises me."

"Ronan has his own demons."

"He despises me with due cause." He didn't realise he was squeezing her fingers so hard. "He never wanted us to marry. He warned me something could happen. He was totally against the marriage, against us being together. He was right, as it turned out."

Emer abruptly took back her hand. "He was not. Sam, he was *not* right. He was wrong, wrong, wrong! He meddled and interfered. He was no help, no help to you and Jackie or to my mother and me afterwards. He was so damned self-righteous, so wrapped up in his own grief and his own rightness that he couldn't give love and compassion where it was most needed." She took a deep breath, startled by the intensity of her raw emotions. "I feel sorry for Ronan, not for Jackie or for you or for me, and certainly not for Avril. She has love in her life, deep love. I'm proud of her, she's a special person and that's down to you. Are you listening, Sam? Jackie would be so proud to see her today, to see her happily in love with a good, dear man, to see her with a beloved child. This is a happy story, Sam, with a happy ending. Avril couldn't be happier than she is now. It doesn't matter where that pair settles in the end, Sam. They're right together and they'll stay together, you can bet on that."

"You are one terrific lady. I never thanked you for all you've done for Avril. All these years you gave her everything a mother would have given. You taught her so much. I never thanked you –"

"You don't need to thank me for loving her, Sam. She has brought happiness and meaning to my life."

"Mine too."

"I want you to move on from this now. Promise me.

Bury that night forever. What's the good in torturing yourself?"

"Those bastards –"

"Don't waste your breath on them. They robbed Jackie's life, don't let them rob yours too. Our time is too precious."

Suddenly and forcibly his excessive self-indulgence appalled him. "Here I am wallowing in self-pity while you are battling for your life. Emer, I'm a stupid old fool."

"Less of the old, please! You're only a few years older than I am and I don't feel old at all. Add some more Coke, will you? The bottle is there on the mantelpiece. You've a very heavy hand with the booze – it reminds me of my mother."

"Another great woman."

Emer saw he might become maudlin. "Isn't Grace an excellent baby? She hasn't stirred at all. Baby-sitting her will be no bother. You'll make a wonderful grandfather. Tell her about me, will you? And tell her about Jackie."

36

The December days were long and dark and Avril, who felt tired most of the time, was busy with the baby and also with looking after Emer who was deteriorating rapidly.

Avril dreaded the thought of this Christmas. The relentless jingle of carols and Yuletide ditties in the shops and on the radio was driving her nuts. There was no escaping it. The enforced jollity and merriment mocked her increasing sadness. The television was as bad with so many programmes devoted to Christmas celebration and preparations: how to decorate with taste, seasonal recipes for a successful dinner party, advice for busy housewives on how to avoid the Christmas rush, choosing presents for your loved ones. Last night there was one programme entirely devoted to showing the viewer how to set the dinner table with grace. Some chance with Grace!

Emer was very weak. She got out of bed for a few hours in the afternoons and sat quietly working on her laptop or reading a book or watching television by the sitting-room fire. Grace, in her carrycot beside the sofa, either slept the sleep of the innocent or gurgled happily in her waking hours. She was an angelic baby. Emer experienced great calmness when she was minding the infant. She was absorbed with the child, enchanted by her every movement and sound and felt she was witnessing the start of something truly remarkable. For her tiny grandniece she foresaw a fulfilled life, a path of wonder and discovery.

"You will have wings," she whispered constantly in the tiny ear. "You will take on all the adventures this life has to offer."

Emer relished these moments alone with the baby and felt she was of some practical help to her niece who could get on with her chores or sometimes even take a siesta.

Avril was in a constant state of alert, always watching for the slightest change in Emer's demeanour. She didn't need her medical training to realise that her aunt was failing on a daily basis. Avril insisted that she was more than capable of looking after her, and that there would be no need for a hospice nurse. She hated the idea of a stranger doing a job she was more than willing and able to do. Emer argued in vain and Avril had her way.

Martin had started to administer morphine in small doses and that had alleviated a lot of Emer's pain. He consulted with Mr Noonan and between them they agreed what was necessary.

What was worse than the pain for Emer was the overwhelming fatigue. She no longer felt able for lengthy visits and Avril discouraged people from staying for more than an hour at a time. It was a difficult balancing act as

Emer loved the company but, while her spirit was willing, her flesh couldn't be weaker. Every day was a struggle.

Avril found these last weeks truly awful – the worst of her life. She was losing her greatest ally and her closest female confidante, day by day, hour by hour, minute by minute, and she didn't feel ready to let her go. Neither could she bear to watch Emer suffer. It was gut-wrenching to watch her aunt's pain, feebleness and flagging energy levels.

Emer kept up a good a 'performance' but conversations with Avril were limited to discussions about the baby or what they'd eat for dinner. More than anything Emer wanted to restore their former closeness but she found it extraordinarily difficult. She was on a journey that nobody else could travel and consequently felt isolated. She wasn't lonely, in fact she'd never had so much company, but the truth was that nobody could really comprehend how she felt and she didn't expect them to.

Martin was a model of tolerance with both of the women. He never lost his cool, was always ready to listen and Emer felt loved, very loved, but nevertheless alone.

She was beaten and bombarded by the persistent aches and discomfort. Some nights the pain was so bad she wished she wouldn't wake the following day. Martin prescribed sleeping pills, which gave her a few hours' respite. They knocked her out but they didn't stop the fretfulness.

The nightmares grew worse, terrible in their intensity, frightening and relentless. They always centred on her parents and on Jackie. The same craggy hill figured in most of them, and it always seemed impossible to climb.

Jackie appeared just within reach – yet unreachable – as she ran away up the grassy knoll, her dark hair streaming after her, her long skirt swirling in the breeze. Emer often found the pillows drenched when she awoke, whether with sweat or tears she could never be sure.

Since his return to work in the New York clinic, Avril missed her father. Although Martin was 'a saint', he was out at work all day. Maggie's visits had also become less frequent and Avril wondered about that. One Thursday afternoon, just after Avril had given her aunt lunch in bed – or what passed for lunch, Emer had barely touched the soup – there was an unexpected knock on the front door. Avril, her daughter in her arms, made her way carefully down the stairs and answered. She was surprised to find a priest on the doorstep.

"May I help you?" she enquired politely, Grace attached to one hip.

"Lovely baby." The priest patted Grace's head. "May I come in, dear?"

"I'm a bit busy." Avril tried to keep her tone friendly but opened the door only a fraction. "I don't have time."

He looked perplexed.

Avril was getting cold, standing in the doorway. The breeze would give Grace a chill. "Time for a chat, I mean. Oh, maybe you're collecting for something? Hold on and I'll get my purse."

The priest laughed aloud. "Oh dear oh dear oh dear! You thought I was here to pay you a courtesy visit, did you? Or you presumed I was collecting, eh? The curse of the clergy, I always say. Once a parishioner sets eyes on you, you must be calling for money or you must want something."

Avril blushed to her roots.

"Not to worry, my dear, let me explain. It's Emer I'm here to visit. I know she's very ill, you don't need to elucidate." He stepped into the hall. He shivered. "Better shut that door, dear. There's a fierce draught getting in." He tickled Grace under the chin. "Isn't she a dote? God bless her."

"Father, is my aunt expecting you?" Avril asked, knowing full well that she wasn't.

He completely ignored the question. "She's in the lilac room at the front of the house, is that right?"

Avril's mouth set. Who was this crazy cleric and what did he want with Emer? Her aunt, above all people, wouldn't relish a visit from a man of the cloth . . . unless, of course, she was having some kind of eleventh hour conversion. Avril seriously doubted it, but how did this man know about the lilac room?

"I'm sorry, dear," he went on. "Allow me to introduce myself which is what I should have done in the first place. I'm Gerald Moore, Noelle's uncle." He put out his hand to shake hers.

Avril struggled with the baby but managed to brush his fingers with hers. "Noelle's uncle?"

He was already on the first step of the stairs. "Yes, dear. I was the one who painted the lilac room. Mind you, I had a lot of help from the lads. I hear she was delighted with the house. The poor creature needs a bit of comfort, doesn't she? That's why I'm here you see, to –"

Grace started to whimper and Avril hoisted her up over her shoulder to be better able to massage her back. "I think Emer may be asleep," she lied.

"Not to worry. I'll sit with her until she wakes. I'm free now for the rest of the afternoon. I have some calls to make later this evening and I've a wedding couple coming to see me tonight but for the next hour or two I'm free and at Emer's disposal."

With that, he was up the stairs like a hare on speed. Avril shrugged. She'd done her best.

"Now, don't be alarmed, it isn't a strictly religious book at all, Emer, it's more in the spiritual line. Noelle warned me you wouldn't appreciate a sermon, as you weren't 'into organised religion' as she put it. This book is totally different from anything I've read. I got it from a Buddhist pal of mine and I found it very useful. Noelle assured me you would too. Weren't you a demon for the books all your life? Now, I'd like to recommend in particular the last few pages but each chapter no doubt will provide food for thought and rest for the soul. It's a beautiful read, warm and intimate and often humorous."

"Humour? I could definitely do with that." Emer took it from him and read the title. *The Tibetan Book of Living and Dying*. "Most unusual coming from a Roman Catholic," she observed wryly.

"The Master is the Master," he replied, not at all perturbed.

She flicked through the pages, stopping here and there to read passages. "This is a bit heavy, Gerald."

"No, Emer. Read a little each day and you will learn a lot."

"Illumination at this stage?"

"Read and see for yourself," he advised. "I believe it

will be of immense help and may show you that what you have been experiencing is normal, no, more than normal, vital for you on the journey you're on."

Emer nodded in relief, glad of his terminology, appreciative of his awareness of her position.

"Now I am also here to help you in pragmatic ways. The biggest lesson you have to learn now is how to accept help – never an easy one for someone as independent as you are."

Emer grimaced. "I'm being forced to accept help – it's inevitable, I'm afraid."

"Don't be afraid, Emer. Asking for help is a blessed act just as much as giving it. So, my dear, what can I do for you?"

"Well, there is one thing that I've been thinking of – I get a lot of time for thinking."

"That's good."

"It is and it isn't. Anyway, this thing has been on my mind for a while now. It's about Christmas, Gerald."

"I presume you will celebrate it here with your family."

"I hope I can. That's what I'd like to ask you. You were so good when you and your group did up this house. It meant so much to me."

He beamed. "It was a pleasure. And now, Emer, what is it you'd like?"

She sat up and sipped water from a glass on the bedside table. "A Christmas tree – could you organise one for us? Avril is in no mood for festivities as I suspect she may feel it inappropriate to be revelling or partying. But celebration is exactly what we need here. There is no point mourning before the event, is there? There'll be time enough after."

"I like your style," the priest said sincerely.

"Avril is up to her eyes with the house and me and the baby and Martin is very busy in the hospital. Normally, I'd do the tree myself but –"

"Say no more, consider it done. I'll have one delivered here for you tomorrow – a nice chunky one that would look a treat in your bay window – and I'll send some of the younger members of the youth choir to put it up and decorate it for you. Have you enough fairy lights?"

"There are three sets in the attic as far as I know."

"In the attic? Well, I can haul myself up there in a moment and check to see if they're functioning."

"We have a Stira."

"Every convenience, what! Oh look, here she comes, the lady with the tray as opposed to the lamp!" He chuckled at his witticism.

Avril did her best to smile as she set the tray down on the end of the bed. "I brought tea, Father. Would you have preferred coffee?"

"Tea is perfect." He grinned at her. "Emer was wide awake, wasn't I lucky?"

Emer accepted a cup of tea and managed a wink at her niece before Gerald noticed. "We're having a nice chat here."

Avril offered Gerald a plate of biscuits.

"Oh lovely, Chocolate Goldgrain, my favourites." He put three on a plate in his lap. "I've a sweet tooth, unfortunately," he confessed.

Avril smiled stiffly and left the bedroom.

"She's not in the best of form, God love her." Gerald took a bite from a biscuit and munched noisily.

"I'm worried about her."

"And she's worried about you. That's the way, Emer. These are hard moments for you all but it's wonderful to see such love in action. As you said, Avril has a lot to manage but she's a strong, healthy young lady."

"Gerald, she's afraid."

His mouth was full so he shook his head in sympathy.

"I'd like to discuss the funeral with her but I don't think she's ready yet. There are things I'd like to organise. All my legal affairs are in order but it's the funeral that's posing the problem. Maybe you can help there? I don't like to impose on your kindness but you're the expert in such matters."

"Funerals are my speciality, I'm reluctant to admit. People are always dying to employ me," he joked.

Emer was lost in thought.

"Have I unnerved you, Emer?"

"Sorry, Gerald?"

"I hope I haven't offended you – my remark about funerals."

"Offended me? Not in the least, you've cheered me up. That particular F word is taboo in this house. At last I can talk freely with someone. There's some paper over there in the wardrobe, third shelf down. You'll find a pen on the dressing table. Maybe we could make a list of things to be done? It must sound morbid but I prefer to have things arranged."

"That's an excellent idea, not in the least morbid. It's all part of the healing process, Emer. You probably think healing is a peculiar word for me to use in your circumstances but –"

"No, Gerald, it is healing for me to be able to discuss this openly with you. I'm glad you called, I genuinely am."

"And I'll be back if you'd like."

Emer put her cup back on the tray. She'd managed only a few sips. "I definitely would."

"Who knows? Maybe I'll succeed in bringing you back to the fold?"

She laughed. "You can try."

37

"Happy birthday, Noelle." Emer, from her armchair, leaned forward and kissed her stooping friend on the cheek. Emer handed her a silver-gift-wrapped box, tied with black ribbon.

"Emer, you're unbelievable – to have remembered and to have bothered." Noelle put the present on the couch and sat down. "How have you been?"

"Open it, I want to see your reaction," Emer urged, ignoring the question.

Noelle vowed never to ask again. It was a stupid question. She untied the ribbon, undid the silver packaging and excitedly opened the box. She gasped. "Oh my God, it's fabulous." She jumped up with delight, fixed the green silk blouse up to her chest and strutted around the room. "It's absolutely gorgeous. I've been admiring it for ages in Brown Thomas, debating about buying it for weeks but I thought it far too extravagant for me. Doh!" Noelle smacked her forehead. "Now I get it. Maggie told you, didn't she? She shouldn't have. It's way too expensive." She kept the blouse tucked under her chin and ran out to the hall mirror to examine her reflection. "It suits me, doesn't it?" she yelled in to Emer.

Emer laughed. "Yes, it does. It's your colour. I gave Avril careful instructions what and where to buy."

Noelle bounced back into the room. "It'll be perfect with my black skirt for the Christmas party I'm giving to the staff at the weekend. Oh, Emer, I love it. You're a pet." She ran over, hugged Emer a bit too roughly. "Sorry, I nearly strangled you." A scarecrow, Noelle thought, skin and bone. She masked her reaction. "Is Grace asleep?"

"She settled down about an hour ago. She's a darling, Noelle, a regular little person in her own right with a real personality. She's bubbly, cute and very alert, watches everything. Every time I come into the room she turns her head and smiles at me. Avril teases me, says it's wind, not a smile but I know my own know."

"A perfect addition to the family."

"Especially now," Emer agreed. She saw Noelle's face fall. "We have to be realistic here, OK?"

"OK."

"It will make things easier for Avril when she has Grace to concentrate on. Babies won't tolerate bereavement. I want Avril to be happy, Noelle."

Noelle went back to admiring the blouse, avoiding Emer's gaze.

"I want you all to be happy."

That was it. Noelle had to speak. Her eyes brimmed as she smiled at her friend. "Have you any idea how much you'll be missed, Emer?" Noelle's voice shook. "Maggie couldn't bear to visit you this evening. I'm meeting her later in town for a few jars. I wish you could come." Noelle's voice perked up. "If I call a taxi, is there any chance you'd join us for an hour or two?"

"Not a snowball's chance in hell," Emer said stoically. "We can celebrate here though. Let's open a bottle now and we'll drink a toast to your good health. Don't look alarmed, Noelle. You're allowed to be healthy. It's not a prerequisite to be ill just because I am."

Noelle lovingly stroked the green blouse. "When I wear this I'll always think of you. I don't need this to remind me, though. I can't imagine your being gone, Emer. I've tried and tried but I can't get my head around it. It's surreal."

"Noelle?"

"Mmh?"

"Gerald Moore gave me a book to read. It's helping me a lot. I think you should read it afterwards. It deals with . . . issues like this. It's insightful."

"Gerald was here? Are you serious? He never said a word."

"I presumed you'd set it up. I was sure you asked him to talk to me and didn't let on because I'd be angry with you."

Noelle crossed her heart. "I never opened my mouth, I swear. Of course he was always asking about you but I never suggested he'd pay you a visit. You don't even know him."

"I do now." Emer laughed. "He's a character."

"Sure is, loves his food."

"I enjoy watching him eat. He does it with such gusto," Emer said.

"Does everything with gusto. He's a ball of energy, that man. Has a great attitude to life."

"And to death," Emer said. "I find his company relaxing. He's been a tremendous help. There are no holds barred when he's here and I like that. He never makes me feel uncomfortable and –"

"And we do? Yes, I expect we do, Emer. None of us knows quite what to say or do. We don't want to make it harder for you."

"I realise that." Emer stretched over and patted her friend's arm. "Gerald deals with death all the time and, nice though he is, he's not emotionally involved with me like you all are. It's a very different ballgame for him. Gerald pacifies me – even when he just sits and eats he calms me down. His presence in the room is enough to appease my worst anxieties. I feel I can say anything to him because he's probably heard it all before. Does that make sense to you? I don't have to pretend."

"Perfect sense. I'm glad he's visiting you, Emer. Gerald won't let you down. He'll be there for you right to . . . the end."

"He's assured me he will. I think that cleared the air a little, didn't it? Don't you dare cry, Noelle. Off with you to the kitchen and get the whiskey. It's in the press to the right of the sink and there's Diet Coke in the fridge. Let's celebrate your fifty-fifth birthday – another landmark. You look lovely, by the way. Your hair is nice clipped up, it frames your face. Get out there and find yourself a good man. That's my advice."

"Bit late for that. One disastrous marriage was enough, thank you very much."

"You don't have to get married but it would be nice to have someone to share your life with. Do it, Noelle. Find someone to love. Don't shut yourself off. We all need love."

"Even if I agreed with that, I'm just not ready for more hurt and pain."

"It needn't be like that."

"It has been in my experience." Noelle got off the couch.

"Well, it's better to love and be hurt than be safe and merely exist. That's living death, Noelle. Whatever our experiences we can learn from them, that's what makes us human. If I had your chances now I'd grab life by the balls."

"A man by the balls, you mean!"

"Indeed. There's a lot to be said for physical passion."

"Like your recent trip? You never talked about it but Maggie told me Ben Fogarty followed you down to Clifden."

"You could put music to that! 'Follow Me Up to Carlow', wasn't that a ballad? I never talked about Ben's trip because I knew you all thought I was disappointed, but the truth is I wasn't. Maybe I was at first, but when I thought about it honestly, I knew it worked out for the best. I enjoyed every lascivious moment and I don't regret it – not one bit. I learned a lot about myself too, how I tend to pre-empt everything, pre-judge and worry about things over which I have no control."

"We all do that," Noelle said, with a sigh.

"Well, I had to learn that it was a mistake and I learned other things too: people react to us because of the vibes we send out. I can see your sceptical expression, Noelle, but it really is true. We have much more to do with our lot in life than we ever realise. We can make things happen or we can destroy them. The pity is that I'm learning this so late."

"Better late than never. More bloody learning – does it ever stop?"

"I reckon that's the principal reason we're put on this earth – why we're here."

"To learn?"

"In a nutshell. I'm on a huge learning curve since I got the diagnosis."

"We all are, Emer. Maggie thought she knew it all, how to handle you, how to handle herself, how to handle her family but it's all falling apart for her."

"Maggie will be fine. She has a lot going for her, especially her marriage. I don't mean to hurt you by saying that, Noelle."

"You're not. I made a mistake that's all – so did Brendan when it comes to it. You're right about learning, Emer. It's hard to judge any marriage from the outside – from the inside too. Maggie is not in a good place at the moment but she'll come out of it. Jesus, how ridiculous is that? Me talking about –"

"Maggie always puts everybody else first, always meets the demands of others. She needs to look after herself."

"Yes, and the irony is that until now she thought she had all the answers. Maggie always accused me of being impulsive and thoughtless but in some ways she's like that herself." Noelle, still standing, folded the blouse back into the wrapping paper. "I'll talk to her tonight. She should be here."

"Should – ought – words we use all the time that inflict so many burdens on ourselves and on those we love. Pity we couldn't wipe out those words altogether. Don't pressurise her, Noelle. She'll come when she can. Now, drinks, please."

Noelle headed off to the kitchen to do Emer's bidding. No matter what Emer said, she was determined to have words with Maggie. She hadn't been in Cabra Road for at least three weeks. And she had been the one rabbiting on about not abandoning Emer – about how important it was that they all stuck together.

Noelle saw a distinct change in Emer this evening – there was something different about her demeanour that Noelle couldn't put her finger on but it scared her. What if something happened now, sooner than they'd expected and Maggie hadn't seen Emer? She'd never forgive herself.

"Holly's refused to go back to school to do her Leaving Cert. I've been up the wall, I really have, that's why I haven't been to see you. I couldn't bring my petty problems here."

"Maggie, your only child is hardly a petty problem. I understand how you must have been worried. Did she give you her reasons?"

Maggie clicked her tongue impatiently. "The usual adolescent garbage: wants to earn her own money so she can be independent of us, enjoys working in Tesco, has no remote interest in study blah-de-blah-de-blah. She's only 'into' her music, discos and dates. Joe finally got involved and talked to her but he didn't do any better than I did. Then, taking the bull by the horns, I made an

310

appointment with the principal and the school counsellor. Holly came too, albeit reluctantly. She sat sulkily throughout the whole interview. My fingers were itching to give her a good slap. How Joe keeps his cool is beyond me. Then she said she felt ignored at home, if you don't mind! When did I ever ignore her, Emer? I've done my best for her and with her, God knows. I think she's selfish."

"Her behaviour is typical, though."

"No, it isn't. Her other pals are staying on at school. They'll study, get good exam results and go to college and she'll be stuck in a dead-end job, stacking shelves and cleaning floors. Holly is clever and she needs something stimulating to challenge her."

"What did Joe say?"

"Told me to let her do as she pleases this year. He rang the Institute of Education and a secretary said they'd accept her next September if she wants to attend there. It costs a lot, but money was never the issue with us. I just feel she'd have been better off to remain with her friends in familiar surroundings and settle down. Joe is too easy with her."

"What did she say about the Institute? Has she agreed to go?"

"We haven't told her about the offer. Joe thinks we should let her work her silly notions out of her system and that she'll finally see sense herself. He gives her three months! Says the harsh reality of working fulltime will wake her up."

"I think he's very wise." Emer closed her eyes and focused on her breathing. Mr Noonan had given her muscle-relaxing exercises to do.

"Emer, you look haggard! You'd need to do something about your appearance."

Emer opened her eyes and stared in astonishment. "I beg your pardon?"

"Look at the state of you! Where's the blue nightdress we got in Marks? That one has seen better days. Honestly, it's depressing looking at you like that. You should let Noelle do something with your hair."

"You want me to be a nice corpse, is that it?"

"Naturally."

Emer was chuffed to have Maggie back – the old Maggie.

38

Emer hoisted herself up in the bed. Avril placed the basin of warm soapy water on the floor and opened the neck of her aunt's nightdress. She painstakingly patted Emer's chest and neck with a fluffy white facecloth. Not wishing to be rough, Avril barely touched her aunt's skin but the patting motion was wonderfully soothing. "So, how was that? Feel better?" She dried her aunt's skin with a warm towel.

"Very refreshing. You have wonderful healing hands; it's a gift."

"Bed baths are my speciality!" Avril smoothed the sheets on Emer's bed, puffed up her pillows and lit a lavender candle on the bedside table. "Will I turn on the television for you?"

"No, thanks, Avril. I'd love a little chat if you've time. Is Grace still asleep?"

"Knocked out after the walk in the park. The air always does that to her. It'll give me time to get dinner on."

"Off you go, then. I don't want to upset your routine."

"You're not, Emer, I've loads of time. Martin won't be in for an hour at least and I'm grilling lamb cutlets tonight and they don't take long. I'll do a salad too." Avril was suddenly ashamed of herself – talking about food and Emer unable to swallow.

Emer hadn't even noticed. Her mind was on other matters.

"I've left this house to you, Avril."

"But . . . but what about Ronan?"

"Ronan has no interest in it, never had. He's done very well for himself and I'm quite sure his children will be well looked after. No, I've made up my mind and the will has been made. It's what my mother would have wanted. You are to get everything. Maybe you could let Maggie and Noelle choose whatever they'd like – I know Maggie is fond of the painting called *The Corridor* in the hall. My grandmother bought that from the Waddington Gallery years ago. Maggie has always admired it."

"She'll have it," Avril assured her.

"I think Noelle would appreciate some of the Waterford Crystal in the china cabinet. She likes cut glass."

"I'll let them both choose whatever they'd like, Emer. Do we have to discuss this now? It's making me uncomfortable."

Emer took a solid gold band from the bedside table. "As you know this was my mother's wedding ring and I'd like you to have it. Her engagement ring is in the bank – the solicitor has all the details. I want you to keep that ring for Grace for when she grows up."

Avril's eyes watered and she couldn't do anything

about it. Although she knew Emer wanted to have this talk she hated every moment of it; hated to hear Emer talk of her possessions and how they were to be doled out. "I really think you should phone Ronan again, Emer."

Emer shook her head.

"He might not have got that message, and he'd want to be here if he knew how ill you were."

"No, darling. I should have contacted Ronan years ago or he should have got in touch with me. It's too late now. Reunions are such ardent affairs and in this case it would be embarrassing and disturbing for us both. I don't have the energy. I just want peace, Avril. Ronan can be spared the trauma of seeing me like this. Too much water has passed under the bridge. Let him remember me as I once was, eh? And I remember him fondly you know – years ago when we were young. He was a good brother and I did love him. He'll know that, in his heart he will know that."

Her sad tone convinced Avril to say no more. She gently smoothed Emer's hair back from her forehead. "You looked very peaceful after you woke from your nap this afternoon."

Emer's eyes sparkled. "I saw her again. She was so near I almost touched her. She called my name over and over and her voice was pure and strong."

"Saw who?"

"Your mother. She had the sweetest smile on her face and her dark eyes danced, positively danced, in her head. She was beaming with happiness and begging me to follow her."

Avril stroked her aunt's hair again. "That was a nice dream."

Emer looked puzzled.

"I'm glad you're having nice dreams, Emer."

Emer, disappointed, nodded and turned on her side.

Martin stacked the dishwasher while Avril finished the mountain of ironing. He felt jaded tonight having had a longer than usual stint in the hospital. He'd lost a patient after a valiant struggle and it had been hard to comfort the widow. The man's children were distraught. All Martin's energy was drained.

"Emer thinks she saw my mother again today." Avril tried to keep her voice nonchalant. "It unnerves me when she talks like that, Martin. I know she's only dreaming but I think she believes that my mother is here with her. It's creepy. One minute she was lucid – really with it – discussing what she wants people to have; the next talking about seeing my mother." She paused. "She told me she was leaving me – us – the house. That's another thing we have to discuss – our future."

"Now is not the time, Avril. We've enough to contend with at the moment."

"Yes," she replied, "but we do have decisions to make. Now, don't pretend you're happy in Dublin, I know you're only here to please me. I did think I wanted us to settle in Ireland but now I realise that with . . . without Emer . . ."

He went over to her, unplugged the iron and took her in his arms. "Let's just get through the coming days with as little anxiety as possible, OK, honey?"

"It really threw me when she talked about my mother. She genuinely believes she sees her." Avril pulled away from him and shuddered. "Maybe she can? What if she really sees her? It's scary."

He drew her back to him and caressed her face. "The cancer is spreading, Avril. I warned you it would eventually reach her brain. Hallucinations are part of it, I'm afraid."

"Is that what this is about then, hallucinations caused by diminishing brain cells?"

Martin kissed her on the nose, went to set the dishwasher for fifty-five minutes, inserted the tablet in its tray and shut the door to start the machine. "It could be the morphine – I upped the dose on Mr Noonan's advice."

"He telephoned today to find out how Emer was. He's very dedicated."

"And he knows his stuff. Don't let Emer's notions bother you, Avril. From now she'll drift in and out of consciousness and she may be liable to say anything. You'll have to steel yourself."

Martin supported Emer in his arms and coaxed her to sip the Complan, which he knew she absolutely abhorred and found impossible to get down, but it would relieve Avril if her aunt swallowed even a mouthful. Emer's shoulders were skeletal. She was literally starving but he had understood all along that this was how it would be. "Just a little sip, that's the girl. It will do you good. That's it, just a sip."

To please him, Emer willed herself to swallow but she couldn't manage it. She let out a long sigh and sank back on the pillows, her eyes closing. "No," she begged.

"OK, my love." Martin gently wiped her mouth with a moist tissue. "Do you think you'll sleep?"

Emer wasn't listening. She was off in a world of her own, staring at a spot on the ceiling above his head. Her expression was perplexed. She continued to stare and presently she smiled – a wonderful warm smile that lit up her whole face. Martin turned to look at what she was staring at but he saw nothing.

He walked over to the window and peered out. The night was starry and a blanket of frost lay on the garden, glistening in the rays from the street lamps. Some of the houses opposite had Christmas lights festooned on trees and bushes in their gardens and others had intricate displays of Rudolph and Santa and elves. The glittery lights and elaborate decorations reminded him of the States. He missed New York and he missed it especially at Christmas. His mother had taken to telephoning him at the hospital, not wishing to disturb him at the house and not wanting to upset her daughter-in-law. Martin's mother missed him and she desperately wanted to see her granddaughter but she understood that they couldn't leave Dublin yet.

He drew the curtains, shutting out the cheerful scene and turned back to the bed to check on his patient. Emer had already fallen into a deep sleep; the mysterious smile still planted on her lips.

39

The postman knocked with the long-awaited parcel one rainy Wednesday afternoon, two weeks before Christmas. Avril signed for it. It was a bulky parcel – unmistakable. Avril, suddenly energised, took the stairs two at a time, calling out excitedly: "Emer, Emer, wake up! It's come. It's arrived. Wake up, Emer!"

She charged into her aunt's bedroom where Emer was coming out of a very heavy sleep.

"Avril? Is that you?" She battled to open her eyes.

Avril gripped the parcel tightly. "It's here!"

"What is?" Emer found it hard to focus. Her eyesight was dimming.

"It's arrived, Emer. The book – your book – has come in the post. May I open it?"

Emer struggled into a sitting position in the bed and rummaged around the duvet for her reading glasses. "Your shouts woke me. I was dreaming."

"Sorry but I knew you'd want to see it. This is exciting."

Avril tore open the envelope and from the inside bubble wrapping five or six copies of the poetry book fell onto the bed. Avril grabbed one and handed another to Emer along with a covering letter from the editor.

"You read it, love." Emer was too tired.

Avril read it aloud: "'*Dear Emer, please find enclosed six copies of your book – hope they please you as much as they delight us. More copies to follow. These were the first off the press! Hoping you are doing OK and hoping the enclosed will bring you cheer on this festive occasion. A very happy Xmas to you and yours, Best wishes, Bill.*'"

Avril squealed. "Look at it, Emer. The cover is so classy. I love it – I absolutely love it! Look, the glossy back is such an excellent background for the bright red poinsettias. Oh, Emer, it's superb."

Emer's spirits surged at the sight of her niece kissing the book, smelling it, scrutinising it.

"It's your baby, Emer. This is your beautiful baby and it's stunning – ideal for Christmas presents. It would look really elegant on any coffee table. I'm going to buy loads!"

Emer took a book in her hands, felt its smoothness and sleekness. She peered in amazement at her name splashed in gold under the title. I've done it, she thought, I've done it. It's real.

"Granny Dorgan would have been so proud," Avril said, her voice choked up.

Emer lay back on the pillows, still clasping the book. "I want all of you to have a copy – then you'll always have a little piece of me."

Avril lay down and stretched out beside her aunt, careful not to hurt her delicate body. She insinuated her arm under Emer's head and held the book open on the dedication page.

For Grace and for the future!

Avril whispered the words. "'*For Grace and for the future!*' When she grows up she'll be so grateful. It's not every little girl who has a book of poetry dedicated to her. It's a beautiful gesture." She kissed her aunt's cheek.

"I'm glad you approve."

"I'm sorry that Grace will never know you."

"She will," Emer reminded her. "She will through my poems, you said so yourself."

"I'll always talk about you, Emer, like you talked to me about my mother. Those talks meant so much to me." Avril's eyes stung. She couldn't cry now. She'd vowed to herself that there would be no more tears in front of Emer.

Emer gently stroked Avril's arm. "We have to focus on the positive, sweetheart. I know you and Martin will give Grace a lovely life and down the line other babies will follow, hopefully. Life, love and death – they're the three great realities and everything else is just so much dross. Pity I didn't realise that when I fretted about stupid things. We waste so much time on worry and useless surmising."

Avril squeezed her aunt's hand.

"And yet it's the silly trivia and mundane minutiae that makes up the bulk of our lives – but we should never lose sight of what's really important. There are moments in time that are special and never repeated. This moment is one of them."

These were the clearest and most lucid words Emer had spoken in weeks. For a few moments her voice was full and strong and she sounded like her old self.

Avril curled up beside her aunt. She held Emer's hand and in the other hand she clasped the precious book to her breast. In the darkening room, the lavender scent wafted around them and the candle flickered and danced, casting billowy shapes that swelled and swayed on the walls and ceiling. Avril could feel her aunt's heartbeat and hear her shallow breathing, the only sound in the silence.

Christmas came and went with visits, exchanges of presents, kisses, hugs, hot mince pies and rum-and-blackcurrant drinks for visitors. Despite the ornate tree with its twinkling lights, decorated by Gerald and his choir, despite the carollers, the Christmas dinner, the pudding, the chocolates – all the fare that Avril usually enjoyed, she found it impossible to keep up the feigned cheer. Christmas was irrelevant.

Emer couldn't eat anything. She couldn't drink. She was a shell of herself, sitting uncomfortably in the armchair for an hour at a time, doing her utmost to converse and be convivial and the rest of the day she had to spend in bed. "I'm the Ghost of Christmas Past," she joked.

None of them could keep up the pretence of revelry for very long. Martin was the best at keeping up the act: he poured drinks, tended to Grace, nursed Emer and kept Avril steady. Maggie was there every morning, her face now ashen with sadness and grief. Noelle was better in practical ways; she tidied up, organised meals and was a great help to Avril with the baby. Gerald Moore's visits brought the most comfort and strength to them all. It was he who truly took charge of Emer and he calmed her in a way none of the rest could. Emer pointed out the irony of this to her niece. "This must be it – the change before death!"

On the day after St Stephen's Day, Emer called her niece to her room.

"Darling, I need to talk to you about my funeral."

Avril couldn't reply.

"I don't want you to worry about anything. Gerald has it all under control and he knows my wishes for the service."

"Please, Emer –"

"Listen for a moment. Gerald helped me choose the readings. They won't be grim. I want the day to be a celebration of my life and to give some cheer to the congregation and to all of you, my friends and family. I want no tears, no mourning, Avril. I know you'll miss me and I'll miss you wherever I am – if I'm anywhere at all and I still have genuine doubts about that – but I believe you all will live happy and worthwhile lives." Emer paused, took as deep a breath as she could to muster her waning strength. "I have one favour to ask."

"Anything."

"I'd love the Gospel Choir to sing if that's possible. Their music is so uplifting. I'll leave it to you and Gerald, and the choir of course, to choose the hymns. Gloria will help you?"

"She'd be honoured."

"My only request is a hymn I love for obvious reasons: 'Amazing Grace'." Emer stretched out from the bed and took Avril's hand.

"It's one of our best," Avril said.

40

The day started out like any other. A January mist rolled in from the Irish Sea and muffled Dublin in a drizzly haze. Avril hated these dark grey days when she had to keep the lights on until the late morning; it was gloomy and unnatural. Her daily maternal routine demanded an early start and the lack of light was no enticement to get out of bed, but babies had their own in-built hunger-waking system that had no respect for the habits of others. These nights she was always on the alert for any sounds from Emer's room and even when she heard nothing she crept in to check on her aunt.

Avril stretched out on the sofa feeding Grace by the cosy gas fire in the sitting room, supporting her in the crook of one arm while managing to sip her green tea with her free hand. Juggling had become second nature to her: it was amazing how many things she now had to do with one pair of hands and she often marvelled at the old days – the pre-Grace days – when she had to ask for help even when fastening a bracelet. Now, Avril felt omnipotent – well, certainly ambidextrous.

The beeps on the radio signalled the 7 a.m. news. She could hear Martin singing in the shower upstairs. Her husband would then look in on Emer before bringing up the first dose of her daily medication. Avril was free to feed and bathe Grace before the baby's morning nap. Then she would sit with Emer for a while, let in visitors, make coffee and prepare lunch. Usually Maggie dropped in for an hour in the afternoon or early evening, depending on her work schedule and this left Avril free for a quick stroll. Noelle came over three nights a week and sat with Emer or baby-sat Grace if she and Martin wanted to get out. Avril was usually too tired to avail of the opportunity but she knew she had no cause to complain. She had point blank rejected Emer's offer to pay for a night nurse. Avril had their schedule down to a fine art.

Maggie had left the house in tears the night before because Emer was barely able to respond to her. Noelle too said she saw a change, but Avril thought they were being alarmists. The day had been particularly strenuous for Emer because after Gerald's visit, Cheryl, from next door, came in for a chat. Avril didn't like that woman; there was something very frosty about her. In any case, Avril would have to monitor visits more carefully.

Grace guzzled noisily, her delicate blue-veined eyelids loosely shut, her puckered lips fastened on her mother's brown nipple. The powerful suction was intensely pleasurable and sensual. The warmth of her baby's body at her breast, the milky smell, the sucking sounds made the experience wondrous for Avril as she glanced down at her daughter's flawless face. The child attached was a continuation of her own body – mother and child one person, one being and yet intrinsically two. Love surged through Avril in a steady flow and seeped into her daughter.

She heard Martin clomping downstairs more hurriedly than usual. Maybe he was due into work earlier today? She unclamped Grace and deftly moved her to the other nipple.

"Avril!"

She turned quickly towards the sitting-room door. Martin's tone was unmistakable.

She stood up quickly, accidentally disturbing Grace who let out an unceremonious squawk at being ripped from the nipple.

Martin crossed the room and took the baby in his arms. "She's very low. I think you should be prepared."

Avril drew in a sharp breath. "You sure?"

"She's failing rapidly."

"Worse than last night?"

"Her pulse is very weak."

"Did she say anything?" Avril closed over her dressing gown. Her breast was full and sore but Grace had stopped whimpering so this feed was over. "Did she say anything?"

"No, she moaned a little but she didn't open her eyes."

"Did she know you were there?"

"I spoke to her but there was no real response. I upped the morphine drip."

Avril's face crumpled.

"You should go up, honey."

She stroked Grace's cheek and cooed at her daughter as if she hadn't heard.

"Go up, love, I'll look after Grace."

"She's sleeping soundly again, aren't you, sweetie-pie?"

"Avril," he persisted.

She nodded vacuously.

"Avril," he prompted again.

"All right," she reluctantly agreed. "Should I send for the priest?"

"Would Emer want that?"

"I think she would like Gerald to be with her. They've become firm friends."

"I'll phone him."

"His number's stored in the phone." Avril hesitated. "You're not overreacting, Martin, are you? I mean she's been weaker than this before. Remember last month? But she rallied when her book arrived."

"I'm not overreacting." He didn't blame her for this denial. It was understandable and he'd expected it. "Avril, even when we know somebody is going to die, when the end comes it's always a shock." He held up their daughter to her. "Grace needs a kiss."

Avril tried very hard not to cry but the sweet skin of her baby's downy cheek as she kissed it drew tears. Her eyes brimmed and she was blinded. She clung onto her husband's arm. "Should you phone Maggie too? And Noelle?" Her voice was choked.

"I'll contact work as well. I'll take a few days off."

Through her tears relief flooded her face. "Thanks, Martin." She pulled a crumpled tissue from her dressing-gown pocket and loudly blew her nose.

"Would you like me to go up with you?"

"No." Avril stuffed the tissue back in her pocket. "I'd prefer to be with her on my own for a while."

Emer lay still and silent, her eyes closed, her breathing very shallow. She could hear in the distance the recitation of prayers. She thought she felt the faintest touch of fingers caressing her brow. The incantation grew louder but Emer couldn't open her eyes, didn't want to open them. The sight before her was too beautiful to obliterate and the rasping sounds around her bed were an intrusion.

Gerald Moore made the sign of the cross on Emer's forehead and anointed her with the holy oils. Avril held her aunt's cold hands between her own and tried to warm them. Maggie sat in the corner praying silently and Noelle stood by the window gazing out at the front garden below. The lilac tree was bare.

Emer's breathing grew raucous and laboured. Maggie gently approached the bed and put her arms around Avril. Both women knelt down and Noelle left the window and joined them. Martin took his place at Emer's head and gently, very gently, applied a damp swab to her dry parched lips. Gerald Moore began the Lord's Prayer and the women joined in.

The chanting murmur got louder, more irritating, more disturbing. It was a dirge, a drone of desperation and Emer didn't want to hear it. She wanted it to stop. She tried to shout stop, to turn it off. She couldn't move her lips. All her energy was sapped. Then mercifully the chant grew fainter and dwindled away.

Avril came closer and bent her lips to Emer's ear: "It's all right, darling. Everything is all right." She took her grandmother's black shiny rosary beads from the dressing table and loosely draped them around Emer's folded hands.

Emer's breathing became more and more laboured and agitated and her chest heaved. The tears rolled down Avril's face. She couldn't abide the sound, the gasping, grating growl of the desperate struggle of the body's fight to live.

A wonderful world of light opened up before Emer. She felt the draw, the overpowering pull to follow it. She must get there. She needed help to get there. Pain dragged her back, terrible excruciating pain. Someone somewhere was crying but she couldn't be diverted now, she had to go on, she had to follow. She must pursue this beautiful burnished beacon – there she would get help, get respite. There everything would become clear, everything would make sense.

Avril had to help her – she had to release Emer. Again she leaned forward, kissed her aunt's cheek and whispered in her ear. "We are here with you, looking after you and loving you always. Maggie and Noelle are here and Martin and me. We love you so much. You're free, my darling Emer. You're free. You can let go. Let go, darling Emer. You're free."

Avril stifled a sob and Maggie hugged the young woman to her breast. Noelle had to bite her lip to stop from crying out. Gerald Moore put the crucifix to Emer's lips, then kissed it himself. Martin gently pressed two fingers to Emer's neck. The pulse was barely palpable. It quivered, flickered off and on and then it stopped. He kissed Emer's forehead, came around the bed and drew his wife into his arms. Avril sobbed into his shoulder. Gerald came to hug Noelle and she in turn grabbed Maggie whose heart was bursting.

"Oh God, I can't bear it, Noelle," she cried. "I can't bear it."

A fire engulfed Emer's body, the heat was intense yet painless. A luminescence infiltrated everything; a magnificent brightness radiated out from her and filled the vacuum. She felt movement, motion, lightness, and airiness. She was weightless, vaporous, ethereal. The light grew stronger, more tangible and she was in it and of it. A sonorous melody hauntingly echoed around her and from the surrounding soft mist a figure, a shadowy welcoming form, beckoned lovingly.

41

Ronan kept watch over Emer. Seven a.m. and he hadn't slept a wink since he'd finally kissed his niece goodnight and sent her to bed a few hours earlier. This was going to be a tough day for them all, especially for Avril. Her devotion to his sister had been absolute.

"I love you, Emu." He stroked his sister's cold face. "It never occurred to me that I wouldn't have the opportunity to make my peace with you. I'd always taken it for granted."

When he'd thought of her over the years, the image had always been of Emer in this house tending the garden or cooking or nursing their mother. He'd always intended to visit, had planned it more than once in his head, how he'd get over the awkwardness, what he'd do and what he'd say, but he'd waited for an excuse to call – a birthday, Christmas, but then it would be the next one and the one after that. Even their Christmas cards had stopped. Now Emer was leaving the house forever and he'd missed his chance to say goodbye.

Removal was such a cruel word.

He'd agreed to accompany Martin to the undertaker this morning to finalise arrangements. He'd have to phone Della at some stage. He searched around the floor for his mobile and switched it on. Nine messages from his wife! He'd let her stew for a while longer. He wasn't sure how he'd handle her but since he'd entered this house last night Ronan had undergone a dramatic change. The sadness, and for him suddenness, of Emer's passing had highlighted what was important and what was not, what had to be accepted and what had not.

He couldn't go on for ever making allowances and excuses, merely existing in a hostile household with a wife who didn't love him. He wasn't sure how long it had been since they'd felt anything other than animosity for each other. Emer's death was a wake-up call. He owed it to himself to waste no more precious time. Each day in his life from now on must count for something.

Della too would be better off out of this sham of a marriage that lacked passion and honesty. Freed from the sense of duty and perceived morality and imposed social beliefs and constraints, she too could find a new and better life. What was moral about living a lie? Neither of them could thrive in a hotbed of anger and regrets.

He'd phone her now and ask her not to attend the church this evening. He couldn't stomach any fake display of sorrow. This was Emer's day.

"He doesn't want me there, Carla, told me in no uncertain terms to keep away from the funeral. The church is a public building, I told him. He can't keep me away just because he says so, can he? The gall of it! Can you believe how vindictive your father is?" Della ranted into the phone. "He stayed in Cabra last night and never bothered to let me know. He switched his phone off so I couldn't contact him. I was worried stiff. He's selfish. He has no feelings for me whatever. He never thinks of my needs. He's cutting me out now and I can't bear it."

Her daughter, at work in her advertising office in Bayswater, fiddled with the latest sketches on her desk. These would not do at all. She'd have to talk to the graphics department as soon as her mother shut up and left her in peace.

"So, I thought if you could fly over this evening you'd make it to the funeral Mass tomorrow," Della went on without drawing a breath.

Carla had to interrupt: "Absolutely impossible, Mum. I can't get away at the moment. We're up to our eyes in a huge campaign for a major department store. I can't say which at the moment as it's all highly confidential, but suffice to say that if we get this contract I'll be sure of that promotion I told you about."

"But, Carla," her mother complained in that whiny voice which always infuriated her daughter, "just for a day – a single day. I know you're busy but surely you could manage one day off. It would mean so much to me – and to your father, naturally."

"Dad wouldn't expect me to be there. It would be embarrassing for everyone. I don't know this Emer. I was barely aware I had an aunt until a few years ago and only then because I discovered her photo by accident in Dad's bureau. Mum, sorry, but I've no intention of coming. I'll ring Dad later and speak to him. I suppose I could send a bouquet but even that seems a bit insincere."

"You should be here," Della said sharply. "It's your duty to the family."

"Have you any idea just how ridiculous that sounds? Mum, I told you I'm not going. The only reason you want me there is for moral support for yourself. By the sound of things you shouldn't go either. Dad obviously doesn't want you there. Is Ian going?"

"No," Della mumbled.

"Well, he's in Dublin so it would be no hassle for him."

"Your brother said he didn't know her and it would be hypocritical but –"

"Ian is right. For whatever reason, we didn't know Dad's sister and it's a bit late turning up now for a family reunion when the poor woman is dead."

Della started to whimper and blubber.

Jesus, Carla thought, she's on the bottle already and it's not even noon. "I have to go, Mum. I've a meeting."

"I'm very disappointed in you, Carla. I'd have expected more."

"I'll call you tomorrow," Carla said firmly and replaced the receiver.

Gerald Moore listened in reverence to the Gospel choir practice. They were in the community centre beside the church having a last run-through. He was transported by their plaintive version of 'Amazing Grace'. Emer would have loved this, he thought. The words never failed to stir: "*I once was lost and now am found*" the choir sang out and Gerald thought how apt those words were for Emer and for all of us when the time came. He'd miss her. Although he had known her only for a few short weeks he'd been deeply impressed by her courage, her love and thoughtfulness for others and her sardonic sense of humour. He'd promised her he'd be there to offer support to Noelle and Maggie in the coming weeks.

Emer had paid him the best compliment he'd ever received by telling him he'd made her passing easier. In a quiet way, a totally unexpected way, the moment she said that was the most significant moment of his life. During all his time spent in the service of others, Gerald had always been praised and flattered, and in some quarters revered, but those words from Emer made sense of his life and – more importantly – of his vocation. He had made her passing easier – the best tribute ever. He felt humbled.

Avril nodded through her tears at the crowd of neighbours and friends who'd assembled at the gate and down the street to accompany Emer to the church. The evening was dry and dusk would soon descend. A blonde curly-haired little girl came forward and shyly handed Avril a colourful bouquet. "I'm Debbie," she whispered. "The flowers are for Emer. I wrote the message myself." Avril bent down and kissed the child on the cheek. As Deborah Dixon backed away to her mother's waiting arms, Avril glanced at the message stuck to the plastic covering the bouquet:

Super speller sending special sentiments skywards. XXX

Deborah Dixon's childish scrawl moved Avril. The innocence and purity of the thought expressed, the effort to still impress Emer with alliteration and assonance was touching. This little girl would forever remember Emer by words, by sounds, by rhyme.

Ronan took the bouquet from Avril and passed it to Cheryl on the front steps. He wondered why she seemed uncomfortable but he was pleased she'd agreed to stay in the house for the duration of the church service and to be there to help with visitors afterwards. It was a sad fact of Dublin life that many house burglaries took place during funerals. Cheryl had turned up today in her best clothes, hair newly blow-dried, as a mark of respect to her neighbour. She'd even managed a weak smile and nod to Avril.

The McDonnells from the other side of the street said they wouldn't delay in the church after the prayers and they'd hurry back to give Cheryl a hand serving refreshments. The house was full of food – sandwiches, quiches, pizzas, salads, cakes and biscuits. Ronan had gone to the off-licence the night before and had bought all the drink. It seemed that everyone Emer had ever known, but for Sam who couldn't make it on time, was here today and hadn't come empty-handed. Martin had never seen the like of it in the States – this was what Avril had been telling him about.

The undertakers came out of the house carrying the coffin. Avril moaned softly and hid her face in her husband's overcoat. This was the saddest part – Emer leaving her home. The finality of it was awful.

Maggie, tears staining her face, clung on to Joe and Noelle. Holly stood beside them, embarrassed by the grief of her mother yet wanting to be there. She fumbled in her pocket and switched off her mobile phone. She'd always liked Emer Dorgan from the time she was a small child. The woman was cool, Holly considered, cool considering she was one of her mother's mates. Some of the crowd made the sign of the cross as the coffin passed them, others prayed silently. Holly lowered her head.

Ronan, after a slight hesitation, knew what he must do. He hugged Avril and went to help carry his sister's coffin to the waiting hearse that would take her on her final journey. Avril had asked him to give the eulogy the following morning, but he'd politely refused. He was the last person entitled to do that. Gerald Moore would make a fine job of it. Who better than he to sum up Emer's life? Who knew her better in her final weeks?

Martin and Avril with Grace in her arms were the first to follow the coffin. The baby was awake, a contented smile on her chubby cheeks. Maggie and Joe and Noelle and Holly came next and then neighbours and friends and many people Avril had never met, including a large group of teenagers in school uniform. Maggie noticed Ben Fogarty at the back.

The procession slowed the traffic on the main road and Noelle smiled to herself at what a kick Emer would have had at that sight. "There are times," Noelle remembered Emer say when someone once had criticised a student protest march as being self-promoting and self-centred, "we have to make a stir. We're entitled to a little attention at some stage."

The procession followed the coffin down the street to the church nearby. Gerald Moore and the parish priest would be there to greet them on the steps. Other mourners would assemble, people from the area and the library staff and clients. Gloria and the choir would be there also to offer solidarity to Avril. The cortège moved on, some silent, some talking in whispers, all showing respect.

From the bare branches of the lilac tree, he perched and watched.

If you enjoyed
After the Rain by Mary McCarthy
why not try
Shame the Devil also published
by Poolbeg?
Here's a sneak preview of chapters one and two

Shame
The
Devil

Mary McCarthy

*"What's gone and what's past help
Should be past grief."*

SHAKESPEARE: *The Winter's Tale*

1

The voice is persistent. It is not a pleasant voice and it is not welcome. For days, weeks and months Amy Kennedy has tried to banish it but the house, conspiratorially, has let it in. It seeps from the ceilings and the walls or from under the floorboards. It is everywhere around; a pervasive malignant influence. The voice is her enemy: a thief creeping slyly inside her to steal her spirit.

Her husband, Maurice, loves this house. He grew up here in the stylish seaside suburb of Blackrock, Co Dublin. In its day it was a fine family residence but over the years it has become run-down. Its once-imposing façade, now shamefaced, suffers its neglect with painful embarrassment. The ancient gates are rusty, the paint peeling pitifully and the almost-pebbleless driveway oozes mud and slime through grooved tyre-tracks. Weeds choke the shrubbery under the large bay window, whose greying nylon curtains shut out the light, rendering the interior dark and dismal.

The spacious hall is shabby, its dark brown carpet faded and threadbare near the front door. Standing haughtily in the corner, the old-fashioned hatstand seems ludicrously out of place beside the bookcase with the broken leg. The mahogany banister cries out for a coat of varnish.

At the end of the hall, down two steps, lies the kitchen, its great green range now redundant, sitting superfluously in the centre – another sorry example of the waste. Pots and unwashed pans cover the draining board. Cobwebbed dust and grime, embedded in the crevices between the presses and the sink, add to the impression of decay: a testimony of negligence which constantly berates Amy.

To the right of the entrance hall, a dark brown door leads into the high-ceilinged living-room that has stayed the same since Maurice inherited all those years ago. A faded dusty red settee and two armchairs, never used, wait in vain for visitors.

It is four o'clock in the afternoon. Upstairs in the front bedroom, Amy Kennedy, partially dressed, lies on top of a creased duvet. Her eyes are half-open, vacantly watching the flickering images on the portable television, conveniently set on a table at the bed's end.

She stares, unfocused and unseeing. She has an ache somewhere – a dull, throbbing ache which she can't identify but which threatens to devour her. It started in her head, she thinks, but it has spread throughout her body, pickling her pores, her muscles, her very bones.

Bones, other bones, disintegrate in the cold clay. The wrinkled flesh must be wasted away from the bones by now. In what condition is the body? Have the worms done their worst? Are the maggots still in there, gouging and gorging? In the deep recesses of her mind these ominous thoughts scratch and scrape. Battle as she might, she cannot blot them out.

Amy stretches out her hand and gropes among the empty biscuit packets and discarded sweet papers on the filthy floor. Panic rises in her chest, palpitations pound. She must have a cigarette. Heart thumping, hands shaking, she clutches at the packet. Not the voice again. She can't bear to hear it now.

Not again.

2

April is the cruellest month, the poet said, and maybe it was true. Five days had passed with no word from Dawn, but she'd done this before, just her way of showing her annoyance, of teaching her mother a lesson. The withdrawal of love – it was a typical female thing, wasn't it? As a child, Dawn would try to hurt her by not eating. Now it was not speaking. Same treatment, different method. Never mind, Amy would phone her at the flat and apologise. Again.

The whirlpool went round and round, at ever-increasing speed, sucking her in.

What have you done now? her mother would ask, in her strident voice. She'd stand, hands on bony hips and shake her head disdainfully. Her mother had always disapproved of her.

April 10th. First anniversary.

This morning Amy had gone to the cemetery, dutifully placed her multicoloured bouquet on the grave, tidied the tiny white pebbles and dug out the weeds. She'd stood there for a long time, staring at the black marble tombstone . . .

Lead, kindly light, to eternal rest the soul of
Elaine Shiels,
beloved wife and mother.

Beloved wife?

Not the epitaph Amy would have chosen, but that's what Claire had proposed and Claire always got what she wanted. Amy's father hadn't interfered. He never did. He was happy to let others take over.

A wave of sadness washed over Amy as she thought about her father. Staring at the grave, she spoke silently to her mother. Unheard words in a one-way conversation – had it always been so?

Dad likes it in the Home, Mother. Says he does anyway. They give him a daily paper and he still does the cryptic crossword, chews his toffees in the day room. No smoking or eating in the bedrooms. No visitors after seven p.m.

Why did you do it, Amy? Put your father in a Home? Have you no shame? No sense of decency? Or honour?

Amy winced. She didn't have to respond to that. She no longer had to justify herself. She could just keep talking.

The house fetched a great price – over £400,000. Prime location. Good amenities. Room for extending. The Dublin property boom. Dad insisted that Claire and I each got £100,000 He convinced us that his pension and insurance policy, added to his share of the sale of the house, would cover his costs.

You obviously didn't need much convincing. Things

have come to a pretty pass. Now your father is forced to pay for his care.

It's not that simple, Mother.

It is to me. Why are you telling me this, Amy? Why did you come here at all? To do your duty? To salve your conscience?

Just thought you'd like to know the details, Mother. You were always a stickler for details.

Go home, Amy. Go home to your husband.

Amy had stood at the grave in the pelting downpour, a year to the day after her mother's demise, and earnestly tried to pray for the repose of that tormented soul; tried to wipe out the years of misery, the constant criticism, the snide remarks. The bitterness. In her heart she wanted to forgive her mother, but the words wouldn't come.

Outside the bedroom window the storm howled. An eerie wind whipped around the corner of the house, wailing banshee-like, and the rain bashed mercilessly against the windowpanes, jeering at her. Pulling the white cotton sheet snugly around her shoulders, Amy turned on her side and reached over to the mahogany bedside table to get her gold watch, the one her husband had given her for their last anniversary. An unusual extravagance for him.

She squinted at the tiny digits. Nine o'clock. He'd be home any minute. Maurice never stayed out late on a weeknight but, with any luck, she'd be asleep by the time he made his way upstairs. He liked to have a brandy at the kitchen table after his long day, glance through the newspaper and, on the rare occasions when she was not in bed, have a chat. She made sure she was up less and less frequently.

Yes, her mother would gloat, *I always knew it would come to this.*

And what had it come to? She raided her brain for the right word. Misery? Too strong. She hadn't the energy for such a demanding emotion. To be truly sad you had to feel something – moved, excited, motivated – *anything.*

Since Dawn's departure to go to college the house was lonely. Amy missed her daughter. She missed female company: the laughter, the loud music, the telephone ringing, the school stories, the friends calling. All her life, it seemed to Amy, she'd been vaguely dissatisfied but certainly not miserable. The right word hovered at the corners of her mind but tauntingly eluded her.

Her headache hammered. She'd slip downstairs and make a cup of tea, have one of the scones she'd made earlier – the hallmark of her day – a few lousy scones.

But then he'd come in and she'd have to stay and chat. Chat, chat, chat: he'd go into minute detail about every case, each injection or eye examination or teeth-scaling, gingivitis or worming or any bloody thing, the worst being when he had to put an animal to sleep.

"I did it as humanely as I could," he'd mumble sadly, "but, all the same . . ."

All the same, her husband would feel guilty – losing a patient was a failure, no matter that it was a dumb creature. Sometimes she thought that he felt more for his beloved animals than he did for her. The best vet for miles around – his reputation sacrosanct.

She'd sit and watch him and nod and agree and he wouldn't notice whether she was smiling or frowning or frothing at the mouth. He never listened to her and if she did make a comment he ignored or dismissed it. No, that wasn't quite fair – she didn't contribute much to any conversation – that was hardly his fault.

There was no need to converse when Maurice was around. He could talk the hind legs off an ass, eat and lower his drink all at the same time. Sometimes she marvelled at how many words could come tumbling out of his mouth in the space of a few minutes. Hundreds and hundreds of words: nouns, adjectives, verbs, adverbs – all spewing out, the interjections adding suspense or horror or surprise – whatever the need of the moment. She'd sit and say "yes" or "no" or "maybe you're right" in the appropriate places.

He was a great one for the midnight chats; came to life at the witching hour; went over the day's events one by one and then filed them away in that tidy mind of his. Order, method and regularity in his house, in his practice and in his life. Meticulous in everything he did – her slovenly ways must enrage him but he was too polite to make a comment. Didn't like rows, either, our Maurice: "All I want is a peaceful life, Amy."

Not too much to look for.

He'd absentmindedly ask for her news. Then the real panic would set in. What would he think if he knew she'd spent half the day in bed, her only effort that day having been to make a batch of twelve pathetic-looking scones? She'd mutter something about having no news.

No news is good news.

Shut up, Mother, shut up.

Amy would stare at her husband and rack her brains for something to tell him, some bit of gossip or trivia or neighbourhood news . . . anything. But what, in her paltry life, could possibly interest him? Where did she go to get any news? What did she do or even *think* that would engage his curiosity?

I think, therefore I am.

Depressed. Down. Going out of my tree. Losing it. They're right, I am losing it. Who cares? Isn't it easier to just go on and on and on, not complain, do my duty and accept my lot? And he can't see how I am, how I really am. He couldn't understand because I'm not sure I do myself. And what does it matter, anyhow?

Why should he care, Amy, if you don't?

She sighed and switched off the light. Squeezing her eyes shut, she prayed for the respite of sleep. Not so tight, Amy, don't squeeze so tight. Relax. Relax. The yellow, purple and red dots would flicker magically under her eyelids if she managed to relax. She loved this: the changing shapes dancing, running together, separating and moulding again into different patterns and more elaborate forms.

From downstairs the grandfather clock ticked and ticked, louder and louder till it reached drum level. Too tired to get out of bed and close the bedroom door. Anyway, he didn't like her door closed, she knew that – it made him feel rejected, shut out. He'd feel shut out; she felt shut in.

Sleep. Sleep. Go to sleep.

Tick, tick, tick, tick, tick.

She couldn't let this tiredness beat her. She'd have to start cleaning the house; it wasn't fair to leave it all to Dawn at the weekends. She'd plan tomorrow: shopping in the morning if she had the energy – a visit to Nancy in the bookshop. Yes, the bookshop.

She'd promised the old lady ages ago that she'd call in and help her tidy up and price the books in the stockroom. Some of those books were first editions and very valuable.

Nancy wasn't getting any younger and sometimes her memory wasn't the best – Amy wondered how many customers took advantage. The shop was ancient and musty but Amy adored that special smell of old books – there was no smell in the world like it. In her Brontë-bred imagination it was redolent of elegant English drawing-rooms, white-aproned serving-girls carrying in highly polished silver teapots on silver trays, hot buttered muffins and a blazing fire. Nancy, with her cultured accent, genteel manner and pristine-clean old-fashioned lace blouses was quaint. Civilised. The bookshop was an oasis of calm, courtesy and civility, incongruous in the surrounding suburban labyrinth of fast-food joints, honky-tonk computer stores, blaring music shops and antiseptic supermarkets. Every time Amy stepped into the bookshop she stepped into an ancient graceful world.

Tomorrow night she might call to see her sister, Claire.

Claire, she who always had news and insisted on inflicting it on the nearest available pair of ears, would be in high spirits as usual – she'd natter on and on and on about her day in the jewellery shop: who came in, who bought a bracelet for his wife's birthday, who was going out with whom, the butcher next door, the newsagent opposite, the woman in the flower shop . . . on and on and on. Claire should have married Maurice. They could have babbled into oblivion.

Claire had dated Maurice for a few months before she had introduced him to the drama club. When Amy had met him that fateful night of the dress rehearsal, she'd thought he was nice. Nice – such a horribly inane word – but that's what her initial impression had been. After a few weeks, he'd asked her out for a drink. Claire hadn't minded, by then she was seeing someone else. How could she explain to her sister now, after twenty-two years, how she felt?

Count your blessings, Amy, she'd say. You have it all – a beautiful, brilliant daughter at college, a fine home and a decent man for a husband. You're not the only one with problems. I'm on my own. I have to make a living and there's always something to be done – last year rewiring and have you seen the state of the windows? I'll have to take out another loan. So, don't tell me you're feeling down. Stop moping and complaining. With a good cleaning and a coat of paint, your house would be grand. Why not get a part-time job? You were better off emotionally and in every other way when you worked in the surgery. If you don't want to work again with Maurice, there are loads of jobs out there for the asking. Take a ride on the Celtic Tiger, Amy. What about the £100,000 you got? My mortgage ate mine. Invest your money in something you'll enjoy: take a holiday, renovate the house, start a business. Do something constructive. You're an intelligent woman. Get up off your arse, go out there and start living again.

No, a visit to Claire would not be helpful. After her diatribe on the importance of a working life, Claire would try to persuade her to take up a hobby. The drama club. A hobby – the panacea for all problems, according to Claire. The elixir.

The last thing she needed was to hear Claire's pedestrian opinions and trite advice. She couldn't betray her deepest feelings to her sister; she'd never been able to do that.

You've little to complain about, Amy.

I know, Mother, I know. He's not a bad man: a good provider, dedicated to his career – not overly giving in the money department, mind you.

Why was he so opposed to her doing up this house? It was in such bad shape. If he loved it so much, why did he neglect it?

She'd given up asking to visit Paris. He kept putting her off, despite her offer to pay – preferred his holidays at home, he said. Didn't like the hassle of air travel. Their last proper holiday had been to Brittany and that was years ago. Maurice hadn't enjoyed it. His excuse nowadays was that he couldn't leave his practice.

Angrily she reached under the pillow and opened another packet of crisps. Comfort eating.

Never marry a mean man, Amy.

Mean? He didn't mind lashing out on Dawn's third-level education; gave the girl a fortune in pocket money; never quibbled about her house-sharing rent in Stillorgan or the price of her books. Dawn had him eating out of her hand – more power to her.

With his wife he was careful. Prudent. It infuriated her but why complain now? Wasn't that one of the reasons she'd married him in the first place – because he was safe? She'd known all along what he was like. You didn't expect a man to change after marriage. If you did you were a fool.

You walked into this with your eyes open, Amy.

Yes, thank you, Mother.

What did you expect, anyway?

Expect? She hadn't expected anything. Maurice had ambled into her life without fuss. They went out together, enjoyed one another's company. She was young and pretty. Clever but not too clever to upset a man's ego. More to the point, Amy was accommodating – a quality a man like Maurice prized. He told her he loved her. Was that the rock she perished on? When a man told a woman he loved her –

wasn't there something deliciously irresistible about it? Did we automatically love where we were loved? Amy thought it might be so. Maurice had a lot going for him in those days. She admired him for his intelligence and his ambition. He was kind. He was good to her – then. Her friends were getting married. Middle twenties – that's what you did – you got married. They decided to tie the knot. It was easy. Inevitable.

And you thought a marriage like that would work?

Yes, Mother, because that's what you had and, on the surface, it worked for you. I don't remember much passion between you and Dad. You were more like polite acquaintances than husband and wife, immersed in your own little world, but you didn't complain because you knew and I know that after years and years together, that's all there is – mutual tolerance . . . if you're lucky.

Enough of this! You've made your bed, Amy.

And then it struck her – the word she was looking for. Overwhelmed. Her life had overwhelmed her. She woke up one day and felt, with a dire certainty, that she was lost. Utterly lost in this big barracks of a house that she'd grown to despise.

I warned you, Amy, but you wouldn't listen. You never listen.

Dear God, make the bitch leave me alone.

If you enjoyed these chapters from
Shame the Devil by Mary McCarthy
why not order the full book online
@ www.poolbeg.com

POOLBEG WISHES TO

THANK YOU

for buying a Poolbeg book.

If you enjoyed this why not
visit our website:
www.poolbeg.com

and get another book delivered
straight to your home or to a
friend's home!

All books despatched within
24 hours.

POOLBEG

WHY NOT JOIN OUR MAILING LIST
@ www.poolbeg.com and get some
fantastic offers on Poolbeg books